I'm adrift, suspended in a pool of senselessness, but something about her keeps tugging, sparking my nerves, errant currents pushing me to the surface of something—an emotional revelation—that trembles into existence only to evaporate, seconds later, as if it might be terrified to exist.

This goes on and on and on and on and on

Lightyears.

Eons.

over

and

over

whispers of clarity

g a s p s   o f   o x y g e n

and I'm tossed back out to sea.

BOOKS BY TAHEREH MAFI

Shatter Me: Series One

BOOK 1: *Shatter Me*

BOOK 2: *Unravel Me*

BOOK 3: *Ignite Me*

BOOK 4: *Restore Me*

BOOK 5: *Defy Me*

BOOK 6: *Imagine Me*

Shatter Me: Series One Novellas

BOOK 1.5: *Destroy Me*

BOOK 2.5: *Fracture Me*

BOOK 4.5: *Shadow Me*

BOOK 5.5: *Reveal Me*

BOOK 6.5: *Believe Me*

Shatter Me: Series One Novella Collections

Unite Me

Find Me

Shatter Me: Series Two

BOOK 1: *Watch Me*

BOOK 2: *Release Me*

The Woven Kingdom Series

BOOK 1: *This Woven Kingdom*

BOOK 2: *These Infinite Threads*

BOOK 3: *All This Twisted Glory*

BOOK 4: *Every Spiral of Fate*

An Emotion of Great Delight

A Very Large Expanse of Sea

DEFY ME

SHATTER ME: SERIES ONE

BOOK FIVE

TAHEREH MAFI

STORYTIDE

An Imprint of HarperCollins*Publishers*

HarperCollins Children's Books,
a division of HarperCollins Publishers,
195 Broadway, New York, NY 10007

HarperCollins Publishers,
Macken House, 39/40 Mayor Street Upper,
Dublin 1, D01 C9W8, Ireland

Storytide is an imprint of HarperCollins Publishers.

Defy Me

harpercollins.com

Library of Congress Control Number: 2019931360
ISBN 978-0-06-349769-6

Typography by Ray Shappell
26 27 28 29 30 RTLO 10 9 8 7 6 5 4 3 2 1

SPECIAL EDITION, 2026

KENJI

She's screaming.

She's just screaming words, I think. They're just *words.* But she's screaming, screaming at the top of her lungs, with an agony that seems almost an exaggeration, and it's causing devastation I never knew possible. It's like she just—imploded.

It doesn't seem real.

I mean, I knew Juliette was strong—and I knew we hadn't discovered the depth of her powers—but I never imagined she'd be capable of this.

Of this:

The ceiling is splitting open. Seismic currents are thundering up the walls, across the floors, chattering my teeth. The ground is rumbling under my feet. People are frozen in place even as they shake, the room vibrating around them. The chandeliers swing too fast and the lights flicker ominously. And then, with one last vibration, three of the massive chandeliers rip free from the ceiling and shatter as they hit the floor.

Crystal flies everywhere. The room loses half its light, bathing the cavernous space in a freakish glow, and it's suddenly hard to see what's happening. I look at Juliette and see her staring, slack-jawed, frozen at the sight of the devastation, and I realize she must've stopped screaming a minute ago. She can't stop this. She already put the energy into the world and now—

It has to go somewhere.

The shudders ripple with renewed fervor across the floorboards, ripping through walls and seats and *people*.

I don't actually believe it until I see the blood. It seems fake, for a second, all the limp bodies in seats with their chests butterflied open. It seems staged—like a bad joke, like a bad theater production. But when I see the blood, thick and heavy, seeping through clothes and upholstery, dripping down frozen hands, I know we'll never recover from this.

Juliette just murdered six hundred people at once.

There's no recovering from this.

I shove my way through the quiet, stunned, still-breathing bodies of my friends. I hear Winston's soft, insistent whimpers and Brendan's steady, reassuring response that the wound isn't as bad as it looks, that he's going to be okay, that he's been through worse than this and survived it—

And I know my priority right now needs to be Juliette.

When I reach her I pull her into my arms, and her cold, unresponsive body reminds me of the time I found her standing over Anderson, a gun aimed at his chest. She was so terrified—*so surprised*—by what she'd done that she could hardly speak. She looked like she'd disappeared into herself somewhere—like she'd found a small room in her brain and had locked herself inside. It took a minute to coax her back out again.

She hadn't even killed anyone that time.

I try to warm some sense into her, begging her now to return to herself, to hurry back to her mind, to the present moment.

"I know everything is crazy right now, but I need you to snap out of this, J. Wake up. Get out of your head. We have to get out of here."

She doesn't blink.

"Princess, please," I say, shaking her a little. "We have to go—*now*—"

And when she still doesn't move, I figure I have no choice but to move her myself. I start hauling her backward. Her limp body is heavier than I expect, and she makes a small, wheezing sound that's almost like a sob. Fear sparks in my nerves. I nod at Castle and the others to go, to move on without me, but when I glance around, looking for Warner, I realize I can't find him anywhere.

What happens next knocks the wind from my lungs.

The room tilts. My vision blackens, clears, and then darkens only at the edges in a dizzying moment that lasts hardly a second. I feel off-center. I stumble.

And then, all at once—

Juliette is gone.

Not figuratively. She's literally gone. Disappeared. One second she's in my arms, and the next, I'm grasping at air. I blink and spin around, convinced I'm losing my mind, but when I scan the room I see the audience members begin to stir. Their shirts are torn and their faces are scratched, but no one appears to be dead. Instead, they begin to stand, confused, and as soon as they start shuffling around, someone shoves me, hard. I look to up to see Ian swearing at me, telling me to get moving while we still have a chance, and I try to push back, try to tell him that we lost Juliette—that I haven't seen Warner—and he doesn't hear me, he just forces me forward, offstage, and when the murmur of the crowd grows into a roar, I know I have no choice.

I have to go.

WARNER

"I'm going to kill him," she says, her small hands forming fists. "I'm going to kill him—"

"Ella, don't be silly," I say, and walk away.

"One day," she says, chasing after me, her eyes bright with tears. "If he doesn't stop hurting you, I swear I'll do it. You'll see."

I laugh.

"It's not funny!" she cries.

I turn to face her. "No one can kill my dad. He's unkillable."

"No one is unkillable," she says.

I ignore her.

"Why doesn't your mum do anything?" she says, and she grabs my arm.

When I meet her eyes she looks different. Scared.

"Why doesn't anyone stop him?"

The wounds on my back are no longer fresh, but, somehow, they still hurt. Ella is the only person who knows about these scars, knows what my dad started doing to me on my birthday two years ago. Last year, when all the families came to visit us in California, Ella had barged into my room, wanting to know where Emmaline and Nazeera had gone off to, and she'd caught me staring at my back in the mirror.

I begged her not to say anything, not to tell anyone what she saw, and she started crying and said that we had to tell someone, that she was going to tell her mom and I said, "If you tell your mom I'll only get into more trouble. Please don't say anything, okay? He won't do it again."

But he did do it again.

And this time he was angrier. He told me I was seven years old now, and that I was too old to cry.

"We have to do something," she says, and her voice shakes a little. Another tear steals down the side of her face and, quickly, she wipes it away. "We have to tell someone."

"Stop," I say. "I don't want to talk about it anymore."

"But—"

"Ella. Please."

"No, we have t—"

"Ella," I say, cutting her off. "I think there's something wrong with my mom."

Her face falls. Her anger fades. "What?"

I'd been terrified, for weeks, to say the words out loud, to make my fears real. Even now, I feel my heart pick up.

"What do you mean?" she says. "What's wrong with her?"

"She's . . . sick."

Ella blinks at me. Confused. "If she's sick we can fix her. My mum and dad can fix her. They're so smart; they can fix anything. I'm sure they can fix your mum, too."

I'm shaking my head, my heart racing now, pounding in my ears. "No, Ella, you don't understand— I think—"

"What?" She takes my hand. Squeezes. "What is it?"

"I think my dad is killing her."

KENJI

We're all running.

Base isn't far from here, and our best option is to go on foot. But the minute we hit the open air, the group of us—myself, Castle, Winston, injured Brendan, Ian, and Alia—go invisible. Someone shouts a breathless *thanks* in my direction, but I'm not the one doing this.

My fists clench.

Nazeera.

These last couple of days with her have been making my head spin. I never should've trusted her. First she hates me, then she hates me even more, and then, suddenly, she decides I'm not an asshole and wants to be my friend? I can't believe I fell for it. I can't believe I'm such an idiot. She's been playing me this whole time. This girl just shows up out of nowhere, magically mimics my exact supernatural ability, and then—right when she pretends to be best friends with Juliette—we're ambushed at the symposium and Juliette sort of murders six hundred people?

No way. I call bullshit.

No way this was all some big coincidence.

Juliette attended that symposium because *Nazeera* encouraged her to go. Nazeera convinced Juliette it was the right thing to do. And then five seconds before Brendan gets shot, Nazeera tells me to run? Tells me we have the same powers?

Bullshit.

I can't believe I let myself be distracted by a pretty face. I should've trusted Warner when he told me she was hiding something.

Warner.

God. I don't even know what happened to him.

The minute we get back to base our invisibility is lifted. I can't know for sure if that means Nazeera went her own way, but we can't slow down long enough to find out. Quickly, I project a new layer of invisibility over our team; I'll have to keep it up just long enough to get us all to a safe space, and just being back on base isn't assurance enough. The soldiers are going to ask questions, and right now I don't have the answers they need.

They're going to be pissed.

We make our way, as a group, to the fifteenth floor, to our home on base in Sector 45. Warner only just finished having this thing built for us. He cleared out this entire top floor for our new headquarters—we'd hardly even settled in—and things have already gone to shit. I can't even allow myself to think about it now, not yet.

It makes me feel sick to my stomach.

Once we're gathered in our largest common room, I do a head count. All original, remaining Omega Point members are present. Adam and James show up to find out what happened, and Sonya and Sara stick around just long enough to gather intel before carting Brendan over to the medical wing. Winston disappears down the hall behind them.

Juliette and Warner never show.

Quickly, we share our own versions of what we saw. It doesn't take long to confirm we all witnessed basically the same thing: blood, mayhem, murdered bodies, and then—a slightly less-bloody version of the same thing. No one seems as surprised by the twisted turn of events as I was, because, according to Ian, "Weird supernatural shit happens around here all the time, it's not that weird," but, more important:

No one saw what happened to Warner and Juliette.

No one but me.

For a few seconds, we all stare at each other. My heart pounds hard and heavy in my chest. I feel like I might be on fire, burning with indignation.

Denial.

Alia is the first to speak. "You don't think they're dead, do you?"

Ian says, "Probably."

And I jump to my feet. "STOP. They're not dead."

"How can you be sure?" Adam says.

"I would know if they were dead."

"What? How w—"

"I would just know, okay?" I cut him off. "I would know. And they're not dead." I take a deep, steadying breath. "We're not going to freak out," I say as calmly as possible. "There has to be a logical explanation. People don't just *disappear,* right?"

Everyone stares at me.

"You know what I mean," I snap, irritated. "We all know that Juliette and Warner wouldn't, like, run away together. They weren't even on speaking terms before the symposium. So it makes the most sense that they would be kidnapped." I pause. Look around again. "Right?"

"Or dead," Ian says.

"If you keep talking like that, Sanchez, I can guarantee that at least one person *will* be dead tonight."

Ian sighs, hard. "Listen, I'm not trying to be an asshole. I know you were close with them. But let's be real: they weren't close with the rest of us. And maybe that makes me less invested in all this, but it also makes me more level-headed."

He waits, gives me a chance to respond.

I don't.

Ian sighs again. "I'm just saying that maybe you're letting emotion cloud your better judgment right now. I know you don't *want* them to be dead, but the possibility that they *are* dead is, like, really high. Warner was a traitor to The Reestablishment. I'm surprised they didn't try to kill him sooner. And Juliette—I mean, that's obvious, right? She murdered Anderson and declared herself ruler of North America." He raises his eyebrows in a knowing gesture. "Those two have had targets on their backs for months."

My jaw clenches. Unclenches. Clenches again.

"So," Ian says quietly. "We have to be smart about this. If they're dead, we need to be thinking about our next moves. Where do we go?"

"Wait—what do you mean?" Adam says, sitting forward. "What next moves? You think we have to leave?"

"Without Warner and Juliette, I don't think we're safe here." Lily takes Ian's hand in a show of emotional support that makes me feel violent. "The soldiers paid their allegiance to the two of them—to Juliette in particular. Without her, I'm not sure they'd follow the rest of us anywhere."

"And if The Reestablishment had Juliette murdered," Ian adds, "they're obviously just getting started. They'll be coming to reclaim Sector 45 any second now. Our best chance of survival is to first consider what's best for our team. Since we're the obvious next targets, I think we should bail. Soon." A pause. "Maybe even tonight."

"Bro, are you insane?" I drop down into my chair too hard, feeling like I might scream. "We can't just bail. We need to look for them. We need to be planning a rescue mission right now!"

Everyone just stares at me. Like *I'm* the one who's lost his mind.

"Castle, sir?" I say, trying and failing to keep the sharp edge out of my voice. "Do you want to chime in here?"

But Castle has sunk down in his chair. He's staring up, at the ceiling, at nothing. He looks dazed.

I don't have the chance to dwell on it.

"Kenji," Alia says quietly. "I'm sorry, but Ian's right. I don't think we're safe here anymore."

"We're not leaving," Adam and I say at exactly the same time.

I spin around, surprised. Hope shoots through me fast

and strong. Maybe Adam feels more for Juliette than he lets on. Maybe Adam will surprise us all. Maybe he'll finally stop hiding, stop cowering in the background. *Maybe,* I think, Adam is back.

"Thank you," I say, and point at him in a gesture that says to everyone:

See? This is loyalty.

"James and I aren't running anymore," Adam says, his eyes going cold as he speaks. "I understand if the rest of you have to leave, but James and I will stay here. I was a Sector 45 soldier. I lived on this base. Maybe they'll give me immunity."

I frown. "But—"

"James and I aren't leaving anymore," Adam says. Loudly. Definitively. "You can make your plans without us. We have to take off for the night, anyway." Adam stands, turns to his brother. "It's time to get ready for bed."

James stares at the floor.

"James," Adam says, a gentle warning in his voice.

"I want to stay and listen," James says, crossing his arms. "You can go to bed without me."

"James—"

"But I have a theory," the ten-year-old says. He says the word *theory* like it's brand-new to him, like it's an interesting sound in his mouth. "And I want to share it with Kenji."

Adam looks so tense that the strain in his shoulders is stressing *me* out. I think I haven't been paying close enough attention to him, because I didn't realize until right now that Adam looks worse than tired. He looks ragged. Like he could collapse, crack in half, at any moment.

James catches my eye from across the room, his own eyes round and eager.

I sigh.

"What's your theory, little man?"

James's face lights up. "I was just thinking: maybe all the fake-killing thing was, like, a distraction."

I raise an eyebrow.

"Like, if someone wanted to kidnap Warner and Juliette," James says. "You know? Like you said earlier. Causing a scene like that would be the perfect distraction, right?"

"Well. Yeah," I say, and frown. "I guess. But why would The Reestablishment need a distraction? When have they ever been secretive about what they want? If a supreme commander wanted to take Juliette or Warner, for example, wouldn't they just show up with a shit ton of soldiers and take what they wanted?"

"Language," Adam says, outraged.

"My bad. Strike the word *shit* from the record."

Adam shakes his head. He looks like he might throttle me. But James is smiling, which is really all that matters.

"No. I don't think they'd rush in like that, not with so many soldiers," James says, his blue eyes bright. "Not if they had something to hide."

"You think they'd have something to hide?" Lily pipes up. "From *us*?"

"I don't know," James says. "Sometimes people hide

things." He steals a split-second glance at Adam as he says it, a glance that sets my pulse racing with fear, and I'm about to respond when Lily beats me to it.

"I mean, it's possible," she says. "But The Reestablishment doesn't have a long history of caring about pretenses. They stopped pretending to care about the opinion of the public a long time ago. They mow people down in the street just because they feel like it. I don't think they're worried about hiding things from us."

Castle laughs, out loud, and we all spin around to stare at him. I'm relieved to finally see him react, but he still seems lost in his head somewhere. He looks angry. I've never really seen Castle get angry.

"They hide a great deal from us," he says sharply. "And from each other." After a long, deep breath, he finally gets to his feet. Smiles, warily, at the ten-year-old in the room. "James, you are wise indeed."

"Thank you," James says, blinking up at him.

"Castle, sir?" I say, my voice coming out harder than I'd intended. "Will you please tell us what the hell is going on? Do you know something?"

Castle sighs. Rubs the stubble on his chin with the flat of his palm. "All right, Nazeera," he says, turning toward nothing, like he's speaking to a ghost. "Go ahead."

When Nazeera appears, as if out of thin air, I'm not the only one who's pissed. Okay, maybe I'm the only one who's pissed.

But everyone else looks surprised, at least.

They're staring at her, at each other, and then all of

them—*all of them*—turn to look at me.

"Bro, did you know about this?" Ian asks.

I scowl.

Invisibility is *my* thing. My thing, goddammit.

No one ever said I had to share that with anyone. Especially not with someone like Nazeera, a lying, manipulative—

Gorgeous. Gorgeous human being.

Shit.

I turn, stare at the wall. I can't be distracted by her anymore. She knows I'm into her—my infatuation is apparently obvious to everyone within a ten-mile radius, according to Castle—and she's clearly been using my idiocy to her best advantage.

Smart. I respect the tactic.

But that also means I have to keep my guard up when she's around. No more staring. No more daydreaming about her. No more thinking about how she looked at me when she smiled. Or the way she laughed, like she meant it, the same night she yelled at me for asking reasonable questions. Which, by the way—

I don't think I was crazy for wondering out loud how the daughter of a supreme commander could get away with wearing an illegal headscarf. She told me later that she wears the scarf symbolically, every once in a while, that she can't get away with wearing it all the time because it's illegal. But when I pointed this out to her, she gave me hell. And then she gave me shit for being confused.

I'm *still* confused.

She's not covering her hair now, either, but no one else

seems to have registered this fact. Maybe they'd already seen her like this. Maybe everyone but me already had that conversation with her, already heard her story about wearing it symbolically, occasionally.

Illegally, when her dad wasn't watching.

"Kenji," she says, and her voice is so sharp I look up, stare at her despite my own very explicit orders to keep my eyes on the wall. All it takes is two seconds of eye contact and my heart hits itself.

That mouth. Those eyes.

"Yeah?" I cross my arms.

She looks surprised, like she wasn't expecting me to be upset, and I don't care. She should know that I'm pissed. I want to her to know that invisibility is my thing. That I know I'm petty and I don't care. Plus, I don't trust her. Also, what is up with these kids of the supreme commanders all being super-good-looking? It's almost like they did it on purpose, like they made these kids in test tubes or someshit.

I shake my head to clear it.

Carefully, Nazeera says, "I really think you should sit down for this."

"I'm good."

She frowns. For a second she looks almost hurt, but before I have a chance to feel bad about it, she shrugs. Turns away.

And what she says next nearly splits me in half.

JULIETTE

I'm sitting on an orange chair in the hallway of a dimly lit building. The chair is made of cheap plastic, its edges coarse and unfinished. The floor is a shiny linoleum that occasionally sticks to the soles of my shoes. I know I've been breathing too loudly but I can't help it. I sit on my hands and swing my legs under my seat.

Just then, a boy comes into view. His movements are so quiet I only notice him when he stops directly in front of me. He leans against the wall opposite me, his eyes focused on a point in the distance.

I study him for a moment.

He seems about my age, but he's wearing a suit. There's something strange about him; he's so pale and stiff he seems close to dead.

"Hi," I say, and try to smile. "Do you want to sit down?"

He doesn't return my smile. He won't even look at me. "I'd prefer to stand," he says quietly.

"Okay."

We're both silent awhile.

Finally, he says, "You're nervous."

I nod. My eyes must be a little red from crying, but I'd been hoping no one would notice. "Are you here to get a new family, too?"

"No."

"Oh." I look away. Stop swinging my feet. I feel my bottom lip tremble and I bite it, hard. "Then why are you here?"

He shrugs. I see him glance, briefly, at the three empty chairs next to me, but he makes no effort to sit down. "My father made me come."

"He made you come here*?"*

"Yes."

"Why?"

He stares at his shoes and frowns. "I don't know."

"Shouldn't you be in school?"

And then, instead of answering me, he says, "Where are you from?"

"What do you mean?"

He looks up then, meets my eyes for the first time. He has such unusual eyes. They're a light, clear green.

"You have an accent," he says.

"Oh," I say. "Yeah." I look at the floor. "I was born in New Zealand. That's where I lived until my mum and dad died."

"I'm sorry to hear that."

I nod. Swing my legs again. I'm about to ask him another question when the door down the hall finally opens. A tall man in a navy suit walks out. He's carrying a briefcase.

It's Mr. Anderson, my social worker.

He beams at me. "You're all set. Your new family is dying to meet you. We have a couple more things to do before you can go, but it won't take too lon—"

I can't hold it in anymore.

I start sobbing right there, all over the new dress he bought me. Sobs rack my body, tears hitting the orange chair, the sticky floor.

Mr. Anderson sets down his briefcase and laughs. "Sweetheart, there's nothing to cry about. This is a great day! You should be happy!"

But I can't speak.

I feel stuck, stuck to the seat. Like my lungs have been stuck together. I manage to calm the sobs but I'm suddenly hiccuping, tears spilling quietly down my cheeks. "I want—I want to go h-home—"

"You are going home," he says, still smiling. "That's the whole point."

And then—

"Dad."

I look up at the sound of his voice. So quiet and serious. It's the boy with the green eyes. Mr. Anderson, I realize, is his father.

"She's scared," the boy says. And even though he's talking to his dad, he's looking at me. "She's really scared."

"Scared?" Mr. Anderson looks from me to his son, then back again. "What's there to be scared of?"

I scrub at my face. Try and fail to stop the tears.

"What's her name?" the boy asks. He's still staring at me, and this time, I stare back. There's something in his eyes, something that makes me feel safe.

"This is Juliette," Mr. Anderson says, and looks me over. "Tragic"—he sighs—"just like her namesake."

KENJI

Nazeera was right. I should've sat down.

I'm looking at my hands, watching a tremor work its way across my fingers. I nearly lose my grip on the stack of photos I'm clutching. The photos. The photos Nazeera passed around after telling us that Juliette is not who we think she is.

I can't stop staring at the pictures.

A little brown girl and a little white girl running in a field, both of them smiling tiny-toothed smiles, long hair flying in the wind, small baskets full of strawberries swinging from their elbows.

Nazeera and Emmaline at the strawberry patch, it read on the back.

Little Nazeera being hugged, on either side, by two little white girls, all three of them laughing so hard they look like they're about to fall over.

Ella and Emmaline and Nazeera, it read.

A close-up of a little girl smiling right into the camera, her eyes huge and blue-green, lengths of soft brown hair framing her face.

Ella on Christmas morning, it read.

"Ella Sommers," Nazeera says.

She says her real name is Ella Sommers, sister to Emmaline Sommers, daughter of Maximillian and Evie Sommers.

"Something is wrong," Nazeera says.

"Something is happening," she says. She says she woke up six weeks ago remembering Juliette—sorry, Ella—

"Remembering her. I was *remembering* her, which means I'd forgotten her. And when I remembered Ella," she says, "I remembered Emmaline, too. I remembered how we'd all grown up together, how our parents used to be friends. I remembered but I didn't understand, not right away. I thought maybe I was confusing dreams with memory. Actually, the memories came back to me so slowly I thought, for a while, that I might've been hallucinating."

She says the hallucinations, as she called them, were impossible to shake, so she started digging, started looking for information.

"I learned the same thing you did. That two girls named Ella and Emmaline were donated to The Reestablishment, and that only Ella was taken out of their custody, so Ella was given an alias. Relocated. Adopted. But what you didn't know was that the parents who gave up their daughters were also members of The Reestablishment. They were doctors and scientists. You didn't know that Ella—the girl you know to be Juliette—is the daughter of Evie Sommers, the current supreme commander of Oceania. She and I grew up together. She, like the rest of us kids, was built to serve The Reestablishment."

Ian swears, loudly, and Adam is so stunned he doesn't complain.

"That can't be possible," Adam says. "Juliette— The girl I went to school with? She was"—he shakes his head—"I knew Juliette for years. She wasn't made like you or Warner. She was this quiet, timid, sweet girl. She was always so *nice*. She never wanted to hurt anyone. All she ever wanted was to, like, connect with people. She was trying to *help* that little boy in the grocery store. But then it just—everything ended so badly and she got sucked into this whole mess and I tried," he says, looking suddenly distraught, "I tried to help her, I tried to keep her safe. I wanted to protect her from this. I wanted t—"

He cuts himself off. Pulls himself together.

"She wasn't like this," he says, and he's staring at the ground now. "Not until she started spending all that time with Warner. After she met him she just— I don't know what happened. She lost herself, little by little. Eventually she became someone else." He looks up. "But she wasn't made to be this way, not like you. Not like Warner. There's no way she's the daughter of a supreme commander—she's not a born murderer. Besides," he says, taking a sharp breath, "if she were from Oceania she would have an *accent*."

Nazeera tilts her head at Adam.

"The girl you knew had undergone severe physical and emotional trauma," she says. "She'd had her native memories forcibly removed. She was shipped across the globe as a specimen and convinced to live with abusive adoptive parents who beat the life out of her." Nazeera shakes her head slowly. "The Reestablishment—and Anderson, in particular—made sure that Ella could never remember why she was suffering, but just because she couldn't remember what happened to her didn't change the fact that it happened. Her body was repeatedly used and abused by a rotating cast of monsters. And that shit leaves its mark."

Nazeera looks Adam straight in the eye.

"Maybe you don't understand," she says. "I read all the reports. I hacked into all my father's files. I found *everything.* What they did to Ella over the course of twelve years is *unspeakable.* So yes, I'm sure you remember a very different person. But I don't think she became someone she wasn't. My guess is she finally gathered the strength to remember who she'd always been. And if you don't get that, I'm glad things didn't work out between the two of you."

In an instant, the tension in the room is nearly suffocating.

Adam looks like he might be on fire. Like fire might literally come out of his eyeballs. Like it might be his new superpower.

I clear my throat. I force myself to say something—anything—to break the silence. "So you guys, uh, you all knew about Adam and Juliette, too, huh? I didn't realize you knew about that. Huh. Interesting."

Nazeera takes her time turning in her seat to look me in the eye. "Are you kidding?" she says, staring at me like I'm worse than an idiot.

I figure it's best not to press the issue.

"Where did you get these photos?" Alia asks, changing the subject more deftly than I did. "How can we trust that they're real?"

At first, Nazeera only looks at her. And she seems resigned when she says, "I don't know how to convince you that the photos are real. I can only tell you that they are."

The room goes silent.

"Why do you even care?" Lily says. "Why are we supposed to believe you care about this? About Juliette—about *Ella*? What do you have to gain from helping us? Why would you betray your parents?"

Nazeera sits back in her seat. "I know you all think the children of the supreme commanders are a bunch of carefree, amoral psychopaths, happy to be the military robots our parents wanted us to be, but nothing is ever that straightforward. Our parents are homicidal maniacs intent on ruling the world; that part is true. But the thing no one seems to understand is that our parents *chose* to be homicidal maniacs. We, on the other hand, were forced to be. And just because we've been trained to be mercenaries doesn't mean we like it. None of us got to choose this life. None of us enjoyed being taught to torture before we could even drive. And it's not insane to imagine that sometimes even horrible people are searching for a way out of their own darkness."

Nazeera's eyes flash with feeling as she speaks, and her words puncture the life vest around my heart. Emotion drowns me again.

Shit.

"Is it really so crazy to think I might care about the girls I once loved as my own sisters?" she's saying. "Or about the lies my parents forced me to swallow, or the innocent people I watched them murder? Or maybe even something simpler than that—that I might've opened my eyes one day and realized that I was part and parcel of a system that was not only ravaging the world but also slaughtering everyone in it?"

Shit.

I can feel it, can feel my heart filling out, filling up. My chest feels tight, like it's swollen, like my lungs don't fit anymore. I don't want to care about Nazeera. Don't want to feel her pain or feel connected to her or feel *anything*. I just want to keep a level head. Be cool.

I force myself to think about a joke James told me the other day, a stupid pun—something to do with muffins—a joke that was so lame I nearly cried. I focus on the memory, the way James laughed at his own lameness, snorting so hard a little food fell out of his mouth. I smile and glance at James, who looks like he might be falling asleep in his seat.

Soon, the tightness in my chest begins to abate.

Now I'm really smiling, wondering if it's weird that I love bad jokes even more than good ones, when I hear Ian say—

"It's not that you seem heartless. It's just that these photos seem so convenient. You had them ready to share." He stares down at the single photo he's holding. "These kids could be anyone."

"Look closely," Nazeera says, standing up to get a better

look at the picture in his hands. "Who do you think that is?"

I lean over—Ian isn't far from me—and peer over his shoulder. There's really no point denying it anymore; the resemblance is insane.

Juliette. *Ella.*

She's just a kid, maybe four or five years old, standing in front of the camera, smiling. She's holding a bouquet of dandelions up to the cameraman, as if to offer him one. And then, just off to the side, there's another figure. A little blond boy. So blond his hair is white. He's staring, intensely, at a single dandelion in his hands.

I nearly fall out of my chair. Juliette is one thing, but this—

"Is that *Warner*?" I say.

Adam looks up sharply. He glances from me to Nazeera, then stalks over to look at the photo. His eyebrows fly up his head.

"No way," he says.

Nazeera shrugs.

"No way," Adam says again. "*No way.* That's impossible. There's no way they knew each other this long. Warner had no idea who Juliette was before she came here." When Nazeera seems unmoved, Adam says, "I'm serious. I know you think I'm full of shit, but I'm not wrong about this. I was *there.* Warner literally interviewed me for the job of being her cellmate in the asylum. He didn't know who she was. He'd never met her. Never seen her face, not up close, anyway. Half the reason he chose me to be her roommate was because she and I had history, because he found that useful. He'd grill me for hours about her."

Nazeera sighs slowly, like she's surrounded by idiots.

"When I found these photos," she says to Adam, "I couldn't understand how I came across them so easily. I didn't understand why anyone would keep evidence like this right under my nose or make it so easy to find. But I know now that my parents never expected me to look. They got lazy. They figured that, even if I found these photos, I'd never know what I was looking at. Two months ago I could've seen these pictures and assumed that this girl"—she plucks a photo of herself, what appears to be a young Haider, and a thin brown-haired girl with bright blue eyes, out of a pile—"was a neighbor kid, someone I used to know but can't be bothered to remember.

"But I do remember," she says. "I remember all of it. I remember the day our parents told us that Ella and Emmaline had drowned. I remember crying myself to sleep every night. I remember the day they took us to a place I thought was a hospital. I remember my mother telling me I'd feel better soon. And then, I remember *remembering* nothing. Like time, in my brain, just folded in on itself." She raises her eyebrows. "Do you get what I'm trying to say to you, Kent?"

He glares at her. "I get that you think I'm an idiot."

She smiles.

"Yes, I get what you're saying," he says, obviously irritated. "You're saying you all had your memories wiped.

You're saying Warner doesn't even know that they knew each other."

She holds up a finger. "*Didn't* know," she says. "He didn't know until just before the symposium. I tried to warn him—and Castle," she says, glancing at Castle, who's looking at the wall. "I tried to warn them both that something was wrong, that something big was happening and I didn't really understand what or why. Warner didn't believe me, of course. I'm not sure Castle did, either. But I didn't have time to give them proof."

"Wait, what?" I say, my eyebrows furrowing. "You told Warner and Castle? *Before* the symposium? You told them all of this?"

"I tried," she says.

"Why wouldn't you just tell Juliette?" Lily asks.

"You mean Ella."

Lily rolls her eyes. "Sure. Ella. Whatever. Why not warn her directly? Why tell everyone else?"

"I didn't know how she'd take the news," Nazeera says. "I'd been trying to take her temperature from the moment I got here, and I could never figure out how she felt about me. I didn't think she really trusted me. And then after everything that happened"—she hesitates—"it never seemed like the right time. She got shot, she was in recovery, and then she and Warner broke up, and she just . . . I don't know. Spiraled. She wasn't in a healthy headspace. She'd already had to stomach a bunch of revelations and she didn't seem to be handling them well. I wasn't sure she could take much more, to be honest, and I was worried what she might do."

"Murder six hundred people, maybe," Ian mutters under his breath.

"Hey," I snap. "She didn't murder anyone, okay? That was some kind of magic trick."

"It was a distraction," Nazeera says firmly. "James was the only one who saw this for what it was." She sighs. "I think this whole thing was staged to make Ella appear volatile and unhinged. That scene at the symposium will no doubt undermine her position here, at Sector 45, by instilling fear in the soldiers who pledged their allegiance to her. She'll be described as unstable. Irrational. Weak. And then—easily captured. I knew The Reestablishment wanted Ella gone, but I thought they'd just burn the whole sector to the ground. I was wrong. This was a far more efficient tactic. They didn't need to kill off a regiment of perfectly good soldiers and a population of obedient workers," Nazeera says. "All they needed to do was to discredit Ella as their leader."

"So what happens now?" Lily says.

Nazeera hesitates. And then, carefully, she says, "Once they've punished the citizens and thoroughly quashed any hope for rebellion, The Reestablishment will turn everyone against you. Put bounties on your heads, or, worse, threaten to murder loved ones if civilians and soldiers don't turn you in. You were right," she says to Lily. "The soldiers and citizens paid allegiance to Ella, and with both her *and* Warner gone, they'll feel abandoned. They have no reason to trust the rest of you." A pause. "I'd say you have about twenty-four hours before they come for your heads."

Silence falls over the room. For a moment, I think everyone actually stops breathing.

"Fuck," Ian says, dropping his head in his hands.

"Immediate relocation is your best course of action," Nazeera says briskly, "but I don't know that I can be much help in that department. Where you go will be up to your discretion."

"Then what are you even doing here?" I say, irritated. I understand her a little better now—I know that she's been trying to help—but that doesn't change the fact that I still feel like shit. Or that I still don't know how to feel about her. "You showed up just to tell us we're all going to die and that's it?" I shake my head. "So helpful, thanks."

"Kenji," Castle says, finally breaking his silence. "There's no need to attack our guest." His voice is a calm, steadying sound. I've missed it. "She really did try to talk to me—to warn me—while she was here. As for a contingency plan," he says, speaking to the room, "give me a little time. I have friends. We're not alone, as you well know, in our resistance. There's no need to panic, not yet."

"Not yet?" Ian says, incredulous.

"Not yet," Castle says. Then: "Nazeera, what of your brother? Were you able to convince him?"

Nazeera takes a steadying breath, losing some of the tension in her shoulders. "Haider knows," she explains to the rest of us. "He's been remembering things about Ella, too, but his memories of her aren't as strong as mine, and he didn't understand what was happening to him until last night when I decided to tell him what I'd discovered."

"Whoa— Wait," Ian says. "You trust him?"

"I trust him enough," she says. "Besides, I figured he had a right to know; he knew Ella and Emmaline, too. But he wasn't entirely convinced. I don't know what he'll decide to do, not yet, but he definitely seemed shaken up about it, which I think is a good sign. I asked him to do some digging, to find out if any of the other kids were beginning to remember things, too, and he said he would. Right now, that's all I've got."

"Where *are* the other kids?" Winston asks, frowning. "Do they know you're still here?"

Nazeera's expression grows grim. "All the kids were supposed to report back as soon as the symposium was over. Haider should be on his way back to Asia by now. I tried to convince my parents I was staying behind to do more reconnaissance, but I don't think they bought it. I'm sure I'll hear from them soon. I'll handle it as it comes."

"So— Wait—" I glance from her to Castle. "You're staying with us?"

"That wasn't really my plan."

"Oh," I say. "Good. That's good."

She raises an eyebrow at me.

"You know what I mean."

"I don't think I do," she says, and she looks suddenly irritated. "Anyway, even though it *wasn't* my plan to stay, I think I might have to."

My eyes widen. "What? Why?"

"Because," she says, "my parents have been lying to me since I was a kid—stealing my memories and rewriting my history—and I want to know why. Besides"—she takes a deep breath—"I think I know where Ella and Warner are, and I want to help."

WARNER

"Goddammit."

I hear the barely restrained anger in my father's voice just before something slams, hard, into something else. He swears again.

I hesitate outside his door.

And then, impatiently—

"What do you want?"

His voice is practically a growl. I fight the impulse to be intimidated. I make my face a mask. Neutralize my emotions. And then, carefully, I step into his office.

My father is sitting at his desk, but I see only the back of his chair and the unfinished glass of Scotch clutched in his left hand. His papers are in disarray. I notice the paperweight on the floor; the damage to the wall.

Something has gone wrong.

"You wanted to see me," I say.

"What?" My father turns in his chair to face me. "See you for what?"

I say nothing. I've learned by now never to remind him when he's forgotten something.

Finally, he sighs. Says, "Right. Yes." And then: "We'll have to discuss it later."

"Later?" This time, I struggle to hide my feelings. "You said

you'd give me an answer today—"

"Something's come up."

Anger wells in my chest. I forget myself. "Something more important than your dying wife?"

My father won't be baited. Instead, he picks up a stack of papers on his desk and says, "Go away."

I don't move.

"I need to know what's going to happen," I say. "I don't want to go to the capital with you—I want to stay here, with Mom—"

"Jesus," he says, slamming his glass down on the desk. "Do you hear yourself?" He looks at me, disgusted. "This behavior is unhealthy. It's disturbing. I've never known a sixteen-year-old boy to be so obsessed with his mother."

Heat creeps up my neck, and I hate myself for it. Hate him for making me hate myself when I say, quietly, "I'm not obsessed with her."

Anderson shakes his head. "You're pathetic."

I take the emotional hit and bury it. With some effort, I manage to sound indifferent when I say, "I just want to know what's going to happen."

Anderson stands up, shoves his hands in his pockets. He looks out the massive window in his office, at the city just beyond.

The view is bleak.

Freeways have become open-air museums for the skeletons of forgotten vehicles. Mountains of trash form ranges along the terrain. Dead birds litter the streets, carcasses still occasionally falling out of the sky. Untamed fires rage in the distance, heavy winds stoking their flames. A thick layer of smog has permanently settled over the city, and the remaining clouds are gray, heavy with rain. We've already begun the process of regulating what passes for livable and unlivable turf, and entire sections of the city have since been shut down. Most of the coastal areas, for example, have been evacuated, the streets and homes flooded, roofs slowly collapsing.

By comparison, the inside of my father's office is a veritable paradise. Everything is still new in here; the wood still smells like wood, every surface shines. The Reestablishment was voted into power just four months ago, and my father is currently the commander and regent of one of our brand-new sectors.

Number 45.

A sudden gust of wind hits the window, and I feel the shudder reverberate through the room. The lights flicker. He doesn't flinch. The world may be falling apart, but The Reestablishment has been doing better than ever. Their plans fell into place more swiftly than they'd expected. And even though my father is already being considered for a huge promotion—to supreme commander of North America—no amount of success seems to soothe him. Lately, he's been more volatile than usual.

Finally, he says, "I have no idea what's going to happen. I don't even know if they'll be considering me for the promotion anymore."

I'm unable to mask my surprise. "Why not?"

Anderson smiles, unhappily, at the window. "A babysitting job gone awry."

"I don't understand."

"I don't expect you to."

"So—we're not moving anymore? We won't be going to the capital?"

Anderson turns back around. "Don't sound so excited. I said I don't know yet. First, I have to figure out how to deal with the problem."

Quietly, I say, "What's the problem?"

Anderson laughs; his eyes crinkle and he looks, for a moment, human. "Suffice it to say that your girlfriend is ruining my goddamn day. As usual."

"My what?" I frown. "Dad, Lena isn't my girlfriend. I don't care what she's telling any—"

"Different girlfriend," Anderson says, and sighs. He won't meet my eyes now. He snatches a file folder from his desk, flips it open, and scans the contents.

I don't have a chance to ask another question.

There's a sudden, sharp knock at the door. At my dad's signal, Delalieu steps inside. He seems more than a little surprised to see me, and, for a moment, says nothing.

"Well?" My dad seems impatient. "Is she here?"

"Y-yes, sir." Delalieu clears his throat. His eyes flit to me again. "Should I bring her up, or would you prefer to meet elsewhere?"

"Bring her up."

Delalieu hesitates. "Are you quite certain, sir?"

I look from my dad to Delalieu. Something is wrong.

My father meets my eyes when he says, "I said, bring her up."

Delalieu nods, and disappears.

My head is a stone, heavy and useless, my eyes cemented to my skull. I maintain consciousness for only seconds at a time. I smell metal, taste metal. An ancient, roaring noise grows loud, then soft, then loud again.

Boots, heavy, near my head.

Voices, but the sounds are muffled, light-years away. I can't move. I feel as though I've been buried, left to rot. A weak orange light flickers behind my eyes and for just a second—just a second—

No.

Nothing.

Days seem to pass. Centuries. I'm only aware enough to know I've been heavily sedated. Constantly sedated. I'm parched, dehydrated to the point of pain. I'd kill for water. Kill for it.

When they move me I feel heavy, foreign to myself. I land hard on a cold floor, the pain ricocheting up my body as if from a distance. I know that, too soon, this pain will catch up to me. Too soon, the sedative will wear off and I'll be alone with my bones and this dust in my mouth.

A swift, hard kick to the gut and my eyes fly open, blackness devouring my open, gasping mouth, seeping into the sockets of my eyes. I feel blind and suffocated at once, and when the shock finally subsides, my limbs give out. Limp.

The spark dies.

KENJI

"Do you want to tell me what the hell is going on?"

I stop, frozen in place, at the sound of Nazeera's voice. I was heading back to my room to close my eyes for a minute. To try to do something about the massive headache ringing through my skull.

We finally, finally, took a break.

A brief recess after hours of exhausting, stressful conversations about next steps and blueprints and something about stealing a plane. It's too much. Even Nazeera, with all her intel, couldn't give me any real assurance that Juliette—sorry, Ella—and Warner were still alive, and just the *chance* that someone out there might be torturing them to death is, like, more than my mind can handle right now. Today has been a shitstorm of shit. A tornado of shit. I can't take it anymore. I don't know whether to sit down and cry or set something on fire.

Castle said he'd brave his way down to the kitchens to see about scrounging up some food for us, and that was the best news I'd heard all day. He also said he'd do his best to placate the soldiers for just a little longer—just long enough for us to figure out exactly what we're going to do next—but I'm not sure how much he can do. It was bad enough when J got shot. The hours she spent in the medical wing were stressful for the rest of us, too. I really thought the soldiers would revolt right then. They kept stopping me in the halls, yelling about how they thought she was supposed to be *invincible,* that this wasn't the plan, that they didn't decide to risk their lives for a *regular* teenage girl who couldn't take a bullet and goddammit she was supposed to be some supernatural phenomenon, something more than human—

It took forever to calm them down.

But now?

I can only imagine how they'll react when they hear what happened at the symposium. It'll be mutiny, most likely.

I sigh, hard.

"So you're just going to ignore me?"

Nazeera is standing inches away from me. I can feel her, hovering. Waiting. I still haven't said anything. Still haven't turned around. It's not that I don't want to talk— I think I might, sort of, want to talk. Maybe some other day. But right now I'm out of gas. I'm out of James's jokes. I'm fresh out of fake smiles. Right now I'm nothing but pain and exhaustion and raw emotion, and I don't have the bandwidth for another serious conversation. I really don't want to do this right now.

I'd nearly made my escape, too. I'm right here, right in front of my door. My hand is on the handle.

I could just walk away, I think.

I could be that kind of guy, a Warner kind of guy. A

jackass kind of guy. Just walk away without a word. Too tired, no thank you, don't want to talk.

Leave me alone.

Instead, I slump forward, rest my hands and forehead against the closed bedroom door. "I'm tired, Nazeera."

"I can't believe you're upset with me."

My eyes close. My nose bumps against the wood. "I'm not upset with you. I'm half asleep."

"You were *mad*. You were mad at me for having the same ability as you. Weren't you?"

I groan.

"Weren't you?" she says again, this time angrily.

I say nothing.

"*Unbelievable.* That is the most petty, ridiculous, *immature—*"

"Yeah, well."

"Do you know how hard it was for me to tell you that? Do you have any idea—" I hear her sharp, angry huff. "Will you at least look at me when I'm talking to you?"

"Can't."

"What?" She sounds startled. "What do you mean you can't?"

"Can't look at you."

She hesitates. "Why not?"

"Too pretty."

She laughs, but angrily, like she might punch me in the face. "Kenji, I'm trying to be serious with you. This is important to me. This is the first time in my whole life I've ever shown other people what I can do. It's the first time I've ever interacted with other people like me. Besides," she says, "I thought we decided we were going to be friends. Maybe that's not a big deal to you, but it's a big deal to me, because I don't make friends easily. And right now you're making me doubt my own judgment."

I sigh so hard I nearly hurt myself.

I push off the door, stare at the wall. "Listen," I say, swallowing hard. "I'm sorry I hurt your feelings. I just— There was a minute back there, before you really started talking, when I thought you'd just, like, lied about things. I didn't understand what was happening. I thought maybe you'd set us up. A bunch of stuff seemed too crazy to be a coincidence. But we've been talking for hours now, and I don't feel that way anymore. I'm not mad anymore. I'm sorry. Can I go now?"

"Of course," she says. "I just . . ." She trails off, like she's confused, and then she touches my arm. No, she doesn't just touch my arm. She takes my arm. She wraps her hand around my bare forearm and tugs, gently.

The contact is hot and immediate. Her skin is soft. My brain feels dim. Dizzy.

"Stop," I say.

She drops her hand.

"Why won't you look at me?" she says.

"I already told you why I won't look at you, and you laughed at me."

She's quiet for so long I wonder if she's walked away.

Finally, she says, "I thought you were joking."

"Well, I wasn't."

More silence.

Then: "Do you always say exactly what you're thinking?"

"Most of the time, yeah." Gently, I bang my head against the door. I don't understand why this girl won't let me wallow in peace.

"What are you thinking right now?" she asks.

Jesus Christ.

I look up, at the ceiling, hoping for a wormhole or a bolt of lightning or maybe even an alien abduction—anything to get me out of here, this moment, this relentless, exhausting conversation.

In the absence of miracles, my frustration spikes.

"I'm thinking I want to go to sleep," I say angrily. "I'm thinking I want to be left alone. I'm thinking I've already told you this, a thousand times, and you won't let me go even though I apologized for hurting your feelings. So I guess what I'm really thinking is *I don't understand what you're doing here*. Why do you care so much about what I think?"

"What?" she says, startled. "I don't—"

Finally, I turn around. I feel a little unhinged, like my brain is flooded. There's too much happening. Too much to feel. Grief, fear, exhaustion. Desire.

Nazeera takes a step back when she sees my face.

She's perfect. Perfect everything. Long legs and curves. Her face is insane. Faces shouldn't look like that. Bright, honey-colored eyes and skin like dusk. Her hair is so brown it's nearly black. Thick, heavy, straight. She reminds me of something, of a feeling I don't even know how to describe. And there's something about her that's made me stupid. Drunk, like I could just stare at her and be happy, float forever in this feeling. And then I realize, with a start, that I'm staring at her mouth again.

I never mean to. It just happens.

She's always touching her mouth, tapping that damn diamond piercing under her lip, and I'm just dumb, my eyes following her every move. She's standing in front of me with her arms crossed, running her thumb absently against the edge of her bottom lip, and I can't stop staring. She startles, suddenly, when she realizes I'm looking. Drops her hands to her sides and blinks at me. I have no idea what she's thinking.

"I asked you a question," I say, but this time my voice comes out a little rough, a little too intense. I knew I should've kept my eyes on the wall.

Still, she only stares at me.

"All right. Forget it," I say. "You keep begging me to talk, but the minute I ask *you* a question, you say nothing. That's just great."

I turn away again, reach for the door handle.

And then, still facing the door, I say:

"You know—I'm aware that I haven't done a good job being smooth about this, and maybe I'll never be that kind of guy. But I don't think you should treat me like this, like I'm some idiot nothing, just because I don't know how to be a douchebag."

"What? Kenji, I don't—"

"*Stop,*" I say, jerking away from her. She keeps touching my arm, touching me like she doesn't even know she's doing it. It's driving me crazy. "Don't do that."

"Don't do what?"

Finally, angrily, I spin around. I'm breathing hard, my chest rising and falling too fast. "Stop messing with me," I say. "You don't know me. You don't know anything about me. You say you want to be my friend, but you talk to me like I'm an idiot. You touch me, constantly, like I'm a child, like you're trying to comfort me, like you have no idea that I'm a grown-ass man who might *feel* something when you put your hands on me like that." She tries to speak and I cut her off. "I don't care what you think you know about me—or how stupid you think I am—but right now I'm exhausted, okay? I'm done. So if you want nice Kenji maybe you should check back in the morning, because right now all I've got is jack shit in the way of pleasantries."

Nazeera looks frozen. Stunned. She stares at me, her lips slightly parted, and I'm thinking this is it, this is how I die, she's going to pull out a knife and cut me open, rearrange my organs, put on a puppet show with my intestines. What a way to go.

But when she finally speaks, she doesn't sound angry. She sounds a little out of breath.

Nervous.

"I don't think you're a child," she says.

I have no idea what to say to that.

She takes a step forward, presses her hands flat against my torso, and I turn into a statue. Her hands seem to sear into my body, heat pressing between us, even through my shirt.

I feel like I might be dreaming.

She runs her hands up my chest and that simple motion feels so good I'm suddenly terrified. I feel magnetized to her, frozen in place. Afraid to wake up.

"What are you doing?" I whisper.

She's still staring at my chest when she says, again, "I don't think you're a child."

"Nazeera."

She lifts her head to meet my eyes, and a flash of feeling, hot and painful, shoots down my spine.

"And I don't think you're stupid," she says.

Wrong.

I'm definitely stupid.

So stupid. I can't even think right now.

"Okay," I say stupidly. I don't know what to do with my hands. I mean, I *know* what to do with my hands, I'm just worried that if I touch her she might laugh and then, probably, kill me.

She smiles then, smiles so big I feel my heart explode, make a mess inside my chest. "So you're not going to make a move?" she says, still smiling. "I thought you liked me. I thought that's what this whole thing was all about."

"*Like* you?" I blink at her. "I don't even know you."

"Oh," she says, and her smile disappears. She begins to

pull away and she can't meet my eyes and then, I don't know what comes over me—

I grab her hand, open my bedroom door, and lock us both inside.

She kisses me first.

I have an out-of-body moment, like I can't believe this is actually happening to me. I can't understand what I did to make this possible, because according to my calculations I messed this up on a hundred different levels and, in fact, I was pretty sure she was pissed at me up until, like, five minutes ago.

And then I tell myself to shut up.

Her kiss is soft, her hands tentative against my chest, but I wrap my arms around her waist and kiss her, really kiss her, and then somehow we're against the wall and her hands are around my neck and she parts her lips for me, sighs in my mouth, and that small sound of pleasure drives me crazy, floods my body with heat and desire so intense I can hardly stand.

We break apart, breathing hard, and I stare at her like an idiot, my brain still too numb to figure out exactly how I got here. Then again, who cares how I got here. I kiss her again and it nearly kills me. She feels so good, so soft. Perfect. She's perfect, fits perfectly in my arms, like we were made for this, like we've done this a thousand times before, and she smells like shampoo, like something sweet. Perfume, maybe. I don't know. Whatever it is, it's in my head now. Killing brain cells.

When we break apart she looks different, her eyes darker, deeper. She turns away and when she turns back again she's smiling at me and for a second I think we might both be thinking the same thing. But I'm wrong, of course, so wrong, because I was thinking about how I'm, like, the luckiest guy on the planet and *she*—

She puts her hand on my chest and says, softly:

"You're really not my type."

That knocks the wind out of me. I drop my arms from around her waist and take a sudden, uncertain step backward.

She cringes, covers her face with both hands. "I don't— wow— I don't mean you're not my *type*." She shakes her head, hard. "I just mean I don't normally— I don't usually do this."

"Do what?" I say, still wounded.

"This," she says, and gestures between us. "I don't— I don't, like, just go around kissing guys I barely know."

"Okay." I frown. "Do you want to leave?"

"No." Her eyes widen.

"Then what do you want?"

"I don't know," she says, and her eyes go soft again. "I kind of just want to look at you for a minute. I meant what I said about your face," she says, and smiles. "You have a great face."

I go suddenly weak in the knees. I literally have to sit down. I walk over to my bed and collapse backward, my head hitting the pillow. It feels too good to be horizontal. If there weren't a gorgeous woman in my room right now, I'd be asleep already.

"Just so you know, this is not a move," I say, mostly to the ceiling. "I'm not trying to get you to sleep with me. I just literally had to lie down. Thank you for appreciating my face. I've always thought I had an underappreciated face."

She laughs, hard, and sits next to me, teetering on the edge of the bed, near my arm. "You're really not what I was expecting," she says.

I peer at her. "What were you expecting?"

"I don't know." She shakes her head. Smiles at me. "I guess I wasn't expecting to like you so much."

My chest goes tight. Too tight. I force myself to sit up, to meet her eyes.

"Come here," I say. "You're too far away."

She kicks off her boots and shifts closer, folding her legs up underneath her. She doesn't say a word. Just stares at me. And then, carefully, she touches my face, the line of my jaw. My eyes close, my mind swimming with nonsense. I lean back, rest my head against the wall behind us. I know it doesn't say much for my self-confidence that I'm so surprised this is happening, but I can't help it.

I never thought I'd get this lucky.

"Kenji," she says softly.

I open my eyes.

"I can't be your girlfriend."

I blink. Sit up a little. "Oh," I say.

It hadn't occurred to me until exactly this moment that I might even want something like that, but now that I'm thinking about it, I know that I do. A girlfriend is exactly what I want. I want a relationship. I want something real.

"It would never work, you know?" She tilts her head, looks at me like it's obvious, like I know as well as she does why things would never work out between us. "We're not—" She motions between our bodies to indicate something I don't understand. "We're so different, right? Plus, I don't even live here."

"Right," I say, but my mouth feels suddenly numb. My whole face feels numb. "You don't even live here."

And then, just as I'm trying to figure out how to pick up the pieces of my obliterated hopes and dreams, she climbs into my lap. Zero to sixty. My body malfunctions. Overheats.

She presses her face into my cheek and kisses me, softly, just underneath my jaw, and I feel myself melt into the wall, into the air.

I don't understand what's happening anymore. She likes me but she doesn't want to be with me. She's not going to be with me but she's going to sit on my lap and kiss me into oblivion.

Sure. Okay.

I let her touch me the way she wants to, let her put her hands on my body and kiss me wherever, however she wants. She touches me in a proprietary way, like I already belong to her, and I don't mind. I kind of love it. And I let her take the lead for as long as I can bear it. She's pulling up my shirt, running her hands across my bare skin and telling me how much she likes my body, and I really feel like—like I can't breathe. I feel too hot. Delirious but sharp, aware of this moment in an almost primal way.

She helps me pull off my shirt and then she just looks at me, first at my face and then at my chest, and she runs her hands across my shoulders, down my arms. "Wow," she says softly. "You're so gorgeous."

That's it for me.

I pick her up off my lap and lay her down, on her back, and she gasps, stares at me like she's surprised. And then, *deep*, her eyes go deep and dark, and she's looking at my mouth but I decide to kiss her neck, the curve of her shoulder.

"Nazeera," I whisper, hardly recognizing the sound of my own voice. "I want you so badly it might kill me."

Suddenly, someone is banging on my door.

"Bro, where the hell did you go?" Ian shouts. "Castle brought dinner up like ten minutes ago."

I sit up too fast. I nearly pull a muscle. Nazeera laughs out loud, and even though she claps a hand over her mouth to muffle the sound, she's not quick enough.

"Uh— Hello?" Ian again. "Kenji?"

"I'll be right there," I shout back.

I hear him hesitate—his footsteps uncertain—and then he's gone. I drop my head into my hands. Suddenly, everything comes rushing back to me. For a few minutes this moment with Nazeera felt like the whole world, a welcome reprieve from all the war and death and struggle. But now, with a little oxygen in my brain, I feel stupid. I don't know what I was thinking.

Juliette might be *dead*.

I get to my feet. I pull my shirt on quickly, careful not to meet her eyes. For some reason, I can't bring myself to look at Nazeera. I have no regrets about kissing her—it's just that I also feel suddenly guilty, like I was doing something wrong. Something selfish and inappropriate.

"I'm sorry," I say. "I don't know what got into me."

Nazeera is tugging on her boots. She looks up, surprised. "What do you mean?"

"What we just"—I sigh, hard—"I don't know. I forgot, for a moment, everything we have to do. The fact that Juliette might be out there, somewhere, being tortured to death. Warner might be dead. We'll have to pack up and run, leave this place behind. God, there's so much happening and I just— My head was in the wrong place. I'm sorry."

Nazeera is standing up now. She looks upset. "Why do you keep apologizing to me? Stop apologizing to me."

"You're right. I'm sorry." I wince. "I mean— You know what I mean. Anyway, we should go."

"Kenji—"

"Listen, you said you didn't want a relationship, right? You didn't want to be my girlfriend? You don't think that this"—I mimic what she did earlier, motioning between us—"could ever work? Well, then—" I take a breath. Run a hand through my hair. "This is what not being my girlfriend looks like. Okay? There are only a few people in my life who actually care about me, and right now my best friend is probably being murdered by a bunch of psychopaths, and I should be out there, doing something."

"I didn't realize you and Warner were so close," she says quietly.

"What?" I frown. "No, I'm talking about Juliette," I say. "Ella. Whatever."

Nazeera's eyebrows go high.

"Anyway, I'm sorry. We should probably just keep this professional, right? You're not looking for anything serious, and I don't know how to have casual relationships anyway. I always end up caring too much, to be honest, so this probably wasn't a good idea."

"Oh."

"Right?" I look at her, hoping, suddenly, that there was something I missed, something more than the cool distance in her eyes. "Didn't you just tell me that we're too different? That you don't even live here?"

She turns away. "Yes."

"And have you changed your mind in the last thirty seconds? About being my girlfriend?"

She's still staring at the wall when she says, "No."

Pain shoots up my spine, gathers in my chest. "Okay then," I say, and nod. "Thanks for your honesty. I have to go."

She cuts past me, walks out the door. "I'm coming, too."

JULIETTE

I've been sitting in the back of a police car for over an hour. I haven't been able to cry, not yet. And I don't know what I'm waiting for, but I know what I did, and I'm pretty sure I know what happens next.

I killed a little boy.

I don't know how I did it. I don't know why it happened. I just know that it was me, my hands, me. I did that. Me.

I wonder if my parents will show up.

Instead, three men in military uniforms march up to my window. One of them flings open the door and aims a machine gun at my chest.

"Get out," he barks. "Out with your hands up."

My heart is racing, terror propelling me out of the car so fast I stumble, slamming my knee into the ground. I don't need to check to know that I'm bleeding; the pain of the fresh wound is already searing. I bite my lip to keep from crying out, force the tears back.

No one helps me up.

I want to tell them that I'm only fourteen, that I don't know a lot about a lot of things, but that I know enough. I've watched TV shows about this sort of thing. I know they can't charge me as an adult. I know that they shouldn't be treating me like this.

But then I remember that the world is different now. We have a new government now, one that doesn't care how we used to do things. Maybe none of that matters anymore.

My heart beats faster.

I'm shoved into the backseat of a black car, and before I know it, I'm deposited somewhere new: somewhere that looks like an ordinary office building. It's tall. Steel gray. It seems old and decrepit—some of its windows are cracked—and the whole thing looks sad.

But when I walk inside I'm stunned to discover a blinding, gleaming interior. I look around, taking in the marble floors, the rich carpets and furnishings. The ceilings are high, the architecture modern but elegant. It's all glass and marble and stainless steel.

I've never been anywhere so beautiful.

And I haven't even had a moment to take it all in before I'm greeted by a thin, older man with even thinner brown hair.

The soldiers flanking me step back as he steps forward.

"Ms. Ferrars?" he says.

"Yes?"

"You are to come with me."

I hesitate. "Who are you?"

He studies me a moment and then seems to make a decision. "You may call me Delalieu."

"Okay," I say, the word disappearing into a whisper.

I follow Delalieu into a glass elevator and watch him use a key card to authorize the lift. Once we're in motion, I find the courage to speak.

"Where am I?" I ask. "What's happening?"

His answer comes automatically. "You are in Sector 45 headquarters. You're here to have a meeting with the chief commander and regent of Sector 45." He doesn't look at me when he speaks, but there's nothing in his tone that feels threatening. So I ask another question.

"Why?"

The elevator doors ping as they open. Delalieu finally turns to look at me. "You'll find out in just a moment."

I follow Delalieu down a hall and wait, quietly, outside a door while he knocks. He peeks his head inside when the door opens, announces his presence, and then motions for me to follow him in.

When I do, I'm surprised.

There's a beautiful man in military uniform—I'm assuming he's the commander—standing in front of a large, wooden desk, his arms crossed against his chest. He's staring me straight in the eye, and I'm suddenly so overwhelmed I feel myself blush.

I've never seen anyone so handsome before.

I look down, embarrassed, and study the laces of my tennis shoes. I'm grateful for my long hair. It serves as a dark, heavy curtain, shielding my face from view.

"Look at me."

The command is sharp and clear. I look up, nervously, to meet his eyes. He has thick, dark brown hair. Eyes like a storm. He looks at me for so long I feel goose bumps rise along my skin. He won't look away, and I feel more terrified by the moment. This man's eyes are full of anger. Darkness. There's something genuinely frightening about him, and my heart begins to hammer.

"You're growing up quickly," he says.

I stare at him, confused, but he's still studying my face.

"Fourteen years old," he says quietly. "Such a complicated age for a young girl." Finally, he sighs. Looks away. "It always breaks

my heart to break beautiful things."

"I don't— I don't understand," I say, feeling suddenly ill.

He looks up again. "You're aware of what you did today?"

I freeze. Words pile up in my throat, die in my mouth.

"Yes or no?" he demands.

"Y-yes," I say quickly. "Yes."

"And do you know why you did it? Do you know how you did it?"

I shake my head, my eyes filling fast with tears. "It was an accident," I whisper. "I didn't know— I didn't know that this—"

"Does anyone else know about your sickness?"

"No." I stare at him, my eyes wide even as tears blur my vision. "I mean, n-not, not really—just my parents—but no one really understands what's wrong with me. I don't even understand—"

"You mean you didn't plan this? It wasn't your intention to murder the little boy?"

"No!" I cry out, and then clap both hands over my mouth. "No," I say, quietly now. "I was trying to help him. He'd fallen to the floor and I— I didn't know. I swear I didn't know."

"Liar."

I'm still shaking my head, wiping away tears with shaking hands. "It was an accident. I swear, I didn't mean to—I d-didn't—"

"Sir." It's Delalieu. His voice.

I didn't realize he was still in the room.

I sniff, hard, wiping quickly at my face, but my hands are still shaking. I try, again, to swallow back the tears. To pull myself together.

"Sir," Delalieu says more firmly, "perhaps we should conduct this interview elsewhere."

"I don't see why that's necessary."

"I don't mean to seem impertinent, sir, but I really feel that you might be better served conducting this interview privately."

I dare to turn, to look up at him. And that's when I notice the third person in the room.

A boy.

My breath catches in my throat with an almost audible gasp. A single tear escapes down my cheek and I brush it away, even as I stare at him. I can't help it—I can't look away. He has the kind of face I've never seen in real life. He's more handsome than the commander. More beautiful. Still, there's something unnerving about him, something cold and alien about his face that makes him difficult to look at. He's almost too perfect. He has a sharp jawline and sharp cheekbones and a sharp, straight nose. Everything about him reminds me of a blade. His face is pale. His eyes are a stunning, clear green, and he has rich, golden hair. And he's staring at me, his eyes wide with an emotion I can't decipher.

A throat clears.

The spell is broken.

Heat floods my face and I avert my eyes, mortified I didn't look away sooner.

I hear the commander mutter angrily under his breath. "Unbelievable," he says. "Always the same."

I look up.

"Aaron," he says sharply. "Get out."

The boy—his name must be Aaron—startles. He stares at the commander for a second, and then glances at the door. But he doesn't move.

"Delalieu, please escort my son from the room, as he seems presently unable to remember how to move his legs."

His son.

Wow. That explains the face.

"Yes, sir, of course, sir."

Aaron's expression is impossible to read. I catch him looking at me, just once more, and when he finds me staring, he frowns. It's not an unkind look.

Still, I turn away.

He and Delalieu move past me as they exit, and I pretend not to notice when I hear him whisper—

"Who is she?"

—as they walk away.

"Ella? Are you all right?"

I blink, slowly clearing the webbing of blackness obscuring my vision. Stars explode and fade behind my eyes and I try to stand, the carpet pressing popcorn impressions into my palms, metal digging into my flesh. I'm wearing manacles, glowing cuffs that emit a soft, blue light that leaches the life from my skin, makes my own hands seem sinister.

The woman at my door is staring at me. She smiles.

"Your father and I thought you might be hungry," she says. "We made you dinner."

I can't move. My feet seem bolted in place, the pinks and purples of the walls and floors assaulting me from every corner. I'm standing in the middle of the bizarre museum of what was likely my childhood bedroom—staring at what might be my biological mother—and I feel like I might throw up. The lights are suddenly too bright, the voices too loud. Someone walks toward me and the movement feels exaggerated, the footsteps thudding hard and fast in my ears. My vision goes in and out and the walls seem to shake. The floor shifts, tilts backward.

I fall, hard, onto the floor.

For a minute, I hear nothing but my heartbeat. Loud, so loud, pressing in on me, assaulting me with a cacophony of sound so disturbing I double over, press my face into the carpet and scream.

I'm hysterical, my bones shaking in my skin, and the woman picks me up, reels me in, and I tear away, still screaming—

"Where is everyone?" I scream. "What's happening to me?" I scream. "Where am I? Where's Warner and Kenji and oh my God—*oh my God*—all those people—all those people I k-killed—"

Vomit inches up my throat, choking me, and I try and fail to suppress the images, the horrible, terrifying images of bodies cleaved open, blood snaking down ridges of poorly torn flesh and something pierces my mind, something sharp and blinding and suddenly I'm on my knees, heaving the meager contents of my stomach into a pink basket.

I can hardly breathe.

My lungs are overworked, my stomach still threatening to betray me, and I'm gasping, my hands shaking hard as I try to stand. I spin around, the room moving more quickly than I do, and I see only flashes of pink, flashes of purple.

I sway.

Someone catches me again, this time new arms, and the man who calls me his daughter holds me like I'm his child and he says, "Honey, you don't have to think about them anymore. You're safe now."

"Safe?" I rear back, eyes wild. "Who *are* you—?"

The woman takes my hand. Squeezes my fingers even as I wrench free from her grip. "I'm your mother," she says. "And I've decided it's time for you to come home."

"What"—I grab two fistfuls of her shirt—"have you done *with my friends*?" I scream. And then I shake her, shake her so hard she actually looks scared for a second, and then I try to pick her up and throw her into the wall but remember, with a start, that my powers have been cut off, that I have to rely on mere anger and adrenaline and I turn around, suddenly furious, feeling more certain by the second that I've begun to hallucinate, hallucinate, when

unexpectedly

she slaps me in the face.

Hard.

I blink, stunned, but manage to stay upright.

"Ella Sommers," she says sharply, "you will pull yourself together." Her eyes flash as she appraises me. "What is this ridiculous, dramatic behavior? Worried about your *friends*? Those people are not your friends."

My cheek burns and half my mouth feels numb but I say, "Yes, yes they're my fr—"

She slaps me again.

My eyes close. Reopen. I feel suddenly dizzy.

"We are your parents," she says in a harsh whisper. "Your father and I have brought you home. You should be grateful."

I taste blood. I reach up, touch my lip. My fingers come away red. "Where's Emmaline?" Blood is pooling in my mouth and I spit it out, onto the floor. "Have you kidnapped her, too? Does she know what you've done? That you donated us to The Reestablishment? Sold our bodies to the world?"

A third, swift slap.

I feel it ring in my skull.

"How dare you." My mother's face flushes crimson. "How *dare* you— You have no idea what we've built, all these years— The sacrifices we made for our *future*—"

"Now, Evie," my dad says, and places a calming hand on her shoulder. "Everything is going to be okay. Ella just needs a little time to settle in, that's all." He glances at me. "Isn't that right, Ella?"

It hits me then, in that moment. Everything. It hits me, all at once, with a frightening, destabilizing force—

I've been kidnapped by a pair of crazy people and I might never see my friends again. In fact, my friends might be dead. My *parents* might've killed them. All of them.

The realization is like suffocation.

Tears fill my throat, my mouth, my eyes—

"Where," I say, my chest heaving, "is Warner? What did you do to him?"

Evie's expression goes suddenly murderous. "You and

that damn boy. If I have to hear his name one more time—"

"*Where's Warner?*" I'm screaming again. "Where is he? Where's Kenji? What did you do with them?"

Evie looks suddenly exhausted. She pinches the bridge of her nose between her thumb and index finger.

"Darling," she says, but she isn't looking at me, she's looking at my father. "Will you handle this, please? I have a terrible headache and several urgent phone calls to return."

"Of course, my love." And he pulls a syringe from his pocket and stabs it, swiftly, into my neck.

KENJI

The common room is really growing on me.

I used to walk by, all the time, and wonder why Warner ever thought we'd need a common room this big. There's tons of seating and a lot of room to spread out, but I always thought it was a waste of space. I secretly wished Warner had used the square footage for our bedrooms.

Now I get it.

When Nazeera and I walk in, ten minutes late to the impromptu pizza party, everyone is here. *Brendan* is here. He's sitting in a corner being fussed over by Castle and Alia, and I nearly tackle him. I don't, of course, because it's obvious he's still in recovery, but I'm relieved to find that he looks okay. Mostly he looks wrung-out, but he's not wearing a sling or anything, so I'm guessing the girls didn't run into any problems when they were patching him up. That's a great sign.

I spot Winston walking across the room and I catch up to him, clap him on the back. "Hey," I say, when he turns around. "You okay?"

He's balancing a couple of paper plates, both of which are already sagging under the weight of too much pizza, and he smiles with his whole face when he says, "I hate today.

Today is a garbage fire. I hate everything about today except for the fact that Brendan is okay and we have pizza. Other than that, today can go straight to hell."

"Yeah. I feel that so much." And then, after a pause, I say quietly: "So I'm guessing you never had that conversation with Brendan, huh?"

Winston goes suddenly pink. "I said I was waiting for the right time. Does this seem like the right time to you?"

"Good point." I sigh. "I guess I was just hoping you had some good news. We could all use some good news right now."

Winston shoots me a sympathetic look. "No word on Juliette?"

I shake my head. Feel suddenly sick. "Has anyone told you her real name is Ella?"

"I heard," Winston says, raising his eyebrows. "That whole story is batshit."

"Yeah," I say. "Today is the worst."

"Fuck today," Winston says.

"Don't forget about tomorrow," I say. "Tomorrow's going to suck, too."

"What? Why?" The paper plates in Winston's hands are going translucent from pizza grease. "What's happening tomorrow?"

"Last I heard we were jumping ship," I say. "Running for our lives. I'm assuming it's going to suck."

"*Shit*." Winston nearly drops his plates. "Seriously? Brendan needs more time to rest." Then, after a beat: "Where are we going to go?"

"The other side of the continent, apparently," Ian says as he walks over.

He hands me a plate of pizza. I murmur a quick thanks and stare at the pizza, wondering whether I'd be able to shove the whole thing in my mouth at once. Probably not.

"Do you know something we don't?" Winston says to Ian, his glasses slipping down the bridge of his nose. Winston tries, unsuccessfully, to shove them back up with his forearm, and Ian steps up to do it for him.

"I know a lot of things you don't know," Ian says. "The first of which is that Kenji was definitely hooking up with Nazeera, like, five seconds ago."

My mouth nearly falls open before I remember there's food in it. I swallow, too quickly, and choke. I'm still coughing as I look around, panicking that Nazeera might be within earshot. Only when I spot her across the room speaking with Sonya and Sara do I finally relax.

I glare at Ian. "What the hell is wrong with you?"

Winston, at least, has the decency to whisper-yell when he says, "You were hooking up with Nazeera? We were only gone a few hours!"

"I did not hook up with Nazeera," I lie.

Ian takes a bite of pizza. "Whatever, bro. No judgment. The world's on fire. Have some fun."

"We didn't"—I sigh, look away—"it wasn't like that. It's not even anything. We were just, like—" I make some random gesture with my hand that means exactly nothing.

Ian raises his eyebrows.

"Okay," Winston says, shooting me a look. "We'll talk

about the Nazeera thing later." He turns to Ian. "What's happening tomorrow?"

"We bail," Ian says. "Be ready to go at dawn."

"Right, I heard that part," Winston says, "but where are we going?"

Ian shrugs. "Castle has the news," he says. "That's all I heard. He was waiting for Kenji and Nazeera to put their clothes back on before he told everyone the details."

I tilt my head at Ian, threatening him with a single look. "Nothing is going on with me and Nazeera," I say. "Drop it."

"All right," he says, picking at his pizza. "Makes sense. I mean she's not even that pretty."

My plate falls out of my hand. Pizza hits the floor. I feel a sudden, unwelcome need to punch Ian in the face. "Are you— Are you out of your mind? Not even— She's, like, the most beautiful woman I've ever seen in my *life*, and you're out here saying she's *not even that pretty*? Have y—"

"See what I'm saying?" Ian cuts me off. He's looking at Winston.

"Wow," Winston says, staring solemnly at the pizza on the ground. "Yeah, Kenji is definitely full of shit."

I drag a hand across my face. "I hate you guys."

"Anyway," Ian says, "I heard Castle's news has something to do with Nouria."

My head snaps back up.

Nouria.

I nearly forgot. This morning, just before the symposium, the twins told me they'd uncovered something—something to do with the poison in the bullets Juliette had been shot with—that led them back to Nouria.

But so much happened today that I never had the chance to follow up. Find out what happened.

"Did you hear about that?" Ian asks me, raising an eyebrow. "She sent a message, apparently. That's what the girls are saying."

"Yeah," I say, and frown. "I heard."

I honestly have no idea how this might shake out.

It's been at least ten years since the last time Castle saw his daughter, Nouria. Darrence and Jabari, his two boys, were murdered by police officers when they refused to let the men into their house without a warrant. This was before The Reestablishment took over.

Castle wasn't home that day, but Nouria was.

She watched it happen. Castle said he felt like he'd lost three children that day. Nouria never recovered. Instead, she grew detached. Listless. She stopped coming home at normal hours and then—one day—she disappeared. The Reestablishment was always picking kids up off the street and shipping them wherever they felt there was a need to fill. Nouria was collected against her will; picked up and packaged for another sector. Castle knew for certain that it happened, because The Reestablishment sent him a receipt for his child. A fucking receipt.

Everyone from Point knew Castle's story. He always made an effort to be honest, to share the hardest, most painful memories from his life so that the rest of us didn't feel like we were suffering alone.

Castle thought he'd never see Nouria again.

So if she's reaching out now—

Just then, Castle catches my eye. He glances at me, then at Nazeera. A hint of a smile touches his lips and then it's gone, his spine straight as he addresses the room. He looks good, I realize. He looks bright, alive like I haven't seen him in years. His locs are pulled back, tied neatly at the base of his neck. His faded blue blazer still fits him perfectly, even after all these years.

"I have news," he says.

But I'm pretty sure I know what's coming next.

Nouria lives in Sector 241, thousands of miles away, and cross-sector communication is nearly unheard of. Only rebel groups are brave enough to risk sending coded messages across the continent. Ian and Winston know this. I know this.

Everyone knows this.

Which means Castle is probably here to tell us that Nouria has gone rogue.

Ha.

Like father, like daughter.

WARNER

"Hi," I say.

She turns at the sound of my voice and startles when she sees my face. Her eyes widen. And I feel it, right away, when her emotions change.

She's attracted to me.

She's attracted to me, and the revelation makes me happy. I don't know why. It's not new. I learned, long ago, that lots of people find me attractive. Men. Women. Especially older women, a phenomenon I still don't understand. But this—

It makes me happy. She finds me attractive.

"Hi," she says, but she won't look at me.

I realize she's blushing. I'm surprised. There's something sweet about her, something gentle and sweet I wasn't really expecting.

"Are you doing all right?" I ask.

It's a stupid question. The girl is clearly in an awful position. Right now she's only in our custody for as long as it takes my father to decide what to do with her. She's currently in a fairly comfortable holding facility here on base, but she'll likely end up in a juvenile detention center. I'm not sure. I've heard my father talk about running more tests on her first. Her parents are apparently hysterical, desperate for us to take her in and deal with her. Offer a diagnosis. They think she killed the little boy on purpose. They think their daughter is insane.

I think she seems just fine.

Better than fine.

I can't stop looking at her. My eyes travel her face more than once, studying her features carefully. She seems so familiar to me, like I might've seen her before. Maybe in a dream.

I'm aware, even as I think it, that my thoughts are ridiculous.

But I was drawn down here, magnetized to her by something beyond my control. I know I shouldn't have come. I have no business talking to her, and if my father found me in here he'd likely murder me. But I've tried, for days, to forget her face, and I couldn't. I try to sleep at night and her likeness materializes in the blackness. I needed to see her again.

I don't know how to defend it.

Finally, she speaks, and I shake free from my reverie. I remind myself that I've asked her a question.

"Yes, thank you," she says, her eyes on the floor. "I'm doing fine."

She's lying.

I want her to look up, to meet my eyes. She doesn't, and I find it frustrating.

"Will you look at me?" I say.

That works well enough.

But when she looks me directly in the eye I feel my heart go suddenly, terrifyingly still. A skipped beat. A moment of death.

And then—

Fast. My heart is racing too fast.

I've never understood my ability to be so aware of others, but it's often served me well. In most cases, it offers me an advantage. In this case, it's nothing short of overwhelming.

Right now, everything is hitting me twice as hard. I feel two sets of emotions—hers and mine, the both of them intertwined. We seem to be feeling the same things at the same time. It's disorienting, so heady I can hardly catch my breath. I feel a surprising desire to touch her. I want—

"Why?" she says.

I blink. "What?"

"Why do you want me to look at you?"

I take a breath. Clear my head, consider my options. I could tell the truth. I could tell a lie. I could be evasive, change the subject.

Finally, I say, "Do I know you?"

She laughs and looks away. "No," she says. "Definitely not."

She bites her lip and I feel her sudden nervousness, hear the spike in her breathing. I draw closer to her almost without realizing it.

She looks up at me then, and I realize, with a thrill, how close we are. There's a palpable heat between our bodies, and her eyes are big and beautiful, blue green. Like the globe, I think. Like the whole world.

She's looking at me and I feel suddenly off-balance.

"What's wrong?" she says.

I have to step away from her. "I don't—" I look at her again. "Are you sure I don't know you?"

And she smiles. Smiles at me and my heart shatters.

"Trust me," she says. "I'd remember you."

KENJI

Delalieu.

I can't believe we forgot about Delalieu.

I thought Castle's news would be about Nouria. I thought he was going to tell us that she reached out to say that she was some fancy resistance leader now, that we'd be welcome to crash at her place for a while. Instead, Castle's news was—

Delalieu.

Homeboy came through.

Castle steps aside and allows the lieutenant to enter the room, and even though he seems stiff and out of place, Delalieu looks genuinely upset. I feel it, like a punch to the gut, the moment I see his face. *Grief.*

He clears his throat two or three times.

When he finally speaks, his voice is steadier than I've ever heard it. "I've come to reassure you," he says, "in person, that I'll make sure your group remains safe here, for as long as I can manage." A pause. "I don't know yet exactly what's happening right now, but I know it can't be good. I'm worried it won't end well if you stay, and I'm committed to helping you while you plan your escape."

Everyone is quiet.

"Um, thank you," I say, breaking the silence. I look around the room when I say, "We really appreciate that. But, uh, how much time do we have?"

Delalieu shakes his head. "I'm afraid I can't guarantee your safety for more than a week. But I'm hoping a few days' reprieve will give you the necessary time to figure out your next steps. Find a safe place to go. In the meantime, I'll provide whatever assistance I can."

"Okay," Ian says, but he looks skeptical. "That's really . . . generous."

Delalieu clears his throat again. "It must be hard to know whether you should trust me. I understand your concerns. But I fear I've stayed silent for t-too long," he says, his voice losing its steadiness. "And now—with— With what's happened to Warner and to Ms. Ferrars—" He stops, his voice breaking on the last word. He looks up, looks me in the eye. "I'm sure Warner told none of you that I am his grandfather."

My jaw drops open. Actually drops open.

Castle is the only person in the room who doesn't look shocked.

"You're Warner's grandfather?" Adam says, getting to his feet. The terrified look in his eyes breaks my heart.

"Yes," Delalieu says quietly. "On his mother's side." He meets Adam's eyes, acknowledging, silently, that he knows. Knows that Adam is Anderson's illegitimate son. That he knows everything.

Adam sits back down, relief apparent on his face.

“I can only imagine what an unhappy life yours must’ve been,” Brendan says. I turn to look at him, surprised to hear his voice. He’s been so quiet all this time. But then, of course Brendan would be compassionate. Even to someone like Delalieu, who stepped aside and said nothing while Anderson set the world on fire. “But I’m grateful—we’re all grateful,” Brendan says, “for your help today.”

Delalieu manages a smile. “It’s the least I can do,” he says, and turns to go.

“Did you know her?” Lily says, her voice sharp. “As Ella?”

Delalieu freezes in place, still half turned toward the exit.

“Because if you’re Warner’s grandfather,” Lily says, “and you’ve been working under Anderson for this long—you must’ve known her.”

Slowly, very slowly, Delalieu turns to face us. He seems tense, nervous like I’ve never seen him. He says nothing, but the answer is written all over his face. The twitch in his hands.

Jesus.

“How long?” I say, anger building inside of me. “How long did you know her and say nothing?”

“I don’t— I d-don’t—”

“How long?” I say, my hand already reaching for the gun tucked in the waistband of my pants.

Delalieu takes a jerky step backward. “Please don’t,” he says, his eyes wild. “Please don’t ask this of me. I can give you aid. I can provide you with weapons and transportation—anything you need—but I can't— You don't underst—"

"Coward," Nazeera says, standing up. She looks stunning, tall and strong and steady. I love watching that girl move. Talk. Breathe. Whatever. "You watched and said nothing as Anderson tortured his own children. Didn't you?"

"No," Delalieu says desperately, his face flushing with emotion I've never seen in him before. "No, that's not—"

Castle picks up a chair with single flick of his hand and drops it, unceremoniously, in front of Delalieu.

"Sit down," he says, a violent, unguarded rage flashing in his eyes.

Delalieu obeys.

"How long?" I say again. "How long have you known her as Ella?"

"I— I've"—Delalieu hesitates, looks around—"I've known Ella s-since she was a child," he says finally.

I feel the blood leave my body.

His clear, explicit confession is too much. It means too much. I sag under the weight of it—the lies, the conspiracies. I sink back into my chair and my heart splinters for Juliette, for all she's suffered at the hands of the people meant to protect her. I can't form the words I need to tell Delalieu he's a spineless piece of shit. It's Nazeera who still has the presence of mind to spear him.

Her voice is soft—lethal—when she speaks.

"You've known Ella since she was a child," Nazeera says. "You've been here, working here, helping Anderson since

Ella was a *child*. That means you helped Anderson put her in the custody of abusive, adoptive parents and you stood by as they tortured her, as Anderson tortured her, over and over—"

"No," Delalieu cries out. "I d-didn't condone any of that. Ella was supposed to grow up in a normal home environment. She was supposed to be given nurturing parents and a stable upbringing. Those were the terms everyone agreed t—"

"Bullshit," Nazeera says, her eyes flashing. "You know as well as I do that her adoptive parents were monsters—"

"Paris changed the terms of the agreement," Delalieu shouts angrily.

Nazeera raises an eyebrow, unmoved.

But something seems to have loosened Delalieu's tongue, something like fear or guilt or pent-up rage, because suddenly the words rush out of him.

"Paris went back on his word as soon as Ella was in his custody," he says. "He thought no one would find out. Back then he and I were about the same, as far as rank went, in The Reestablishment. We often worked closely together because of our family ties, and I was, as a result, privy to the choices he made."

Delalieu shakes his head.

"But I discovered too late that he purposely chose adoptive parents who exhibited abusive, dangerous behavior. When I confronted him about it he argued that any abuse Ella suffered at the hands of her surrogate parents would only encourage her powers to manifest, and he had the statistics to support his claim. I tried to voice my concerns—I reported him; I told the council of commanders that he was hurting her, *breaking* her—but he made my concerns sound like the desperate histrionics of someone unwilling to do what was necessary for the cause."

I can see the color creeping up Delalieu's neck, his anger only barely contained.

"I was repeatedly overruled. Demoted. I was punished for questioning his tactics.

"But I knew Paris was wrong," he says quietly. "Ella withered. When I first met her she was a strong girl with a joyful spirit. She was unfailingly kind and upbeat." He hesitates. "It wasn't long before she grew cold and closed-off. Withdrawn. Paris moved up in rank quickly, and I was soon relegated to little more than his right hand. I was the one he sent to check on her at home, at school. I was ordered to monitor her behavior, write the reports outlining her progress.

"But there were no results. Her spirit had been broken. I begged Paris to put her elsewhere—to, at the very least, return her to a regular facility, one that I might oversee personally—and still he insisted, over and over again, that the abuse she suffered would spur results." Delalieu is on his feet now, pacing. "He was hoping to impress the council, hoping his efforts would be rewarded with yet another promotion. It soon became his single task to wait, to have me watch Ella closely for developments, for any sign that she'd changed. Evolved." He stops in place. Swallows, hard. "But Paris was careless."

Delalieu drops his head into his hands.

The room around us has gone so quiet I can almost hear the seconds pass. We're all waiting for him to keep going, but he doesn't lift his head. I'm studying him—his shaking hands, the tremble in his legs, his general loss of composure—and my heart hammers in my chest. I feel like he's about to break. Like he's close to telling us something important.

"What do you mean?" I say quietly. "Careless how?"

Delalieu looks up, his eyes red-rimmed and wild.

"I mean *it was his one job,*" he says, slamming his fist against the wall. He hits it, hard, his knuckles breaking through the plaster, and for a moment, I'm genuinely stunned. I didn't think Delalieu had it in him.

"You don't understand," he says, losing the fire. He stumbles back, sags against the wall. "My greatest regret in life has been watching those kids suffer and doing nothing about it."

"Wait," Winston says. "Which kids? Who are you talking about?"

But Delalieu doesn't seem to hear him. He only shakes his head. "Paris never took Ella's assignment seriously. It was his fault she lost control. It was his fault she didn't know better, it was his fault she hadn't been prepared or trained or properly guarded. It was his fault she killed that little boy," he says, now so broken his voice is shaking. "What she did that day nearly destroyed her. Nearly ruined the entire operation. Nearly exposed us to the world."

He closes his eyes, presses his fingers to his temples. And then he sinks back down into his chair. He looks unmoored.

Castle and I share a knowing glance from across the room. Something is happening. Something is about to happen.

Delalieu is a resource we never realized we had. And for all his protests, he actually seems like he wants to talk. Maybe Delalieu is the key. Maybe he can tell us what we need to know about—about everything. About Juliette, about Anderson, about The Reestablishment. It's obvious a dam broke open in Delalieu. I'm just hoping we can keep him talking.

It's Adam who says, "If you hated Anderson so much, why didn't you stop him when you had the chance?"

"Don't you understand?" Delalieu says, his eyes big and round and sad. "I *never* had the chance. I didn't have the authority, and we'd only just been voted into power. Leila—my daughter—was sicker every day and I was— I wasn't myself. I was unraveling. I suspected foul play in her illness but had no proof. I spent my work hours overseeing the crumbling mental and physical health of an innocent young woman, and I spent my free hours watching my daughter die."

"Those are excuses," Nazeera says coldly. "You were a coward."

He looks up. "Yes," he says. "That's true. I was a coward." He shakes his head, turns away. "I said nothing, even when Paris spun Ella's tragedy into a victory. He told everyone that what Ella did to that boy was a blessing in disguise. That, in fact, it was exactly what he'd been working toward. He argued that what she did that day, regardless of the consequences, was the exact manifestation of her powers he'd been hoping for all along." Delalieu looks suddenly sick. "He got away with everything. Everything he ever wanted, he was given. And he was always reckless. He did lazy work, all the while using Ella as a pawn to fulfill his own sadistic desires."

"Please be more specific," Castle says coolly. "Anderson had a great deal of sadistic desires. Which are you referring to?"

Delalieu goes pale. His voice is lower, weaker, when he says, "Paris has always been perversely fond of destroying his own son. I never understood it. I never understood his need to break that boy. He tortured him a thousand different ways, but when Paris discovered the depth of Aaron's emotional connection to Ella, he used it to drive that boy near to madness."

"That's why he shot her," I say, remembering what Juliette—Ella—told me after Omega Point was bombed. "Anderson wanted to kill her to teach Warner a lesson. Right?"

But something changes in Delalieu's face. Transforms him, sags him down. And then he laughs—a sad, broken laugh. "You don't understand, you don't understand, *you don't understand,*" he cries, shaking his head. "You think these recent events are everything. You think Aaron fell in love with your friend of several months, a rebel girl named Juliette. You don't know. You don't know. You don't know that Aaron has been in love with Ella for the better part of his entire life. They've known each other since childhood."

Adam makes a sound. A stunned sound of disbelief.

"Okay, I have to be honest— I don't get it," Ian says. He steals a wary glance at Nazeera before he says, "Nazeera said Anderson has been wiping their memories. If that's true, then how could Warner be in love with her for so long? Why would Anderson wipe their memories, tell them all about how they know each other, and then wipe their memories again?"

Delalieu is shaking his head. A strange smile begins to form on his face, the kind of shaky, terrified smile that isn't a smile at all. "No. *No*. You don't—" He sighs, looks away. "Paris has never told either of them about their shared history. The reason he had to keep wiping their memories was because it didn't matter how many times he reset the story or remade the introductions— Aaron always fell in love with her. Every time.

"In the beginning Paris thought it was a fluke. He found it almost funny. Entertaining. But the more it happened, the more it began to drive Paris insane. He thought there was something wrong with Aaron—that there was something wrong with him on a genetic level, that he'd been plagued by a sickness. He wanted to crush what he saw as a weakness."

"Wait," Adam says, holding up his hands. "What do you mean, *the more it happened*? How many times did it happen?"

"At least several times."

Adam looks shell-shocked. "They met and fell in love *several* times?"

Delalieu takes a shaky breath. "I don't know that they always fell in love, exactly. Paris seldom let them spend that much time alone. But they were always drawn together. It was obvious, every time he put them in the same room, they were like"—Delalieu claps his hands—"magnets."

Delalieu shakes his head at Adam.

"I'm sorry to be the one to tell you all this. I'm sure it's painful to hear, especially considering your history with Ella. It's not fair that you were pulled into Paris's games. He never should've p—"

"Whoa, whoa— Wait. What games?" Adam says, stunned. "What are you talking about?"

Delalieu runs a hand across his sweaty forehead. He looks like he's melting, crumbling under pressure. Maybe someone should get him some water.

"There's too much," he says wearily. "Too much to tell. Too much to explain." He shakes his head. "I'm sorry, I—"

"I need you to try," Adam says, his eyes flashing. "Are you saying our relationship was fake? That everything she said—everything she felt was fake?"

"No," Delalieu says quickly, even as he uses his shirt-sleeve to wipe the sweat from his face. "No. As far as I'm aware, her feelings for you were as real as anything else. You came into her life at a particularly difficult time, and your kindness and affection no doubt meant a great deal to her." He sighs. "I only mean that it wasn't coincidence that both of Paris's boys fell in love with the same girl. Paris liked toying with things. He liked cutting things open to study them. He liked experiments. And Paris pit you and Warner against each other on *purpose*.

"He planted the soldier at your lunch table who let slip that Warner was monitoring a girl with a lethal touch. He sent another to speak with you, to ask you about your history with her, to appeal to your protective nature by discussing Aaron's plans for her— Do you remember? You were persuaded, from every angle, to apply for the position. When you did, Paris pulled your application from the pile and encouraged Aaron to interview you. He then made it clear that you should be chosen as her cellmate. He let Aaron think he was making all his own decisions as CCR of Sector 45—but Paris was always there, manipulating everything. I watched it happen."

Adam looks so stunned it takes him a moment to speak. "So . . . he knew? My dad always knew about me? Knew where I was—what I was doing?"

"Knew?" Delalieu frowns. "Paris *orchestrated* your lives. That was the plan, from the beginning." He looks at Nazeera. "All the children of the supreme commanders were to become case studies. You were engineered to be soldiers. You and James," he says to Adam, "were unexpected, but he made plans for you, too."

"What?" Adam goes white. "What's his plan for me and James?"

"This, I honestly don't know."

Adam sits back in his chair, looking suddenly ill.

"Where is Ella now?" Winston says sharply. "Do you know where they're keeping her?"

Delalieu shakes his head. "All I know is that she can't be dead."

"What do you mean she *can't* be dead?" I ask. "Why not?"

"Ella's and Emmaline's powers are critical to the regime," he says. "Critical to the continuation of everything we've been working toward. The Reestablishment was built with the promise of Ella and Emmaline. Without them, Operation Synthesis means nothing."

Castle bolts upright. His eyes are wide. "Operation Synthesis," he says breathlessly, "has to do with *Ella*?"

"The Architect and the Executioner," Delalieu says. "It—"

Delalieu falls back with a small, surprised gasp, his head hitting the back of his chair. Everything, suddenly, seems to slow down.

I feel my heart rate slow. I feel the world slow. I feel formed from water, watching the scene unfold in slow motion, frame by frame.

A bullet between his eyes.

Blood trickling down his forehead.

A short, sharp scream.

"You traitorous son of a bitch," someone says.

I'm seeing it, but I don't believe it.

Anderson is here.

JULIETTE

I'm given no explanations.

My father doesn't invite me to dinner, like Evie promised. He doesn't sit me down to offer me long histories about my presence or his; he doesn't reveal groundbreaking information about my life or the other supreme commanders or even the nearly six hundred people I just murdered. He and Evie are acting like the horrors of the last seventeen years never happened. Like *nothing* strange has ever happened, like I never stopped being their daughter—not in the ways that matter, anyway.

I don't know what was in that needle, but the effects are unlike anything I've experienced. I feel both awake and asleep, like I'm spinning in place, like there's too much grease turning the wheels in my brain and I try to speak and realize my lips no longer move on command. My father carries my limp body into a blindingly silver room, props me up in a chair, straps me down, and panic pours into me, hot and terrifying, flooding my mind. I try to scream. Fail. My brain is slowly disconnecting from my body, like I'm being removed from myself. Only basic, instinctual functions seem to work. Swallowing. Breathing.

Crying.

Tears fall quietly down my face and my father whistles a tune, his movements light and easy even as he sets up an IV drip. He moves with such startling efficiency I don't even realize he's removed my manacles until I see the scalpel.

A flash of silver.

The blade is so sharp he meets no resistance as he slices clean lines into my forearms and blood, blood, heavy and warm, spills down my wrists and into my open palms and it doesn't seem real, not even when he stabs several electrical wires into my exposed flesh.

The pain arrives just seconds later.

Pain.

It begins at my feet, blooms up my legs, unfurls in my stomach and works its way up my throat only to explode behind my eyes, *inside my brain*, and I cry out, but only in my mind, my useless hands still limp on the armrests, and I'm so certain he's going to kill me—

but then he smiles.

And then he's gone.

I lie in agony for what feels like hours.

I watch, through a delirious fog, as blood drips off my fingertips, each drop feeding the crimson pools growing in the folds of my pants. Visions assault me, memories of a girl I might've been, scenes with people I might've known. I want to believe they're hallucinations, but I can't be certain of anything anymore. I don't know if Max and Evie are planting things in my mind. I don't know that I can trust anything I might've once believed about myself.

I can't stop thinking about Emmaline.

I'm adrift, suspended in a pool of senselessness, but something about her keeps tugging, sparking my nerves, errant currents pushing me to the surface of something—an emotional revelation—that trembles into existence only to evaporate, seconds later, as if it might be terrified to exist.

This goes on and on and on and on and on

Lightyears.

Eons.

over

and

over

whispers of clarity

g a s p s   o f   o x y g e n

and I'm tossed back out to sea.

Bright, white lights flicker above my head, buzzing in unison with the low, steady hum of engines and cooling units. Everything smells sharp, like antiseptic. Nausea makes my head swim. I squeeze my eyes shut, the only command my body will obey.

Me and Emmaline at the zoo

Me and Emmaline, first trip on a plane
Me and Emmaline, learning to swim
Me and Emmaline, getting our hair cut

Images of Emmaline fill my mind, moments from the first years of our lives, details of her face I never knew I could conjure. I don't understand it. I don't know where they're coming from. I can only imagine that Evie put these images here, but why Evie would want me to see *this,* I don't understand. Scenes play through my head like I might be flipping through a photo album, and they make me miss my sister. They make me remember Evie as my mother. Make me remember I had a family.

Maybe Evie wants me to reminisce.

My blood has hit the floor. I hear it, the familiar drip, the sound like a broken faucet, the slow

tap

tap

of tepid fluid on tile.

Emmaline and I held hands everywhere we went, often wearing matching outfits. We had the same long brown hair, but her eyes were pure blue, and she was a few inches taller than me. We were only a year apart, but she looked so much older. Even then, there was something in her eyes that looked hard. Serious. She held my hand like she was trying to protect me. Like maybe she knew more than I did.

Where are you? I wonder. *What did they do to you?*

I have no idea where I am. No idea what they've done

to me. No idea of the hour or the day, and pain blisters everywhere. I feel like a live wire, like my nerves have been stapled to the outside of my body, sensitive to every minute change in environment. I exhale and it hurts. Twitch and it takes my breath away.

And then, in a flash of movement, my mother returns.

The door opens and the motion forces a gentle rush of air into the room, a whisper of a breeze, gentle even as it grazes my skin, and somehow the sensation is so unbearable I'm certain I'll scream.

I don't.

"Feeling better?" she says.

Evie is holding a silver box. I try to look more closely but the pain is in my eyes now. Searing.

"You must be wondering why you're here," she says softly. I hear her working on something, glass and metal touching together, coming apart, touching together, coming apart. "But you must be patient, little bird. You might not even get to stay."

I close my eyes.

I feel her cold, slender fingers on my face just seconds before she yanks my eyelids back. Swiftly, she replaces her fingers with sharp, steel clamps, and I muster only a low, guttural sound of agony.

"Keep your eyes open, Ella. Now's not the time to fall asleep."

Even then, in that painful, terrifying moment, the words sound familiar. Strange and familiar. I can't figure out why.

"Before we make any concrete plans to keep you here, I need to make sure"—she tugs on a pair of latex gloves—"that you're still viable. See how you've held up after all these years."

Her words send waves of dread coursing through me.

Nothing has changed.

Nothing has changed.

I'm still no more than a receptacle. My body exchanges hands exchanges hands in exchange for what

My mother has no love for me.

What has she done to my sister.

"Where is Emmaline?" I try to scream, but the words don't leave my mouth. They expand in my head, explosive and angry, pressing against the ridges of my mind even as my lips refuse to obey me.

Dying.

The word occurs to me suddenly, as if it were something I've just remembered, the answer to a question I forgot existed.

I don't comprehend it.

Evie is standing in front of me again.

She touches my hair, sifts through the short, coarse strands like she might be panning for gold. The physical contact is excruciating.

"Unacceptable," she says. "This is unacceptable."

She turns away, makes notes in a tablet she pulls out of

her lab coat. Roughly, she takes my chin in her hand, lifts my face toward hers.

Evie counts my teeth. Runs the tip of one finger along my gums. She examines the insides of my cheeks, the underside of my tongue. Satisfied, she rips off the gloves, the latex making harsh snapping sounds that collide and echo, shattering the air around me.

A mechanical purr fills my ears and I realize Evie is adjusting my chair. I was previously in a reclining position, now I'm flat on my back. She takes a pair of shears to my clothes, cutting straight through my pants, my shirt, my sleeves.

Fear threatens to rip my chest open, but I only lie there, a perfect vegetable, as she strips me down.

Finally, Evie steps back.

I can't see what's happening. The hum of an engine builds into a roar. Sounds like scissors, slicing the air. And then: Sheets of glass materialize at the edges of my vision, move toward me from all sides. They lock into place easily, seams sealing shut with a cool *click* sound.

I'm being burned alive.

Heat like I've never known it, fire I can't see or stop. I don't know how it's happening but I feel it. I *smell* it. The scent of charred flesh fills my nose, threatens to upend the contents of my stomach. The top layer of skin is being slowly singed off my body. Blood beads along my body like morning dew, and a fine mist follows the heat, cleansing and cooling. Steam fogs up the glass around me and then, just when I think I might die from the pain, the glass fissures open with a sudden gasp.

I wish she would just kill me.

Instead, Evie is meticulous. She catalogs my every physical detail, making notes, constantly, in her pocket tablet. For the most part, she seems frustrated with her assessment. My arms and legs are too weak, she says. My shoulders too tense, my hair too short, my hands too scarred, my nails too chipped, my lips too chapped, my torso too long.

"We made you too beautiful," she says, shaking her head at my naked body. She prods at my hips, the balls of my feet. "Beauty can be a terrifying weapon, if you know how to wield it. But all this seems deeply unnecessary now." She makes another note.

When she looks at me again, she looks thoughtful.

"I gave this to you," she says. "Do you understand? This container you live in. I grew it, shaped it. You belong to me. Your life belongs to me. It's very important that you understand that."

Rage, sharp and hot, sears through my chest.

Carefully, Evie cracks open the silver box. Inside are dozens of slim glass cylinders. "Do you know what these are?" she says, lifting a few vials of shimmering, white liquid. "Of course you don't."

Evie studies me awhile.

"We did it wrong the first time," she finally says. "We didn't expect emotional health to supersede the physical in such dramatic fashion. We expected stronger minds, from both you. Of course—" Evie hesitates. "She was the superior specimen, your sister. Infinitely superior. You were always a bit doe-eyed as a child. A little moonier than I'd have liked. Emmaline, on the other hand, was pure fire. We never dreamed she'd deteriorate so quickly. Her failures have been a great personal disappointment."

I inhale sharply and choke on something hot and wet in my throat. Blood. So much blood.

"But then," Evie says with a sigh, "such is the situation. We must be adaptable to the unexpected. Amenable to change when necessary."

Evie hits a switch and something seizes inside of me. I feel my spine straighten, my jaw go slack. Blood is now bubbling up my throat in earnest, and I don't know whether to let it up or swallow it down. I cough, violently, and blood spatters across my face. My arms. Drips down my chest, my fresh pink skin.

My mother drops into a crouch. She takes my chin in her hand and forces me to look at her. "You are far too full of emotion," she says softly. "You feel too much for this world. You call people your friends. You imagine yourself in love." She shakes her head slowly. "That was never the plan for you, little bird. You were meant for a solitary existence. We put you in isolation on purpose." She blinks. "Do you understand?"

I'm hardly breathing. My tongue feels rough and heavy, foreign in my mouth. I swallow my own blood and it's revolting, thick and lukewarm, gelatinous with saliva.

"If Aaron were anyone else's son," she says, "I would've had him executed. I'd have him executed right now, if I could. Unfortunately, I alone do not have the authority."

A force of feeling seizes my body.

I'm half horror, half joy. I didn't know I had any hope left that Warner was alive until just this moment.

The feeling is explosive.

It takes root inside of me. Hope catches fire in my blood, a feeling more powerful than these drugs, more powerful than myself. I cling to it with my whole heart, and, suddenly, I'm able to feel my hands. I don't know why or how but I feel a quiet strength surge up my spine.

Evie doesn't notice.

"I regret our mistakes," she's saying. "I regret the oversights that seem so obvious now. We couldn't have known so many years ago that things would turn out like this. We didn't expect to be blindsided by something so flimsy as your emotions. We couldn't have known, at the onset, that things would escalate in this way.

"Paris," she says, "had convinced everyone that bringing you on base in Sector 45 would be beneficial to us all, that he'd be able to monitor you in a new environment rife with experiences that would motivate your powers to evolve. Your father and I thought it was a stupid plan, stupider still for placing you under the direct supervision of a nineteen-year-old boy with whom your history was . . . complicated." She looks away. Shakes her head. "But Anderson delivered results. With Aaron you made progress at a rate we'd only dreamed of, and we were forced to let it be. Still," she says. "It backfired."

Her eyes linger, for a moment, on my shaved head.

"There are few people, even in our inner circle, who really understand what we're doing here. Your father understands. Ibrahim understands. But Paris, for security reasons, was never told everything about you. He wasn't yet a supreme commander when we gave him the job, and we decided to keep him informed on a need-to-know basis. Another mistake," Evie says, her voice both sad and terrifying.

She presses the back of her hand to her forehead.

"Six months and everything falls apart. You run away. You join some ridiculous gang. You drag Aaron into all of this and Paris, the oblivious fool, tries to *kill* you. Twice. I nearly slit his throat for his idiocy, but my mercy may as well have been for nothing, what with your attempt to murder him. Oh, Ella," she says, and sighs. "You've caused me a great deal of trouble this year. The paperwork alone." She closes her eyes. "I've had the same splitting headache for six months."

She opens her eyes. Looks at me for a long time.

"And now," she says, gesturing at me with the tablet in her hand, "there's this. Emmaline needs to be replaced, and we're not even sure you're a suitable substitute. Your body is operating at *maybe* sixty-five percent efficiency, and your mind is a complete disaster." She stops. A vein jumps in her forehead. "Perhaps it's impossible for you to understand how I'm feeling right now. Perhaps you don't care to know the depth of my disappointments. But you and Emmaline are my life's work. I was the one who found a way to isolate the gene that was causing widespread transformations in the population. I was the one who managed to re-create the transformation. I was the one who rewrote your genetic code." She frowns at me, looking, for the first time, like a real person. Her voice softens. "I *remade* you, Ella. You and your sister were the greatest accomplishments of my career. Your failures," she whispers, touching the tips of her fingers to my face, "are my failures."

I make a harsh, involuntary sound.

She stands up. "This is going to be uncomfortable for you. I won't pretend otherwise. But I'm afraid we have no choice. If this is going to work, I'll need you to have a healthy, unpolluted headspace. We have to start fresh. When we're done, you won't remember anything but what I tell you to remember. Do you understand?"

My heart picks up and I hear its wild, erratic beats amplified on a nearby monitor. The sounds echo around the room like a siren.

"Your temperature is spiking," Evie says sharply. "There's no need to panic. This is the merciful option. Paris is still clamoring to have you killed, after all. But Paris"—she hesitates—"Paris can be melodramatic. We've all known how much he's hated you for your effect on Aaron. He blames you, you know." Evie tilts her head at me. "He thinks you're part of the reason Aaron is so weak. Honestly, sometimes I wonder if he's right."

My heart is beating too fast now. My lungs feel fit to burst. The bright lights above my head bleed into my eyes, into my brain—

"Now. I'm going to download this information"—I hear her tap the silver box—"directly into your mind. It's a lot of data to process, and your body will need some time to accept it all." A long pause. "Your mind might try to reject this, but it's up to you to let things take their course, do you understand? We don't want to risk splicing the past and present. It's only painful in the first few hours, but if you can survive those first hours, your pain receptors will begin to fail, and the rest of the data should upload without incident."

I want to scream.

Instead, I make a weak, choking sound. Tears spill fast down my cheeks and my mother stands there, her fingers small and foreign on my face, and I see, but cannot feel, the enormous needle going into the soft flesh at my temple. She empties and refills the syringe what feels like a thousand times, and each time it's like being submerged underwater, like I'm slowly drowning, suffocating over and over again and never allowed to die. I lie there, helpless and mute, caught in an agony so excruciating I no longer breathe, but rasp, as she leans over me to watch.

"You're right," she says softly. "Maybe this is cruel. Maybe it would've been kinder to simply let you die. But this isn't about you, Ella. This is about me. And right now," she says, stroking my hair, "this is what I need."

KENJI

The whole thing happens so quickly it takes me a second to register exactly what went down.

Delalieu is dead.

Delalieu is dead and Anderson is alive.

Anderson is back from the dead.

I mean, right now he's flat on the ground, buried under the weight of every single piece of furniture in this room. Castle stares, intently, from across the space, and when I hear Anderson wheezing, I realize Castle isn't trying to kill him; he's only using the furniture to contain him.

I inch closer to the crowd forming around Anderson's gasping figure. And then I notice, with a start, that Adam is pressed up against the wall like a statue, his face frozen in horror.

My heart breaks for him.

I'm so glad Adam dragged James off to bed hours ago. So glad that kid doesn't have to see any of this right now.

Castle finally makes his way across the room. He's standing a few feet away from Anderson's prone figure when he asks the question we're all thinking:

"How are you still alive?"

Anderson attempts a smile. It comes out crooked. Crazy. "You know what's always been so great about you, Castle?"

He says Castle's name like it's funny, like he's saying it out loud for the first time. He takes a tight, uneven breath. "You're so predictable. You like to collect strays. You love a good sob story."

Anderson cries out with a sudden, rough exhalation, and I realize Castle probably turned up the pressure. When Anderson catches his breath, he says, "You're an idiot. You're an idiot for trusting so easily."

Another harsh, painful gasp.

"Who do you think called me here?" he says, struggling to speak now. "Who do you think has been keeping me apprised"—another strained breath—"of every single thing you've been discussing?"

I freeze.

A horrible, sick feeling gathers in my chest.

We all turn, as a group, to face Nazeera. She's standing apart from everyone else, the personification of calm, collected intensity. She has no expression on her face. She looks at me like I might be a wall.

For a split second I feel so dizzy I think I might actually pass out.

Wishful thinking.

That's it—that's the thing that does it. A room full of extremely powerful people and yet, it's this moment, this brief, barely there moment of shock that ruins us all. I feel the needle in my neck before I even register what's happening, and I have only a few seconds to scan the room—glimpsing the horror on my friends' faces—before I fall.

WARNER

I'm sitting in my office listening to an old record when I get the call. I worry, at first, that it might be Lena, begging me to come back to her, but my feeling of revulsion quickly transforms to hate when I hear the voice on the line. My father. He wants me downstairs.

The mere sound of his voice fills me with a feeling so violent it takes me a minute to control myself.

Two years away.

Two years becoming the monster my father always wanted me to be. I glance in the mirror, loathing myself with a new, profound intensity I'd never before experienced. Every morning I wake up hoping only to die. To be done with this life, with these days.

He knew, when he made that deal, what he was asking me to do. I didn't. I was sixteen, still young enough to believe in hope, and he took advantage of my naiveté. He knew what it would do to me. He knew it would break me. And it was all he'd ever wanted.

My soul.

I sold my soul for a few years with my mother, and now, after everything, I don't even know if it'll be worth it. I don't know if I'll be able to save her. I've been away too long. I've missed too much. My mother is doing so much worse now, and no doctor has been able to help her. Nothing has helped. My efforts have been worse than futile.

I gave up everything—for nothing.

I wish I'd known how those two years would change me. I wish I'd known how hard it would be to live with myself, to look in the mirror. No one warned me about the nightmares, the panic attacks, or the dark, destructive thoughts that would follow. No one explained to me how darkness works, how it feasts on itself or how it festers. I hardly recognize myself these days. Becoming an instrument of torture destroyed what was left of my mind.

And now, this: I feel empty, all the time. Hollowed out.

Beyond redemption.

I didn't want to come back here. I wanted to walk directly into the ocean. I wanted to fade into the horizon. I wanted to disappear.

Of course, he'd never let that happen.

He dragged me back here and gave me a title. I was rewarded for being an animal. Celebrated for my efforts as a monster. Never mind the fact that I wake up in the middle of every night strangled by irrational fears and a sudden, violent urge to upend the contents of my stomach.

Never mind that I can't get these images out of my head.

I glance at the expensive bottle of bourbon my father left for me in my room and feel suddenly disgusted. I don't want to be like him. I don't want his opiate, his preferred form of oblivion.

At least, soon, my father will be gone. Any day now, he'll be gone, and this sector will become my domain. I'll finally be on my own.

Or something close to it.

Reluctantly, I pull on my blazer and take the elevator down.

When I finally arrive in his quarters as he requested, he spares me only the briefest look.

"Good," he says. "You've come."

I say nothing.

He smiles. "Where are your manners? You're not going to greet our guest?"

Confused, I follow his line of sight. There's a young woman sitting on a chair in the far corner of the room, and, at first, I don't recognize her.

When I do, the blood drains from my face.

My father laughs. "You kids remember each other, right?"

She was sitting so quietly, so still and small that I almost hadn't noticed her at all. My dead heart jumps at the sight of her slight frame, a spark of life trying, desperately, to ignite.

"Juliette," I whisper.

My last memory of her was from two years ago, just before I left home for my father's sick, sadistic assignment. He ripped her away from me. Literally ripped her out of my arms. I'd never seen that kind of rage in his eyes, not like that, not over something so innocent.

But he was wild.

Out of his mind.

She and I hadn't done anything more than talk to each other. I'd started stealing down to her room whenever I could get away, and I'd trick the cameras' feeds to give us privacy. We'd talk, sometimes for hours. She'd become my friend.

I never touched her.

She said that after what happened with the little boy, she was afraid to touch anyone. She said she didn't understand what was happening to her and didn't trust herself anymore. I asked her if she wanted to touch me, to test it out and see if anything would happen, and she looked scared and I told her not to worry. I promised it'd be okay. And when I took her hand, tentatively, waiting for disaster—

Nothing happened.

Nothing happened except that she burst into tears. She threw herself into my arms and wept and told me she'd been terrified that there was something wrong with her, that she'd turned into a monster—

We only had a month, altogether.

But there was something about her that felt right to me, from the very beginning. I trusted her. She felt familiar, like I'd always known her. But I also knew it seemed a dramatic sort of thought, so I kept it to myself.

She told me about her life. Her horrible parents. She'd shared her fears with me, so I shared mine. I told her about my mom, how I didn't know what was happening to her, how worried I was that she was going to die.

Juliette cared about me. Listened to me the way no one else did.

It was the most innocent relationship I'd ever had, but it meant more to me than anything. For the first time in years, I felt less alone.

The day I found out she was finally being transferred, I pulled her close. I pressed my face into her hair and breathed her in and she cried. She told me she was scared and I promised I'd try to do something—I promised to talk to my dad even though I knew he wouldn't care—

And then, suddenly, he was there.

He ripped her out of my arms, and I noticed then that he was wearing gloves. "What the hell are you doing?" he cried. "Have you lost your mind? Have you lost yourself entirely?"

"Dad," I said, panicking. "Nothing happened. I was just saying good-bye to her."

His eyes widened, round with shock. And when he spoke, his words were whispers. "You were just— You were saying good-bye *to her?"*

"She's leaving," I said stupidly.

"You think I don't know that?"

I swallowed, hard.

"Jesus," he said, running a hand across his mouth. "How long have you been doing this? How long have you been coming down here?"

My heart was racing. Fear pulsed through me. I was shaking my head, unable to speak.

"What did you do?" my dad demanded, his eyes flashing. "Did you touch her?"

"No." Anger surged through me, giving me back my voice even as my face flushed with embarrassment. "No, of course not."

"Are you sure?"

"Dad, why are you"—I shook my head, confused—"I don't understand why you're so upset. You've been pushing me and Lena together for months, even though I've told you a hundred times that I don't like her, but now, when I actually—" I hesitated, looking at Juliette, her face half hidden behind my dad. "I was just getting to know her. That's all."

"You were just getting to know her?" He stared at me, disgusted. "Of all the girls in the world, you fall for this one? The child-murderer bound for prison? The likely insane test tube experiment? What is wrong *with you?"*

"Dad, please— Nothing happened. We're just friends. We just talk sometimes."

"Just friends," he said, and laughed. The sound was demented. "You know what? I'll let you take this with you. I'll let you keep this one while you're gone. Let it sit with you. Let it teach you a lesson."

"What? Take what with me?"

"A warning." He leveled me with a lethal look. "Try something like this again," he said, "and I'll kill her. And I'll make sure you get to watch."

I stared at him, my heart beating out of my chest. This was insane. We hadn't even done anything. I'd known that my dad would probably be angry, but I never thought he'd threaten to kill her. If I'd known, I never would've risked it. And now—

My head was spinning. I didn't understand. He was dragging her down the hall and I didn't understand.

Suddenly, she screamed.

She screamed and I stood there, helpless as he dragged her away. She called my name—cried out for me—and he shook her, told her to shut up, and I felt something inside of me die. I felt it as it happened. Felt something break apart inside of me as I watched her go.

I'd never hated myself so much. I'd never been more of a coward.

And now, here we are.

That day feels like a lifetime ago. I never thought I'd see her again.

Juliette looks up at me now, and she looks different. Her eyes are glassy with tears. Her skin has lost its pallor; her hair has lost its sheen. She looks thinner. She reminds me of myself.

Hollow.

"Hi," I whisper.

Tears spill, silently, down her cheeks.

I have to force myself to remain calm. I have to force myself not to lose my head. My mother warned me, years ago, to hide my heart from my father, and every time I slipped—every time I let myself hope he might not be a monster—he punished me, mercilessly.

I wasn't going to let him do that to me again. I didn't want him to know how much it hurt to see her like this. How painful it was to sit beside her and say nothing. Do nothing.

"What is she doing here?" I ask, hardly recognizing my own voice.

"She's here," he says, "because I had her collected for us."

"Collected for what? You said—"

"I know what I said." He shrugs. "But I wanted to see this moment. Your reunion. I'm always interested in your reunions. I find the dynamics of your relationship fascinating."

I look at him, feel my chest explode with rage and somehow, fight it back. "You brought her back here just to torture me?"

"You flatter yourself, son."

"Then what?"

"I have your first task for you," he says, pushing a stack of files across his desk. "Your first real mission as chief commander and regent of this sector."

My lips part, surprised. "What does that have to do with her?"

My father's eyes light up. "Everything."

I say nothing.

"I have a plan," he says. "One that will require your assistance.

In these files"—he nods at the stack in front of me—"is everything you need to know about her illness. Every medical report, every paper trail. I want you to reform the girl. Rehabilitate her. And then I want you to weaponize her abilities for our own use."

I meet his eyes, failing to conceal my horror at the suggestion. "Why? Why would you come to me with this? Why would you ask me to do something like this, when you know our history?"

"You are uniquely suited to the job. It seems silly to waste my time explaining this to you now, as you won't remember most of this conversation tomorrow—"

"What?" I frown. "Why wouldn't I—"

"—but the two of you seem to have some kind of immutable connection, one that might, I hope, inspire her abilities to develop more fully. More quickly."

"That doesn't make any sense."

He ignores me. Glances at Juliette. Her eyes are closed, her head resting against the wall behind her. She seems almost asleep, except for the tears still streaking softly down her face.

It kills me just to look at her.

"As you can see," my father says, "she's a bit out of her mind right now. Heavily sedated. She's been through a great deal these last two years. We had no choice but to turn her into a sort of guinea pig. I'm sure you can imagine how that goes."

He stares at me with a slight smile on his face. I know he's waiting for something. A reaction. My anger.

I refuse to give it to him.

His smile widens.

"Anyhow," he says happily, "I'm going to put her back in

isolation for the next six months—maybe a year, depending on how things develop. You can use that opportunity to prepare. To observe her."

But I'm still fighting back my anger. I can't bring myself to speak.

"Is there a problem?" he says.

"No."

"You remember, of course, the warning I gave you the last time she was here."

"Of course," I say, my voice flat. Dead.

And then, as if out of nowhere: "How is Lena, by the way? I hope she's well."

"I wouldn't know."

It's barely there, but I catch the sudden shift in his voice. The anger when he says, "And why is that?"

"I broke things off with her last week."

"And you didn't think to tell me?"

Finally, I meet his eyes. "I never understood why you wanted us to be together. She's not right for me. She never was."

"You don't love her, you mean."

"I can't imagine how anyone would."

"That," he says, "is exactly why she's perfect for you."

I blink at him, caught off guard. For a moment, it almost sounded like my father cared about me. Like he was trying to protect me in some perverse, idiotic way.

Eventually, he sighs.

He picks up a pen and a pad of paper and begins writing something down. "I'll see what I can do about repairing the damage you've done. Lena's mother must be hysterical. Until then, get to work." He nods at the stack of files he's set before me.

Reluctantly, I pick a folder off the top.

I glance through the documents, scanning the general outline of the mission, and then I look up at him, stunned. "Why does the paperwork make it sound like this was my idea?"

He hesitates. Puts down his pen. "Because you don't trust me."

I stare at him, struggling to understand.

He tilts his head. "If you knew this was my idea, you'd never trust it, would you? You'd look too closely for holes. Conspiracies. You'd never follow through the way I'd want you to. Besides," he says, picking up his pen again. "Two birds. One stone. It's time to finally break the cycle."

I replace the folder on the pile. I'm careful to temper the tone of my voice when I say, "I have no idea what you're talking about."

"I'm talking about your new experiment," he says coolly. "Your little tragedy. This," he says, gesturing between me and Juliette. "This needs to end. And she is unlikely to return your affections when she wakes up to discover you are not her friend but her oppressor. Isn't she?"

And I can no longer keep the fury or the hysteria out of my voice when I say, "Why are you doing this to me? Why are you purposely torturing me?"

"Is it so crazy to imagine that I might be trying to do you a favor?" My father smiles. "Look more closely at those files, son. If you've ever wanted a chance at saving your mother—this might be it."

I've become obsessed with time.

Still, I can only guess at how long I've been here, staring

at these walls without reprieve. No voices, only the occasional warped sounds of faraway speech. No faces, not a single person to tell me where I am or what awaits me. I've watched the shadows chase the light in and out of my cell for weeks, their motions through the small window my only hope for marking the days.

A slim, rectangular slot in my door opens with sudden, startling force, the aperture shot through with what appears to be artificial light on the other side.

I make a mental note.

A single, steaming bun—no tray, no foil, no utensils—is shoved through the slot and my reflexes are still fast enough to catch the bread before it touches the filthy floor. I have enough sense to understand that the little food I'm given every day is poisoned. Not enough to kill me. Just enough to slow me down. Slight tremors rock my body, but I force my eyes to stay open as I turn the soft bun around in my hand, searching its flaky skin for information. It's unmarked. Unextraordinary. It could mean nothing.

There's no way to be sure.

This ritual happens exactly twice a day. I am fed an insignificant, tasteless portion of food twice a day. For hours at a time my thoughts slur; my mind swims and hallucinates. I am slow. Sluggish.

Most days, I fast.

To clear my head, to cleanse my body of the poison, and to collect information. I have to find my way out of here before it's too late.

Some nights, when I'm at my weakest, my imagination runs wild; my mind is plagued by horrible visions of what might've happened to her. It's torture not knowing what they've done with her. Not knowing where she is, not knowing how she is, not knowing if someone is hurting her.

But the nightmares are perhaps the most disconcerting.

At least, I think they're nightmares. It's hard to separate fact from fiction, dreams from reality; I spend too much time with poison running through my veins. But Nazeera's words to me before the symposium—her warning that Juliette was someone else, that Max and Evie are her true, biological parents . . .

I didn't want to believe it then.

It seemed a possibility too perverse to be real. Even my father had lines he wouldn't cross, I told myself. Even The Reestablishment had some sense of invented morality, I told myself.

But I saw them as I was carried away—I saw the familiar faces of Evie and Maximillian Sommers—the supreme commander of Oceania and her husband. And I've been thinking of them ever since.

They were the key scientists of our group, the quiet brains of The Reestablishment. They were military, yes, but they were medical. The pair often kept to themselves. I had few memories of them until very recently.

Until *Ella* appeared in my mind.

But I don't know how to be sure that what I'm seeing is real. I have no way of knowing that this isn't simply another part of the torture. It's impossible to know. It's agony, boring a hole through me. I feel like I'm being assaulted on both sides—mental and physical—and I don't know where or how to begin fighting back. I've begun clenching my teeth so hard it's causing me migraines. Exhaustion feasts, slowly, on my mind. I'm fairly certain I've got at least two fractured ribs, and my only hours of rest are achieved standing up, the single position that eases the pain in my torso. It'd be easy to give up. Give in. But I can't lose myself to these mind games.

I won't.

So I compile data.

I spent my whole life preparing for moments like these by people like this and they will take full advantage of that knowledge. I know they'll expect me to prove that I deserve to survive, and—unexpectedly—knowing this brings me a much-needed sense of calm. I feel none of my usual anxiety here, being carefully poisoned to death.

Instead, I feel at home. Familiar.

Fortified by adrenaline.

Under any other circumstances I'd assume my meals were offered once in the morning and once at night—but I know better than to assume anything anymore. I've been charting the shadows long enough to know that I'm never fed at regular hours, and that the erratic schedule is intentional. There must be a message here: a sequence of numbers, a pattern of information, something I'm not grasping—because I know that this, like everything else, is a test.

I am in the custody of a supreme commander.

There can be no accidents.

I force myself to eat the warm, flavorless bun, hating the way the gummy, overly processed bread sticks to the roof of my mouth. It makes me wish for a toothbrush. They've given me my own sink and toilet, but I have little else to keep my standards of hygiene intact, which is possibly the greatest indignity here. I fight a wave of nausea as I swallow the last bite of bread and a sudden, prickling heat floods my body. Beads of sweat roll down my back and I clench my fists to keep from succumbing too quickly to the drugs.

I need a little more time.

There's a message here, somewhere, but I haven't yet decided where. Maybe it's in the movements of the shadows. Or in the number of times the slot opens and closes. It might be in the names of the foods I'm forced to eat, or in the exact number of footsteps I hear every day—or perhaps it's in the occasional, jarring knock at my door that accompanies silence.

There's something here, something they're trying to tell me, something I'm supposed to decipher—I gasp, reach out blindly as a shock of pain shoots through my gut—

I can figure this out, I think, even as the drug drags me down. I fall backward, onto my elbows. My eyes flutter open and closed and my mind drowns even as I count the sounds outside my door—

one hard step

two dragging steps

one hard step

—and there's something there, something deliberate in the movement that speaks to me. I know this. I know this language, I know its name, it's right there at the tip of my tongue but I can't seem to grasp it.

I've already forgotten what I was trying to do.

My arms give out. My head hits the floor with a dull thud. My thoughts melt into darkness.

The nightmares take me by the throat.

KENJI

I thought I'd spent time in some pretty rough places in my life, but this shit is like nothing else. Perfect darkness. No sounds but the distant, tortured screams of other prisoners. Food is disgusting slop shoved through a slot in the door. No bathrooms except that they open the doors once a day, just long enough for you to kill yourself trying to find the disgusting showers and toilets. I know what this is. I remember when Juliette—

Ella. *Ella.*

Ella used to tell me about this place.

Some nights we'd stay up for hours talking about it. I wanted to know. I wanted to know everything. And those conversations are the only reason I knew what the open door means.

I don't really know how long I've been here—a week? Maybe two? I don't understand why they won't just kill me. I try to tell myself, every minute of every damn day, that they're just doing this to mess with our heads, that the tortured mind is a worse fate than a bullet in the brain, but I can't lie. This place is starting to get to me.

I feel myself starting to go weird.

I'm starting to hear things. See things. I'm beginning to freak myself out about what might've happened to my friends or whether I'll ever get out of here.

I try not to think about Nazeera.

When I think about Nazeera I want to punch myself in the face. I want to shoot myself in the throat.

When I think about Nazeera I feel a rage so acute I'm actually convinced, for a minute, that I might be able to break out of these neon handcuffs with nothing but brute force. But it never happens. These things are unbreakable, even as they strip me of my powers. And they emit a soft, pulsing blue glow, the only light I ever see.

J told me her cell had a window. Mine doesn't.

A harsh buzzing sound fills my cell. I hear a smooth click in the heavy metal door. I jump to my feet.

The door swings open.

I feel my way down the dripping corridor, the dim, pulsing light of my cuffs doing little to guide my way.

The shower is quick and cold. Awful in every way. There are no towels in this shithole, so I'm always freezing until I can get back to my room and wrap myself in the threadbare blanket. I'm thinking about that blanket now, trying to keep my thoughts focused and my teeth from chattering as I wend my way down the dark tunnels.

I don't see what happens next.

Someone comes up on me from behind and puts me in a choke hold, suffocating me with a technique so perfect I don't even know if it's worth a struggle. I'm definitely about to die.

Super weird way to go, but this is it. I'm done.

Shit.

~~JULIETTE~~
ELLA

Mr. Anderson says I can have lunch at his house before I meet my new family. It wasn't his idea, but when Aaron, his son—that was the boy's name—suggested it, Mr. Anderson seemed okay with it.

I'm grateful.

I'm not ready to go live with a bunch of strangers yet. I'm scared and nervous and worried about so many things, I don't even know where to start. Mostly, I feel angry. I'm angry with my parents for dying. Angry with them for leaving me behind.

I'm an orphan now.

But maybe I have a new friend. Aaron said that he was eight years old—about two years older than me—so there isn't any chance we'd be in the same grade, but when I said that we'd probably be going to the same school anyway, he said no, we wouldn't. He said he didn't go to public school. He said his father was very particular about these kinds of things and that he'd been homeschooled by private tutors his whole life.

We're sitting next to each other in the car ride back to his house when he says, quietly, "My dad never lets me invite people over to our house. He must like you."

I smile, secretly relieved. I really hope that this means I'll have a new friend. I'd been so scared to move here, so scared to be somewhere new and to be all alone, but now, sitting next to this strange blond boy with the light green eyes, I'm beginning to feel like things might be okay.

At least now, even if I don't like my new parents, I'll know I'm not completely alone. The thought makes me both happy and sad.

I look over at Aaron and smile. He smiles back.

When we get to his house, I take a moment to admire it from the outside. It's a big, beautiful old house painted the prettiest blue. It has big white shutters on the windows and a white fence around the front yard. Pink roses are growing around the edges, peeking through the wooden slats of the fence, and the whole thing looks so peaceful and lovely that I feel immediately at home.

My worries vanish.

I'm so grateful for Mr. Anderson's help. So grateful to have met his son. I realize, then, that Mr. Anderson might've brought his son to my meeting today just to introduce me to someone my own age. Maybe he was trying to make me feel at home.

A beautiful blond lady answers the front door. She smiles at me, bright and kind, and doesn't even say hello to me before she pulls me into her arms. She hugs me like she's known me forever, and there's something so comfortable about her arms around me that I embarrass everyone by bursting into tears.

I can't even look at anyone after I pull away from her—she told me her name was Mrs. Anderson, but that I could call her Leila, if I wanted—and I wipe at my tears, ashamed of my overreaction.

Mrs. Anderson tells Aaron to take me upstairs to his room while she makes us some snacks before lunch.

Still sniffling, I follow him up the stairs.

His room is nice. I sit on his bed and look at his things. Mostly it's pretty clean except that there's a baseball mitt on his nightstand and there are two dirty baseballs on the floor. Aaron catches me staring and scoops them up right away. He seems embarrassed as he tucks them in his closet, and I don't understand why. I was never very tidy. My room was always—

I hesitate.

I try to remember what my old bedroom looked like but, for some reason, I can't. I frown. Try again.

Nothing.

And then I realize I can't remember my parents' faces.

Terror barrels through me.

"What's wrong?"

Aaron's voice is so sharp—so intense—that I look up, startled. He's staring at me from across the room, the fear on his face reflected in the mirrors on his closet doors.

"What's wrong?" he says again. "Are you okay?"

"I— I don't—" I falter, feeling my eyes refill with tears. I hate that I keep crying. Hate that I can't stop crying. "I can't remember my parents," I say. "Is that normal?"

Aaron walks over, sits next to me on his bed. "I don't know," he says.

We're both quiet for a while. Somehow, it helps. Somehow, just sitting next to him makes me feel less alone. Less terrified.

Eventually, my heart stops racing.

After I've wiped away my tears, I say, "Don't you get lonely, being homeschooled all the time?"

He nods.

"Why won't your dad let you go to a normal school?"

"I don't know."

"What about birthday parties?" I ask. "Who do you invite to your birthday parties?"

Aaron shrugs. He's staring into his hands when he says, "I've never had a birthday party."

"What? Really?" I turn to face him more fully. "But birthday parties are so fun. I used to—" I blink, cutting myself off.

I can't remember what I was about to say.

I frown, trying to remember something, something about my old life, but when the memories don't materialize, I shake my head to clear it. Maybe I'll remember later.

"Anyway," I say, taking a quick breath, "you have to have a birthday party. Everyone has birthday parties. When is your birthday?"

Slowly, Aaron looks up at me. His face is blank even as he says, "April twenty-fourth."

"April twenty-fourth," I say, smiling. "That's great. We can have cake."

The days pass in a stifled panic, an excruciating crescendo toward madness. The hands of the clock seem to close around my throat and still, I say nothing, do nothing.

I wait.

Pretend.

I've been paralyzed here for two weeks, stuck in the prison of this ruse, this compound. Evie doesn't know that her plot to bleach my mind failed. She treats me like a foreign object, distant but not unkind. She instructed me to call her *Evie*, told me she was my doctor, and then proceeded to lie, in great detail, about how I'd been in a terrible accident, that I'm suffering from amnesia, that I need to stay in bed in order to recover.

She doesn't know that my body won't stop shaking, that my skin is slick with sweat every morning, that my throat burns from the constant return of bile. She doesn't know what's happening to me. She could never understand the sickness plaguing my heart. She couldn't possibly understand this agony.

Remembering.

The attacks are relentless.

Memories assault me while I sleep, jolting me upright, my chest seizing in panic over and over and over until, finally, I meet dawn on the bathroom floor, the smell of vomit clinging to my hair, the inside of my mouth. I can only drag myself back to bed every morning and force my face to smile when Evie checks on me at sunrise.

Everything feels wrong.

The world feels strange. Smells confuse me. Words don't feel right in my mouth anymore. The sound of my own name feels at once familiar and foreign. My memories of people and places seem warped, fraying threads coming together to form a ragged tapestry.

But Evie. *My mother.*

I remember her.

"Evie?"

I pop my head out of the bathroom, clutching a robe to my wet body. I search my room for her face. "Evie, are you there?"

"Yes?" I hear her voice just seconds before she's suddenly standing before me, holding a set of fresh sheets in her hands. She's stripping my bed again. "Did you need something?"

"We're out of towels."

"Oh—easily rectified," she says, and hurries out the door. Not seconds later she's back, pressing a warm, fresh towel into my hands. She smiles faintly.

"Thanks," I say, forcing my own smile to stretch, to spark life in my eyes. And then I disappear into the bathroom.

The room is steaming; the mirrors fogged, perspiring. I grip the towel with one hand, watching as beads of water race down my bare skin. Condensation wears me like a suit; I wipe at the damp metal cuffs locked around my wrists and ankles, their glowing blue light my constant reminder that I am in hell.

I collapse, with a heavy breath, onto the floor.

I'm too hot to put on clothes, but I'm not ready to leave the privacy of the bathroom yet, so I sit here, wearing nothing but these manacles, and drop my head into my hands.

My hair is long again.

I discovered it like this—long, heavy, dark—one morning, and when I asked her about it, I nearly ruined everything.

"What do you mean?" Evie said, narrowing her eyes at me. "Your hair has always been long."

I blinked at her, remembering to play dumb. "I know."

She stared at me awhile longer before she finally let it go, but I'm still worried I'll pay for that slip. Sometimes it's hard to remember how to act. My mind is being attacked, assaulted every day by emotion I never knew existed. My memories were supposed to be erased. Instead, they're being replenished.

I'm remembering everything:

My mother's laugh, her slender wrists, the smell of her shampoo, and the familiarity of her arms around me.

The more I remember, the less this place feels foreign to me. The less these sounds and smells—these mountains in the distance—feel unknown. It's as if the disparate parts of my most desperate self are stitching back together, as if the gaping holes in my heart and head are healing, filling slowly with sensation.

This compound was my home. These people, my family. I woke up this morning remembering my mother's favorite shade of lipstick.

Bloodred.

I remember watching her paint her lips some evenings. I remember the day I snuck into her room and stole the glossy metal tube; I remember when she found me, my hands and mouth smeared in red, my face a grotesque reimagining of herself.

The more I remember my parents, the more I begin to finally make sense of myself—my many fears and insecurities, the myriad ways in which I've often felt lost, searching for something I could not name.

It's devastating.

And yet—

In this new, turbulent reality, the one person I recognize anymore is *him*. My memories of him—memories of us—have done something to me. I've changed somewhere deep inside. I feel different. Heavier, like my feet have been more firmly planted, liberated by certainty, free to grow roots here in my own self, free to trust unequivocally in the strength and steadiness of my own heart. It's an empowering discovery, to find that I can trust myself—even when I'm not myself—to make the right choices. To know for certain now that there was at least one mistake I never made.

Aaron Warner Anderson is the only emotional through line in my life that ever made sense. He's the only constant. The only steady, reliable heartbeat I've ever had.

Aaron, Aaron, Aaron, Aaron

I had no idea how much we'd lost, no idea how much of him I'd longed for. I had no idea how desperately we'd been fighting. How many years we'd fought for moments—minutes—to be together.

It fills me with a painful kind of joy.

But when I remember how I left things between us, I want to *scream*.

I have no idea if I'll ever see him again.

Still, I'm holding on to the hope that he's alive, out there, somewhere. Evie said she couldn't kill him. She said that she alone didn't have the authority to have him executed. And if Aaron is still alive, I will find a way to get to him. But I have to be careful. Breaking out of this new prison won't be easy— As it is, Evie almost never lets me out of my room. Worse, she sedates me during the day, allowing me only a couple of lucid hours. There's never enough time to *think*, much less to plan an escape, to assess my surroundings, or to wander the halls outside my door.

Only once did she let me go outside.

Sort of.

She let me onto a balcony overlooking the backyard. It wasn't much, but even that small step helped me understand a bit about where we were and what the layout of the building might look like.

The assessment was chilling.

We appeared to be in the center of a settlement—a small city—in the middle of nowhere. I leaned over the edge of the balcony, craning my neck to take in the breadth of it, but the view was so vast I couldn't see all the way around. From where I stood I saw at least twenty different buildings, all connected by roads and navigated by people in miniature, electric cars. There were loading and unloading docks, massive trucks filing in and out, and there was a landing strip in the distance, a row of jets parked neatly in a concrete lot. I understood then that I was living in the middle of a massive operation—something so much more terrifying than Sector 45.

This is an international base.

This has to be one of the capitals. Whatever this is—whatever they do here—it makes Sector 45 look like a joke.

Here, where the hills are somehow still green and beautiful, where the air is fresh and cool and everything seems alive. My accounting is probably off, but I think we're nearing the end of April—and the sights outside my window are unlike anything I've ever seen in Sector 45: vast, snow-capped mountain ranges; rolling hills thick with vegetation; trees heavy with bright, changing leaves; and a massive, glittering lake that looks close enough to run to. This land looks healthy. Vibrant.

I thought we'd lost a world like this a long time ago.

Evie's begun to sedate me less these days, but some days my vision seems to fray at the edges, like a satellite image glitching, waiting for data to load.

I wonder, sometimes, if she's poisoning me.

I'm wondering this now, remembering the bowl of soup she sent to my room for breakfast. I can still feel the gluey residue as it coated my tongue, the roof of my mouth.

Unease churns my stomach.

I haul myself up off the bathroom floor, my limbs slow and heavy. It takes me a moment to stabilize. The effects of this experiment have left me hollow.

Angry.

As if out of nowhere, my mind conjures an image of Evie's face. I remember her eyes. Deep, dark brown. Bottomless. The same color as her hair. She has a short, sharp bob, a heavy curtain constantly whipping against her chin. She's a beautiful woman, more beautiful at fifty than she was at twenty.

Coming.

The word occurs to me suddenly, and a bolt of panic shoots up my spine. Not a second later there's a sharp knock at my bathroom door.

"Yes?"

"Ella, you've been in the bathroom for almost half an hour, and you know how I feel about wasting ti—"

"*Evie.*" I force myself to laugh. "I'm almost done," I say. "I'll be right out."

A pause.

The silence stretches the seconds into a lifetime. My heart jumps up, into my throat. Beats in my mouth.

"All right," she says slowly. "Five more minutes."

I close my eyes as I exhale, pressing the towel to the racing pulse at my neck. I dry off quickly before wringing the remaining water from my hair and slipping back into my robe.

Finally, I open the bathroom door and welcome the cool morning temperature against my feverish skin. But I hardly have a chance to take a breath before she's in my face again.

"Wear this," she says, forcing a dress into my arms. She's smiling but it doesn't suit her. She looks deranged. "You love wearing yellow."

I blink as I take the dress from her, feeling a sudden, disorienting wave of déjà vu. "Of course," I say. "I love wearing yellow."

Her smile grows thinner, threatens to turn her face inside out.

"Could I just—?" I make an abstract gesture toward my body.

"Oh," she says, startled. "Right." She shoots me another smile and says, "I'll be outside."

My own smile is brittle.

She watches me. She always watches me. Studies my reactions, the timing of my responses. She's scanning me, constantly, for information. She wants confirmation that I've been properly hollowed out. *Remade.*

I smile wider.

Finally, she takes a step back. "Good girl," she says softly.

I stand in the middle of my room and watch her leave, the yellow dress still pressed against my chest.

There was another time when I'd felt trapped, just like this. I was held against my will and given beautiful clothes and three square meals and demanded to be something I wasn't and I fought it—fought it with everything I had.

It didn't do me any good.

I swore that if I could do it again I'd do it differently. I said if I could do it over I'd wear the clothes and eat the food and play along until I could figure out where I was and how to break free.

So here's my chance.

This time, I've decided to play along.

KENJI

I wake up, bound and gagged, a roaring sound in my ears. I blink to clear my vision. I'm bound so tightly I can't move, so it takes me a second to realize I can't see my legs.

No legs. No arms, either.

The revelation that I'm invisible hits me with full, horrifying force.

I'm not doing this.

I didn't bring myself here, bind and gag myself, and make myself invisible.

There's only one other person who would.

I look around desperately, trying to gauge where I am and what my chances might be for escape, but when I finally manage to heave my body to one side—just long enough to crane my neck—I realize, with a terrifying jolt, that I'm on a plane.

And then—voices.

It's Anderson and Nazeera.

I hear them discussing something about how we'll be landing soon, and then, minutes later, I feel it when we touch ground.

The plane taxis for a while and it seems to take forever before the engines finally turn off.

I hear Anderson leave. Nazeera hangs back, saying something about needing to clean up. She shuts down the plane and its cameras, doesn't acknowledge me.

Finally, I hear her footsteps getting closer to my head. She uses one foot to roll me onto my back, and then, just like that, my invisibility is gone. She stares at me for a little while longer, says nothing.

Finally, she smiles.

"Hi," she says, removing the gag from my mouth. "How are you holding up?"

And I decide right then that I'm going to have to kill her.

"Okay," she says, "I know you're probably upset—"

"UPSET? YOU THINK I'M UPSET?" I jerk violently against the ties. "Jesus Christ, woman, get me out of these goddamn restraints—"

"I'll get you out of the restraints when you calm down—"

"HOW CAN YOU EXPECT ME TO BE CALM?"

"I'm trying to save your life right now, so, actually, I expect a lot of things from you."

I'm breathing hard. "Wait. What?"

She crosses her arms, stares down at me. "I've been trying to explain to you that there was really no other way to do this. And don't worry," she says. "Your friends are okay. We should be able to get them out of the asylum before any permanent damage is done."

"What? What do you mean *permanent damage*?"

Nazeera sighs. "Anyway, this was the only way I could think of stealing a plane without attracting notice. I needed to track Anderson."

"So you knew he was alive, that whole time, and you said nothing about it."

She raises her eyebrows. "Honestly, I thought you knew."

"How the hell was I supposed to know?" I shout. "How was I supposed to know *anything*?"

"Stop shouting," she says. "I went to all this trouble to save your life but I swear to God I will kill you if you don't stop shouting right now."

"Where," I say, "THE HELL," I say, "ARE WE?"

And instead of killing me, she laughs. "Where do you think we are?" She shakes her head. "We're in Oceania. We're here to find Ella."

WARNER

"We can live in the lake," she says simply.

"What?" I almost laugh. "What are you talking about?"

"I'm serious," she says. "I heard my mum talking about how to make it so people can live underwater, and I'm going to ask her to tell me, and then we can live in the lake."

I sigh. "We can't live in the lake, Ella."

"Why not?" She turns and looks at me, her eyes wide, startlingly bright. Blue green. Like the globe, I think. Like the whole world. "Why can't we live in the lake? My mum says th—"

"Stop it, Ella. Stop—"

I wake suddenly, jerking upward as my eyes fly open, my lungs desperate for air. I breathe in too fast and cough, choking on the overcorrection of oxygen. My body bows forward, chest heaving, my hands braced against the cold, concrete floor.

Ella.

Ella.

Pain spears me through the chest. I stopped eating the poisoned food two days ago, but the visions linger even when I'm lucid. There's something hyperreal about this one in particular, the memory barreling into me over and over, shooting swift, sharp pains through my gut. It's breathtaking, this disorienting rush of emotion.

For the first time, I'm beginning to believe.

I thought nightmares. Hallucinations, even. But now I know.

Now it seems impossible to deny.

I heard my mum talking about how to make it so people can live underwater

I didn't understand right away why Max and Evie were keeping me captive here, but they must blame me for something—maybe something my father is responsible for. Something I unknowingly took part in.

Maybe something like torturing their daughter Emmaline.

When I was sent away for two years, I was never told where I was going. The details of my location were never disclosed, and during that time period I lived in a veritable prison of my own, never allowed to step outside, never allowed to know more than was absolutely necessary about the task at hand. The breaks I was given were closely guarded, and I was required to wear a blindfold as I was ushered on and off the jet, which always made me think I must've been working somewhere easily identifiable. But those two years also comprised some of the darkest, saddest days of my life; all I knew was my desperate need for oblivion. I was so buried in self-loathing that it seemed only right to find solace in the arms of someone who meant nothing to me. I hated myself every day. Being with Lena was both relief and torture.

Even so, I felt numb, all the time.

After two weeks here, I'm beginning to wonder if this prison isn't one I've known before. If this isn't the same place I spent those two horrible years of my life. It's hard to explain the intangible, irrational reasons why the view outside my window is beginning to feel familiar to me, but two years is a long time to grow familiar with the rhythms of a land, even one you don't understand.

I wonder if Emmaline is here, somewhere.

It makes sense that she'd be here, close to home—close to her parents, whose medical and scientific advances are the only reason she's even alive. Or something close to alive, anyway.

It makes sense that they'd bring Juliette—*Ella,* I remind myself—back here, to her home. The question is—

Why bring her here? What are they hoping to do with her?

But then, if her mother is anything like my father, I think I can imagine what they might have in mind.

I push myself off the floor and take a steadying breath. My body is running on mere adrenaline, so starved for sleep and sustenance that I have to—

Pain.

It's swift and sudden and I gasp even as I recognize the familiar sting. I have no idea how long it'll take for my ribs to fully heal. Until then, I clench my teeth as I stand, feeling blindly for purchase against the rough stone. My hands shake as I steady myself and I'm breathing too hard again, eyes darting around the familiar cell.

I turn on the sink and splash ice-cold water on my face.

The effect is immediate. Focusing.

Carefully, I strip down to nothing. I soak my undershirt under the running water and use it to scrub my face, my neck, the rest of my body. I wash my hair. Rinse my mouth. Clean my teeth. And then I do what little I can for the rest of my clothes, washing them by hand and wringing them dry. I slip back into my underwear even though the cotton is still slightly damp, and I fight back a shiver in the darkness. Hungry and cold is at least better than drugged and delirious.

This is the end of my second week in confinement, and my third day this week without food. It feels good to have a clear head, even as my body slowly starves. I'd already been leaner than usual, but now the lines of my body feel unusually sharp, even to myself, all necessary softness gone from my limbs. It's only a matter of time before my muscles atrophy and I do irreparable damage to my organs, but right now I have no choice. I need access to my mind.

To *think*.

And something about my sentencing feels off.

The more I think about it, the less sense it makes that Max and Evie would want me to suffer for what I did to Emmaline. They were the ones who donated their daughters to The Reestablishment in the first place. My work overseeing Emmaline was assigned to me—in fact, it was likely a job they'd approved. It would make more sense that I were here for treason. Max and Evie, like any other commanders, would want me to suffer for turning my back on The Reestablishment.

But even this theory feels wrong. Incongruous.

The punishment for treason has always been public execution. Quick. Efficient. I should be murdered, with only a little fanfare, in front of my own soldiers. But this—locking people up like this—slowly starving them while stripping them of their sanity and dignity—this is uncivilized. It's what The Reestablishment does to others, not to its own.

It's what they did to Ella. They tortured her. Ran tests on her. She wasn't locked up to inspire penitence. She was in isolation because she was part of an ongoing experiment.

And I am in the unique position to know that such a prisoner requires constant maintenance.

I figured I'd be kept here for a few days—maybe a week—but locking me up for what seems to be an indeterminate amount of time—

This must be difficult for them.

For two weeks they've managed to remain just slightly ahead of me, a feat they accomplished by poisoning my food. In training I'd never needed more than a week to break my way out of high-security prisons, and they must've known this. By forcing me to choose between sustenance and clarity every day, they've given themselves an advantage.

Still, I'm unconcerned.

The longer I'm here, the more leverage I gain. If they

know what I'm capable of, they must also know that this is unsustainable. They can't use shock and poison to destabilize me indefinitely. I've now been here long enough to have taken stock of my surroundings, and I've been filing away information for nearly two weeks—the movements of the sun, the phases of the moon, the manufacturer of the locks, the sink, the unusual hinges on the door. I suspected, but now know for certain, that I'm in the southern hemisphere, not only because I know Max and Evie hail from Oceania, but because the northern constellations outside my window are upside down.

I must be on their base.

Logically, I know I must've been here a few times in my life, but the memories are dim. The night skies are clearer here than they were in Sector 45. The stars, brighter. The lack of light pollution means we are far from civilization, and the view out the window proves that we are surrounded, on all sides, by the wild landscape of this territory. There's a massive, glittering lake not far in the distance, which—

Something jolts to life in my mind.

The memory from earlier, expanded:

She shrugs and throws a rock in the lake. It lands with a dull splash. "Well, we'll just run away," she says.

"We can't run away," I say. "Stop saying that."

"We can, too."

"There's nowhere to go."

"There are plenty of places to go."

I shake my head. "You know what I mean. They'd find us wherever we went. They watch us all the time."

"We can live in the lake," she says simply.

"What?" I almost laugh. "What are you talking about?"

"I'm serious," she says. "I heard my mum talking about how to make it so people can live underwater, and I'm going to ask her to tell me, and then we can live in the lake."

I sigh. "We can't live in the lake, Ella."

"Why not?" She turns and looks at me, her eyes wide, startlingly bright. Blue green. Like the globe, I think. Like the whole world. "Why can't we live in the lake? My mum says th—"

"Stop it, Ella. Stop—"

A cold sweat breaks out on my forehead. Goose bumps rise along my skin. *Ella.*

Ella Ella Ella

Over and over again.

Everything about the name is beginning to sound familiar. The movement of my tongue as I form the word, familiar. It's as if the memory is in my muscle, as if my mouth has made this shape a thousand times.

I force myself to take a steadying breath.

I need to find her. *I have to find her.*

Here is what I know:

It takes just under thirty seconds for the footsteps to disappear down the hall, and they're always the same—same stride, same cadence—which means there's only one person attending to me. The paces are long and heavy, which means my attendant is tall, possibly male. Maybe Max himself, if they've deemed me a high-priority prisoner. Still, they've left me unshackled and unharmed—*why?*—and though I've been given neither bed nor blanket, I have access to water from the sink.

There's no electricity in here; no outlets, no wires. But there must be cameras hidden somewhere, watching my every move. There are two drains: one in the sink, and one underneath the toilet. There's one square foot of window—likely bulletproof glass, maybe eight to ten centimeters thick—and a single, small air vent in the floor. The vent has no visible screws, which means it must be bolted from inside, and the slats are too narrow for my fingers, the steel blades visibly welded in place. Still, it's only an average level of security for a prison vent. A little more time and clarity, and I'll find a way to remove the screen and repurpose the parts. Eventually, I'll find a way to dismantle everything in this room. I'll take apart the metal toilet, the flimsy metal sink. I'll make my own tools and weapons and find a way to slowly, carefully disassemble the locks and hinges. Or perhaps I'll damage the pipes and flood the room and its adjoining hallway, forcing someone to come to the door.

The sooner they send someone to my room, the better. If they've left me alone in my cell this long, it's been for their own protection, not my suffering. I excel at hand-to-hand combat.

I know myself. I know my capacity to withstand complicated physical and mental torture. If I wanted to, I could give myself two—maybe three—weeks to forgo the poisoned meals and survive on water alone before I lost my mind or mobility. I know how resourceful I can be, given the opportunity, and this—this effort to contain me—must be exhausting. Great care went into selecting these sounds and meals and rituals and even this vigilant lack of communication.

It doesn't make sense that they'd go to all this trouble for treason. No. I must be in purgatory for something else.

I rack my brain for a motive, but my memories are surprisingly thin when it comes to Max and Evie. Still forming.

With some difficulty, I'm able to conjure up flickers of images.

A brief handshake with my father.

A burst of laughter.

A cheerful swell of holiday music.

A laboratory and my mother.

I stiffen.

A laboratory and my mother.

I focus my thoughts, homing in on the memory—*bright lights, muffled footsteps, the sound of my own voice asking my father a question* and then, painfully—

My mind goes blank.

I frown. Stare into my hands.

Nothing.

I know a great deal about the other commanders and their families. It's been my business to know. But there's an unusual dearth of information where Oceania is concerned, and for the first time, it sends a shock of fear through me. There are two timelines merging in my mind—a life with Ella, and a life without her—and I'm still learning to sift through the information for something real.

Still, thinking about Max and Evie now seems to strain something in my brain. It's as if there's something there, something just out of reach, and the more I force my mind to recall them—their faces, their voices—the more it hurts.

Why all this trouble to imprison me?

Why not simply have me killed?

I have so many questions it's making my head spin.

Just then, the door rattles. The sound of metal on metal is sharp and abrasive, the sounds like sandpaper against my nerves.

I hear the bolt unlock and feel unusually calm. I was built to handle this life, its blows, its sick, sadistic ways. Death has never scared me.

But when the door swings open, I realize my mistake.

I imagined a thousand different scenarios. I prepared for a myriad of opponents. But I had not prepared for this.

"Hi birthday boy," he says, laughing as he steps into the light. "Did you miss me?"

And I'm suddenly unable to move.

~~JULIETTE~~
ELLA

"Stop—stop it, oh my God, that's disgusting," Emmaline cries. "Stop it. Stop touching each other! You guys are so gross."

Dad pinches Mum's butt, right in front of us.

Emmaline screams. "Oh my God, I said stop!"

It's Saturday morning, and Saturday morning is when we make pancakes, but Mum and Dad don't really get around to cooking anything because they won't stop kissing each other. Emmaline hates it.

I think it's nice.

I sit at the counter and prop my face in my hands, watching. I prefer watching. Emmaline keeps trying to make me work, but I don't want to. I like sitting better than working.

"No one is making pancakes," Emmaline cries, and she spins around so angrily she knocks a bowl of batter to the ground. "Why am I doing all the work?"

Dad laughs. "Sweetheart, we're all together," he says, scooping up the fallen bowl. He grabs a bunch of paper towels and says, "Isn't that more important than pancakes?"

"No," Emmaline says angrily. "We're supposed to make pancakes. It's Saturday, which means we're supposed to make pancakes, and you and Mum are just kissing, and Ella is being lazy—"

"Hey—" I say, and stand up.

"—and no one is doing what they're supposed to be doing and

instead I'm doing it all by myself—"

Mum and Dad are both laughing now.

"It's not funny!" Emmaline cries, and now she's shouting, tears streaking down her face. "It's not funny, and I don't like it when no one listens to me, and I don't—"

Two weeks ago, I was lying on an operating table, limp, naked, and leaking blood through an aperture in my temple the size of a gunshot wound. My vision was blurred. I couldn't hear much more than the sound of my own breathing, hot and heavy and everywhere, building in and around me. Suddenly, Evie came into view. She was staring at me; she seemed frustrated. She'd been trying to complete the process of *physical recalibration,* as she called it.

For some reason, she couldn't finish the job.

She'd already emptied the contents of sixteen syringes into my brain, and she'd made several small incisions in my abdomen, my arms, and my thighs. I couldn't see exactly what she did next, but she spoke, occasionally, as she worked, and she claimed that the simple surgical procedures she was performing would strengthen my joints and reinforce my muscles. She wanted me to be stronger, to be more resilient on a cellular level. It was a preventative measure, she said. She was worried my build was too slight; that my muscles might degenerate prematurely in the face of intense physical challenges. She didn't say it, but I felt it: she wanted me to be stronger than my sister.

"Emmaline," I whispered.

It was lucky that I was too exhausted, too broken, too

sedated to speak clearly. It was lucky that I only lay there, eyes fluttering open and closed, my chapped lips making it impossible to do more than mutter the name. It was lucky that I couldn't understand, right away, that I was still *me*. That I still remembered everything despite Evie's promises to dissolve what was left of my mind.

Still, I'd said the wrong thing.

Evie stopped what she was doing. She leaned over my face and studied me, nose to nose.

I blinked.

Don't

The words appeared in my head as if they'd been planted there long ago, like I was remembering, remembering

Evie jerked backward and immediately started speaking into a device clenched in her fist. Her voice was low and rough and I couldn't make out what she was saying.

I blinked again. Confused. I parted my lips to say something, when—

Don't

The thought came through more sharply this time.

A moment later Evie was in my face again, this time drilling me with questions.

who are you
where are you

what is your name
where were you born
how old are you
who are your parents
where do you live

I was suddenly aware enough to understand that Evie was checking her work. She wanted to make sure my brain had been wiped clean. I wasn't sure what I was supposed to say or do, so I said nothing.

Instead, I blinked.

Blinked a lot.

Evie finally—reluctantly—stepped away, but she didn't seem entirely convinced of my stupidity. And then, when I thought she might murder me just to be safe, she stopped. Stared at the wall.

And then she left.

I was trembling on the operating table for twenty minutes before the room was swarmed by a team of people. They unstrapped my body, washed and wrapped my open wounds.

I think I was screaming.

Eventually the combination of pain, exhaustion, and the slow drip of opiates caught up with me, and I passed out.

I never understood what happened that day.

I couldn't ask, Evie never explained, and the strange, sharp voice in my head never returned. But then, Evie sedated me so much in my first weeks on this compound that it's possible there was never even a chance.

Today, for the first time since that day, I hear it again.

I'm standing in the middle of my room, this gauzy yellow dress still bunched in my arms, when the voice assaults me.

It knocks the wind out of me.

Ella

I spin around, my breaths coming in fast. The voice is louder than it's ever been, frightening in its intensity. Maybe I was wrong about Evie's experiment, maybe this is part of it, maybe hallucinating and hearing voices is a precursor to oblivion—

No

"Who are you?" I say, the dress dropping to the floor. It occurs to me, as if from a distance, that I'm standing in my underwear, screaming at an empty room, and a violent shudder goes through my body.

Roughly, I yank the yellow dress over my head, its light, breezy layers like silk against my skin. In a different lifetime, I would've loved this dress. It's both beautiful and comfortable, the perfect sartorial combination. But there's no time for that kind of frivolity anymore.

Today, this dress is just a part of the role I must play.

The voice in my head has gone quiet, but my heart is still racing. I feel propelled into motion by instinct alone, and, quickly, I slip into a pair of simple white tennis shoes, tying the laces tightly. I don't know why, but today, *right now*, for some reason— I feel like I might need to run.

Yes

My spine straightens.

Adrenaline courses through my veins and my muscles feel tight, burning with an intensity that feels brand-new to me; it's the first time I've felt any positive effects of Evie's procedures. This strength feels like it's been grafted to my bones, like I could launch myself into the air, like I could scale a wall with one hand.

I've known superstrength before, but that strength always felt like it was coming from elsewhere, like it was something I had to harness and release. Without my supernatural abilities—when I turned off my powers—I was left with an unimpressive, flimsy body. I'd been undernourished for years, forced to endure extreme physical and mental conditions, and my body suffered for it. I'd only begun to learn proper forms of exercise and conditioning in the last couple of months, and while the progress I made was helpful, it was only the first step in the right direction.

But this—

Whatever Evie did to me? This is different.

Two weeks ago I was in so much pain I could hardly move. The next morning, when I could finally stand on my own, I saw no discernible difference in my body except that I was seven shades of purple from top to bottom. Everything was bruised. I was walking agony.

Evie told me, as my doctor, that she kept me sedated so that I'd be forced to remain still in order to heal more quickly, but I had no reason to believe her. I still don't. But this is the first time in two weeks that I feel almost normal. The bruises have nearly faded. Only the incision sites, the most painful entry points, still look a little yellow.

Not bad.

I flex my fists and feel powerful, truly powerful, even with the glowing manacles clamped around my wrists and ankles. I've desperately missed my powers, missed them more than I ever thought I could miss something I'd spent so many years hating about myself. But for the first time in weeks, I feel strong. I know Evie did this to me—did this to my muscles—and I know I should distrust it, but it feels so good to feel good that I almost can't help but revel in it.

And right now, I feel like I could—

Run

I go still.

RUN

"What?" I whisper, turning to scan the walls, the ceiling. "Run where?"

Out

The word thunders through me, reverberates along my rib cage. *Out.* As if it were that simple, as if I could turn the doorknob and be rid of this nightmare. If it were that easy to leave this room, I would've done it already. But Evie reinforces the locks on my door with multiple layers of security. I only saw the mechanics of it once, when she returned me to my room after allowing me to look outside for a few minutes. In addition to the discreet cameras and retina displays, there's a biometric scanner that reads Evie's fingerprints to allow her access to the room. I've spent hours trying to get my bedroom door open, to no avail.

Out

Again, that word, loud and harsh inside my head. There's something terrifying about the hope that snakes through me at the thought of escape. It clings and tugs and tempts me to be crazy enough to listen to the absurd hallucinations attacking my mind.

This could be a trap, I think.

This could all be Evie's doing. I could be playing directly into her hand.

Still.

I can't help myself.

I cross the room in a few quick strides. I hesitate, my hand hovering over the handle, and, with a final exhalation, I give in.

The door swings opens easily.

I stand in the open doorway, my heart racing harder. A

heady rush of feeling surges through me and I look around desperately, studying the many hallways stretching out before me.

This seems impossible.

I have no idea where to go. No idea if I'm crazy for listening to a manipulative voice in my head after my psychotic mother spent hours injecting things into my mind.

It's only when I remember that I first heard this voice the night I arrived—just moments before Evie began torturing me—that I begin to doubt my doubt.

Dying

That was what the voice said to me that first night. *Dying.*

I was lying on an operating table, unable to move or speak. I could only shout inside my head and I wanted to know where Emmaline was. I tried to scream it.

Dying, the voice had said.

A cold, paralyzing fear fills my blood.

"Emmaline?" I whisper. "Is that you?"

Help

I take a certain step forward.

WARNER

“I’m a little early,” he says. “I know your birthday is tomorrow, but I just couldn’t wait any longer.”

I stare at my father as though he might be a ghost. Worse, a poltergeist. I can’t bring myself to speak, and for some reason he doesn’t seem to mind my silence.

Then—

He smiles.

It’s a true smile, one that softens his features and brightens his eyes. We’re in something that looks like a sitting room, a bright, open space with plush couches, chairs, a round table, and a small writing desk in the corner. There’s a thick carpet underfoot. The walls are a pleasant, pale yellow, sun pouring in through large windows. My father’s figure is backlit. He looks ethereal. Glowing, like he might be an angel.

This world has a sick sense of humor.

He tossed me a robe when he walked into my cell, but hasn’t offered me anything else. I haven’t been given a chance to change. I haven’t been offered food or water. I feel underdressed—vulnerable—sitting across from him in nothing but cold underwear and a thin robe. I don’t even have socks. Slippers. *Something.*

And I can only imagine what I must look like right now, considering it's been a couple of weeks since I've had a shave or a haircut. I managed to keep myself clean in prison, but my hair is a bit longer now. Not like it used to be, but it's getting there. And my face—

I touch my face almost without thinking.

Touching my face has become a bit of a habit these last couple of weeks. I have a beard. It's not much of a beard, but it's enough to surprise me, every time. I have no idea how I must look right now.

Untamed, perhaps.

Finally, I say, "You're supposed to be dead."

"Surprise," he says, and smiles.

I only stare at him.

My father leans against the table and stuffs his hands into his pants' pockets in a way that makes him look boyish. Charming.

It makes me feel ill.

I look away, scanning the room for help. Details. Something to root me, something to explain *him*, something to arm me against what might be coming.

I come up short.

He laughs. "You know, you could stand to show a bit more emotion. I actually thought you might be happy to see me."

That gets my attention. "You thought wrong," I say. "I was happy to hear you were dead."

"Are you sure?" He tilts his head. "You're sure you didn't

shed a single tear for me? Didn't miss me even the tiniest bit?"

All it takes is a moment of hesitation. The half-second delay during which I remember the weeks I spent caught in a prison of half grief, hating myself for mourning him, and hating that I ever cared at all.

I open my mouth to speak and he cuts me off, his smile triumphant. "I know this must be a bit unsettling. And I know you're going to pretend you don't care. But we both know that your bleeding heart has always been the source of all our problems, and there's no point trying to deny that now. So I'll be generous and offer to overlook your treasonous behavior."

My spine stiffens.

"You didn't think I'd just forget, did you?" My father is no longer smiling. "You try to overthrow *me*—my government, my continent—and then you stand aside like a perfect, pathetic piece of garbage as your girlfriend attempts to *murder* me—and you thought I'd never mention it?"

I can't look at him anymore. I can't stand the sight of his face, so like my own. His skin is still perfect, unscarred. As if he'd never been injured. Never taken a bullet to the forehead.

I don't understand it.

"No? You still won't be inspired to respond?" he says. "In that case, you might be smarter than I gave you credit for."

There. That feels more like him.

"But the fact remains that we're at an important crossroads right now. I had to call in a number of favors to have you transported here unharmed. The council was going to vote to have you executed for treason, and I was able to convince them otherwise."

"Why would you even bother?"

His eyes narrow as he appraises me. "I save your life," he says, "and this is your reaction? Insolence? Ingratitude?"

"This," I say sharply, "is your idea of saving my life? Throwing me in prison and having me poisoned to death?"

"That should've been a picnic." His gaze grows cold. "You really would be better off dead if those circumstances were enough to break you."

I say nothing.

"Besides, we had to punish you somehow. Your actions couldn't go unchecked." My father looks away. "We've had a lot of messes to clean up," he says finally. "Where do you think I've been all this time?"

"As I said, I thought you were dead."

"Close, but not quite. Actually," he says, taking a breath, "I spent a great deal of time convalescing. *Here.* I was airlifted back here, where the Sommerses have been reviving me." He pulls up the hem of his pants and I glimpse the silver gleam of metal where his ankle should be. "I've got new feet," he says, and laughs. "Can you believe it?"

I can't. I can't believe it.

I'm stunned.

He smiles, obviously satisfied with my reaction. "We

let you and your friends think you'd had a victory just long enough to give me time to recover. We sent the rest of the kids down to distract you, to make it seem like The Reestablishment might actually accept its new, self-appointed commander." He shakes his head. "A seventeen-year-old child declaring herself the ruler of North America," he says, almost to himself. And then, looking up: "That girl really was a piece of work, wasn't she?"

Panic gathers in my chest. "What did you do to her? Where is she?"

"No." My father's smile disappears. "Absolutely not."

"What does that mean?"

"It means *absolutely not*. That girl is done. She's gone. No more afternoon specials with your buddies from Omega Point. No more running around naked with your little girlfriend. No more sex in the afternoon when you should be working."

I feel both ill and enraged. "Don't you dare— Don't *ever* talk about her like that. You have no right—"

He sighs, long and loud. Mutters something foul. "When are you going stop this? When will you grow out of this?"

It takes everything I've got to bite back my anger. To sit here, calmly, and say nothing. Somehow, my silence makes things worse.

"Dammit, Aaron," he says, getting to his feet. "I keep waiting for you to move on. To get over her. To *evolve*," he says, practically shouting at me now. "It's been over a decade of the same bullshit."

Over a decade.

A slip.

"What do you mean," I say, studying him carefully. "'Over a decade'?"

"I'm exaggerating," he says, biting off the words. "Exaggerating to make a point."

"Liar."

For the first time, something uncertain flashes through my father's eyes.

"Will you admit it?" I say quietly. "Will you admit to me what I already know?"

He sets his jaw. Says nothing.

"Admit it," I say. "Juliette was an alias. Juliette Ferrars is actually Ella Sommers, the daughter of Evie and Maximillian Som—"

"How—" My father catches himself. He looks away and then, too soon, he looks back. He seems to be deciding something.

Finally, slowly, he nods.

"You know what? It's better this way. Better for you to know," he says quietly. "Better for you to understand exactly why you're never going to see her again."

"That's not up to you."

"Not up to me?" Rage flashes in and out of his eyes, his cool mask quickly crumbling. "That girl has been the bane of my existence for *twelve years,*" he says. "She's caused me more problems than you can even begin to understand, not the least of which has been to distract my idiot son for the better part of the last decade. Despite my every effort to break you apart—to remove this cancer from our lives—you've insisted, over and over again, on falling in love with her." He looks me in the eye, his own eyes wild with fury. "She was never meant for you. She was never meant for any of this. That girl was sentenced to death," he says viciously, "the moment I named her Juliette."

My heart is beating so hard it feels as though I'm dreaming. This must be a nightmare. I have to force myself to speak. To say:

"What are you talking about?"

My father's mouth twists into an imitation of a smile.

"Ella," he says, "was designed to become a tool for war. She and her sister both, right from the beginning. Decades before we took over, sicknesses were beginning to ravage the population. The government was trying to bury the information, but we knew. I saw the classified files. I tracked down one of the secret bunkers. People were malfunctioning, metamorphosing—so much so that it felt almost like the next phase of evolution. Only Evie had the presence of mind to see the sickness as a tool. She was the one who first began studying the Unnaturals. She was the reason we created the asylums—she wanted access to more varieties of the illness—and she was the one who learned how to isolate and reproduce the alien DNA. It was her idea to use the findings to help our cause. Ella and Emmaline," he says angrily, "were only ever meant to be Evie's science experiments. Ella was never meant for you. Never meant for *anyone*," he shouts. "Get her out of your head."

I feel frozen as the words settle around me. Within me. The revelation isn't entirely new and yet—the pain is fresh. Time seems to slow down, speed up, spin backward. My eyes fall closed. My memories collect and expand, exploding with renewed meaning as they assault me, all at once—

Ella through the ages.

My childhood friend.

Ella, ripped away from me when I was seven years old. Ella and Emmaline, who they'd said had drowned in the lake. They told me to forget, to forget the girls ever existed and, finally, tired of answering my questions, they told me they'd make things easier for me. I followed my father into a room where he promised he'd explain everything.

And then—

I'm strapped to a chair, my head held in place with heavy metal clamps. Bright lights flash and buzz above me.

I hear the monitors chirping, the muffled sounds of voices around me. The room feels large and cavernous, gleaming. I hear the loud, disconcerting sounds of my own breathing and the hard, heavy beats of my heart. I jump, a little, at the unwelcome feel of my father's hand on my arm, telling me I'll feel better soon.

I look up at him as if emerging from a dream.

"What is it?" he says. "What just happened?"

I part my lips to speak, wonder if it's safe to tell him the truth.

I decide I'm tired of the lies.

"I've been remembering her," I say.

My father's face goes unexpectedly blank, and it's the only reaction I need to understand the final, missing piece.

"You've been stealing my memories," I say to him, my voice unnaturally calm. "All these years. You've been tampering with my mind. It was you."

He says nothing, but I see the tension in his jaw, the sudden jump of a vein under skin. "What are you remembering?"

I shake my head, stunned as I stare at him. "I should've known. After everything you've done to me—" I stop, my vision shifts, unfocused for a moment. "Of course you wouldn't let me be master of my own mind."

"What, exactly, are you remembering?" he says, hardly able to control the anger in his voice now. "What else do you know?"

At first, I feel nothing.

I've trained myself too well. Years of practice have taught me to bury my emotions as a reflex—especially in his presence—and it takes a few seconds for the feelings to emerge. They form slowly, infinite hands reaching up from infinite graves to fan the flames of an ancient rage I've never really allowed myself to touch.

"You stole my memories of her," I say quietly. "Why?"

"Always so focused on the girl." He glares at me. "She's not the center of everything, Aaron. I stole your memories of lots of things."

I'm shaking my head. I get to my feet slowly, at once out of my mind and perfectly calm, and I worry, for a moment, that I might actually expire from the full force of everything I feel for him. Hatred so deep it might boil me alive.

"Why would you do something like this except to torture me? You knew how I felt about her. You did it on purpose. Pushing us together and pulling us apart—" I stop suddenly. Realization dawns, bright and piercing and I look at him, unable to fathom the depth of his cruelty.

"You put Kent under my command on purpose," I say.

My father meets my eyes with a vacant expression. He says nothing.

"I find it hard to believe you didn't know the whereabouts of your illegitimate children," I say to him. "I don't believe for a second that you weren't having Kent's every move monitored. You must've known what he was doing with his life. You must've been notified the moment he enlisted.

"You could've sent him anywhere," I say. "You had the power to do that. Instead, you let him remain in Sector 45—under *my* jurisdiction—on purpose. Didn't you? And when you had Delalieu show me those files—when he came to me, convinced me that Kent would be the perfect cellmate for Juliette because here was proof that he'd known her, that they'd gone to school together—"

Suddenly, my father smiles.

"I've always tried to tell you," he says softly. "I've tried to tell you to stop letting your emotions rule your mind. Over and over, I tried to teach you, and you never listened. You never learned." He shakes his head. "If you suffer now, it's because you brought it upon yourself. You made yourself an easy target."

I'm stunned.

Somehow, even after everything, he manages to shock me. "I don't understand how you can stand there, defending your actions, after you spent twenty years torturing me."

"I've only ever been trying to teach you a lesson, Aaron. I didn't want you to end up like your mother. She was weak, just like you."

I need to kill him.

I picture it: what it would be like to pin him to the ground, to stab him repeatedly through the heart, to watch the light go out of his eyes, to feel his body go cold under my hands.

I wait for fear.

Revulsion.

Regret.

They don't come.

I have no idea how he survived the last attempt on his life, but I no longer care to know the answer. I want him dead. I want to watch his blood pool in my hands. I want to rip his throat out.

I spy a letter opener on the writing desk nearby, and in the single second I take to swipe it, my father laughs.

Laughs.

Out loud. Doubled over, one hand holding his side.

When he looks up, there are actual tears in his eyes.

"Have you lost your mind?" he says. "Aaron, don't be ridiculous."

I step forward, the letter opener clutched loosely in my fist, and I watch, carefully, for the moment he understands that I'm going to kill him. I want him to know that it's going to be me. I want him to know that he finally got what he wanted.

That he finally broke me.

"You made a mistake sparing my life," I say quietly. "You made a mistake showing your face. You made a mistake thinking you could ask me to come back, after all you've done—"

"You misunderstand me." He's standing straight again, the laughter gone from his face. "I'm not asking you to come back. You don't have a choice."

"Good. That makes this easier."

"Aaron." He shakes his head. "I'm not unarmed. I'm entirely willing to kill you if you step out of line. And though I can't claim that murdering my son is my favorite way to spend a morning, that doesn't mean I won't do it. So you need to stop and think, for just a moment, before you step forward and commit suicide."

I study him. My fingers flex around the weapon in my hand. "Tell me where she is," I say, "and I'll consider sparing your life."

"You fool. Have you not been listening to me? *She's gone.*"

I stiffen. Whatever he means by that, he's not lying. "Gone where?"

"Gone," he says angrily. "Disappeared. The girl you knew no longer exists."

He pulls a remote out of his jacket pocket and points it at the wall. An image appears instantly, projected from elsewhere, and the sound that fills the room is so sudden—so jarring and unexpected—it nearly brings me to my knees.

It's Ella.

She's screaming.

Blood drips down her open, screaming mouth, the agonizing sounds punctured only by the heaving sobs that pull ragged, aching breaths from her body. Her eyes are half open, delirious, and I watch as she's unstrapped from a chair and dragged onto a stretcher. Her body spasms, her arms and legs jerking uncontrollably. She's in a white hospital gown, the insubstantial ties coming undone, the thin fabric damp with her own blood.

My hands shake uncontrollably as I watch, her head whipping back and forth, her body straining against her restraints. She screams again and a bolt of pain shoots through me, so excruciating it nearly bends me in half. And then, quickly, as if out of nowhere, someone steps forward and stabs a needle in her neck.

Ella goes still.

Her body is frozen, her face captured in a single moment of agony before the drug kicks in, collapsing her. Her screams dissolve into smaller, steadier whimpers. She cries, even as her eyes close.

I feel violently ill.

My hands are shaking so hard I can no longer form a

fist, and I watch, as if from afar, as the letter opener falls to the floor. I hold still, forcing back the urge to vomit, but the action provokes a shudder so disorienting I almost lose my balance. Slowly, I turn to face my father, whose eyes are inscrutable.

It takes two tries before I'm able to form a single, whispered word:

"What?"

He shakes his head, the picture of false sympathy. "I'm trying to get you to understand. This," he says, nodding at the screen, "this is what she's destined for. Forever. Stop imagining your life with her. Stop thinking of her as a *person—*"

"This can't be real," I say, cutting him off. I feel wild. Unhinged. "This— Tell me this isn't real. What are you doing to me? Is this—"

"Of course it's real," he says. "Juliette is gone. Ella is gone. She's as good as dead. She had her mind wiped *weeks* ago. But you," he says, "you still have a life to live. Are you listening to me? You have to pull yourself together."

But I can't hear him over the sound of Ella sobbing.

She's still weeping—the sounds softer, sadder, more desperate. She looks terrified. Small and helpless as foreign hands bandage the open wounds on her arms, the backs of her legs. I watch as glowing metal cuffs are shackled to her wrists and ankles. She whimpers once more.

And I feel insane.

I must be. Listening to her scream—watching her fight

for her life, watching her choke on her own blood while I stand here, powerless to help her—

I'll never be able to forget the sound.

No matter what happens, no matter where I run, these screams—her screams—will haunt me forever.

"You wanted me to watch this?" I'm whispering now; I can hardly speak. "Why would you want me to watch this?"

He says something to me. Shouts something at me. But I feel suddenly deaf.

The sounds of the world seem warped, faraway, like my head has been submerged underwater. The fire in my brain has been snuffed out, replaced by a sudden, absolute calm. A sense of certainty. I know what I need to do now. And I know that there's nothing—nothing I won't do to get to her.

I feel it, feel my thin morals dissolving. I feel my flimsy, moth-eaten skin of humanity begin to come apart, and with it, the veil keeping me from complete darkness. There are no lines I won't cross. No illusions of mercy.

I wanted to be better for her. For her happiness. For her future.

But if she's gone, what good is goodness?

I take a deep, steadying breath. I feel oddly liberated, no longer shackled by an obligation to decency. And in one simple move, I pick up the letter opener I dropped on the floor.

"Aaron," he says, a warning in his voice.

"I don't want to hear you speak," I say. "I don't want you to talk to me ever again."

I throw the knife even before the words have left my

mouth. It flies hard and fast, and I enjoy the second it soars through the air. I enjoy the way the second expands, exploding in the strangeness of time. It all feels like slow motion. My father's eyes widen in a rare display of unmasked shock, and I smile at the sound of his gasp when the weapon finds its mark. I was aiming for his jugular, and it looks like my aim was true. He chokes, his eyes bulging as his hands move, shakily, to yank the letter opener from its home in his neck.

He coughs, suddenly, blood spattering everywhere, and with some effort, he's able to pull the thing free. Fresh blood gushes down his shirt, seeps from his mouth. He can't speak; the blade has penetrated his larynx. Instead, he gasps, still choking, his mouth opening and closing like a dying fish.

He falls to his knees.

His hands grasp at air, his veins jumping under his skin, and I step toward him. I watch him as he begs, silently, for something, and then I pat him down, pocketing the two guns I find concealed on his person.

"Enjoy hell," I whisper, before walking away.

Nothing matters anymore.

I have to find her.

~~JULIETTE~~

ELLA

Left.

Right.

Straight.

Left.

The commands keep my feet moving safely down the hall. This compound is vast. Enormous. My bedroom was so ordinary that the truth of this facility is jarring. An open framework reveals many dozens of floors, hallways and staircases intertwining like overpasses and freeways. The ceiling seems miles away, high and arched and intricate. Exposed steel beams meet clean white walkways centered around an open, interior courtyard. I had no idea I was so high up. And, somehow, for such a huge building, I haven't yet been spotted.

Things are growing more eerie by the minute.

I encounter no one as I go; I'm ordered to run, detour, or hide just in time to avoid passersby. It's uncanny. Still, I've been walking for at least twenty minutes, and I don't seem to be getting closer to anything. I have no idea where I am in the scheme of things, and there are no windows nearby. The whole facility feels like a gilded prison.

A long stretch of silence between myself and my imaginary friend starts making me nervous. I think this voice might be Emmaline's, but she still hasn't confirmed it. And though I want to say something, I feel silly speaking out loud. So I speak only inside my mind when I say:

Emmaline? Are you there?

No response.

My nervousness reaches its peak and I stop walking.

Where are you taking me?

This time, the answer comes quickly:

Escape

Are we getting closer? I ask.

Yes

I take a deep breath and forge ahead, but I feel a creeping dread infiltrate my senses. The longer I walk—down hallways and infinite staircases—the closer I seem to be getting to *something*—something that fills me with fear. I can't explain it.

It's clear I'm going underground.

The lights are growing dimmer as I go. The halls are

beginning to narrow. The windows and staircases are beginning to disappear. And I know I'm only getting closer to the bowels of the building when the walls change. Gone are the smooth, finished white walls of the upper floors. Here, everything is unfinished cement. It smells cold and wet. Earthy. The lights buzz and hum, occasionally snapping.

Fear continues to pulse up my spine.

I shuffle down a slight slope, my shoes slipping a little as I go. My lungs squeeze. My heartbeat feels loud, too loud, and a strange sensation begins to fill my arms and legs. Feeling. Too much feeling. It makes my skin crawl, makes my bones itch. I feel suddenly restless and anxious. And just as I'm about to lose hope in this crazy, meandering escape route—

Here

I stop.

I'm standing in front of a massive stone door. My heart is racing in my throat. I hesitate, fear beginning to fissure my certainty.

Open

"Who are you?" I ask again, this time speaking out loud. "This doesn't look like an escape route."

Open

I squeeze my eyes shut; fill my lungs with air.

I came all this way, I tell myself. I have no other options at the moment. I may as well see it through.

But when I open the door I realize it's only the first of several. Wherever I'm headed is protected by multiple layers of security. The mechanisms required to open each door are baffling—there are no knobs or handles, no traditional hinges—but all I have to do is touch the door for it to swing open.

It's too easy.

Finally, I'm standing in front of a steel wall. There's nothing here to indicate there might be a room beyond.

Touch

Tentatively, I touch my fingers to the metal.

More

I press my whole hand firmly against the door, and within seconds, the wall melts away. I look around nervously and step forward.

Immediately, I know I've been led astray.

I feel sick as I look around, sick and terrified. This place is so far from an escape I almost can't believe I fell for it. I'm in a laboratory.

Another laboratory.

Panic collapses something inside me, bones and organs knocking together, blood rushing to my head. I run for the door and it seals shut, the steel wall forming easily, as if from air.

I pull in a few sharp breaths, begging myself to stay calm.

"Show yourself," I shout. "Who are you? What do you want with me?"

Help

My heart shudders to a stop. I feel my fear expand and contract.

Dying

Goosebumps rise along my skin. My breath catches; my fists clench. I take a step farther into the room, and then a few more. I'm still wary, worried this is all yet another part of the trick—

Then I see it.

A glass cylinder as tall and wide as the wall, filled to the hilt with water. There's a creature floating inside of it. Something greater than fear is driving me forward, greater than curiosity, greater than wonder.

Feeling washes over me.

Memories crash into me.

A spindly arm reaches through the murky water, shaky fingers forming a loose fist that pounds, weakly, against the glass.

At first, all I see is her hand.

But the closer I get, the more clearly I'm able to see what

they've done to her. And I can't hide my horror.

She inches closer to the glass and I catch sight of her face. She no longer has a face, not really. Her mouth has been permanently sealed around a regulator, skin spider-webbing over silicone. Her hair is a couple feet long, dark and wild and floating around her head like wispy tentacles. Her nose has melted backward into her skull and her eyes are permanently closed, long dark lashes the only indication they ever used to open. Her hands and feet are webbed. She has no fingernails. Her arms and legs are mostly bone and sagging, wrinkled skin.

"Emmaline," I whisper.

Dying

The tears come hot and fast, hitting me without warning, breaking me from within.

"What did they do to you?" I say, my voice ragged. "How could they do this to you?"

A dull, metallic sound. Twice.

Emmaline is floating closer. She presses her webbed fingers against the barrier between us and I reach up, hastily wiping my eyes before I meet her there. I press my palm to the glass and somehow, impossibly, I feel her take my hand. Soft. Warm. Strong.

And then, with a gasp—

Feeling pulses through me, wave after wave of *feeling*, emotions as infinite as time. Memories, desires, long-extinguished hopes and dreams. The force of everything sends my head spinning; I slump forward and grit my teeth, steadying myself by pressing my forehead against the barrier between us. Images fill my mind like stilted frames from an old movie.

Emmaline's life.

She wants me to know. I feel like I'm being pulled into her, like she's reeling me into her own body, immersing me in her mind. Her memories.

I see her younger, much younger, eight or nine years old. She was spirited, furious. Difficult to control. Her mind was stronger than she could handle and she didn't know how to feel about her powers. She felt cursed, strangled by them. But unlike me, she was kept at home, here, in this exact laboratory, forced to undergo test after test administered by her own parents. I feel her rage pierce through me.

For the first time, I realize I had the luxury of forgetting.

She didn't.

Max and Evie—and even Anderson—tried to wipe Emmaline's memory multiple times, but each time, Emmaline's body prevailed. Her mind was so strong that she was able to convince her brain to reverse the chemistry meant to dissolve her memories. No matter what Max and Evie tried, Emmaline could never forget them.

Instead, she watched as her own parents turned on her.

Turned her inside out.

Emmaline is telling me everything without saying a word. She can't speak. She's lost four of her five senses.

She went blind first.

She lost her sense of smell and sensation a year later, both at the same time. Finally, she lost the ability to speak. Her tongue and teeth disintegrated. Her vocal cords eroded. Her mouth sealed permanently shut.

She can only hear now. But poorly.

I see the scenes change, see her grow a little older, a little more broken. I see the fire go out of her eyes. And then, when she realizes what they have planned for her— The entire reason they wanted her, so desperately—

Violent horror takes my breath away.

I fall, kneecaps knocking the floor. The force of her feelings rips me open. Sobs break my back, shudder through my bones. I feel everything. Her pain, her endless pain.

Her inability to end her own suffering.

She wants this to end.

End, she says, the word sharp and explosive.

With some effort, I manage to lift my head to look at her. "Was it you this whole time?" I whisper. "Did you give me back my memories?"

Yes

"How? Why?"

She shows me.

I feel my spine straighten as the vision moves through me. I see Evie and Max, hear their warped conversations from inside the glass prison. They've been trying to make Emmaline stronger over the years, trying to find ways to enhance Emmaline's telekinetic abilities. They wanted her skills to evolve. They wanted her to be able to perform mind control.

Mind control of the masses.

It backfired.

The more they experimented on her—the further they pushed her—the stronger and weaker she became. Her mind was able to handle the physical manipulations, but her heart couldn't take it. Even as they built her up, they were breaking her down.

She'd lost the will to live. To fight.

She no longer had complete control over her own body; even her powers were now regulated through Max and Evie. She'd become a puppet. And the more listless she became, the more they misunderstood. Max and Evie thought Emmaline was growing compliant.

Instead, she was deteriorating.

And then—

Another scene. Emmaline hears an argument. Max and Evie are discussing *me*. Emmaline hasn't heard them mention me in years; she had no idea I was still alive. She hears that I've been fighting back. That I've been resisting, that I tried to kill a supreme commander.

Emmaline feels hope for the first time in years.

I clap my hands over my mouth. Take a step back.

Emmaline has no eyes, but I feel her staring at me. Watching me for a reaction. I feel unsteady, alert but overcome.

I finally understand.

Emmaline has been using her last gasp of strength to contact me—and not just me, but all the other children of the supreme commanders.

She shows me, inside my own mind, how she's taken advantage of Max and Evie's latest effort to expand her capabilities. She'd never been able to reach out to people individually before, but Max and Evie got greedy. In Emmaline they laid the foundation for their own demise.

Emmaline thinks we're the last hope for the world. She wants us to stand up, fight, save humanity. She's been slowly returning our minds to us, giving back what our parents once stole. She wants us to see the truth.

Help, she says.

"I will," I whisper. "I promise I will. But first I'm going to get you out of here."

Rage, hot and violent, sends me reeling. Emmaline's anger is sharp and terrifying, and a resounding

NO

fills my brain.

I go still. Confused.

"What do you mean?" I say. "I have to help you get out of here. We'll escape together. I have friends—healers—who can restore y—"

NO

And then, in a flash—

She fills my mind with an image so dark I think I might be sick.

"No," I say, my voice shaking. "I won't do it. I'm not going to kill you."

Anger, hot, ferocious anger, attacks my mind. Image after image assaults me, her failed suicide attempts, her inability to turn her own powers against herself, the infinite fail-safes Max and Evie put in place to make sure Emmaline couldn't take her own life, and that she couldn't harm theirs—

"Emmaline, please—"

HELP

"There has to be another way," I say desperately. "This can't be it. You don't have to die. We can get through this together."

She bangs her open palm against the glass. Tremors rock her emaciated body.

Already

dying

I step forward, press my hands to her prison. "It wasn't supposed to end like this," I say, the words broken. "There has to be another way. Please. I want my sister back. I want you to live."

More anger, hot and wild, begins to bloom in my mind and then—

a spike of fear.

Emmaline goes rigid in her tank.

Coming

I look around, steeling myself. Adrenaline spikes in my veins.

Wait

Emmaline has wrapped her arms around her body, her face pinched in concentration. I can still feel her with an immediacy so intimate it feels almost like her thoughts are my own.

And then, unexpectedly—

My shackles pop open.

I spin around as they fall to the floor with a rich clatter. I rub at my aching wrists, my ankles. “How did you—?”

Coming

I nod.

“Whatever happens today,” I whisper, “I’m coming back for you. This isn’t over. Do you hear me? Emmaline, I won’t let you die here.”

For the first time, Emmaline seems to relax.

Something warm and sweet fills my head, affection so unexpected it pricks my eyes.

I fight back the emotion.

Footsteps.

Fear has fled my body. I feel unusually calm. I’m stronger than I’ve ever been. There’s strength in my bones, strength in my mind. And now that the cuffs are off, my powers are back on and a familiar feeling is surging through me; it’s like being joined by an old friend.

I meet Evie’s eyes as she walks through the door.

She’s already pointing a gun at me. Not a gun—something that looks like a gun. I don’t know what’s in it.

“What are you doing here?” she says, her voice only slightly hysterical. “What have you done?”

I shake my head.

I can’t look at her face anymore without feeling blind rage. I can’t even think her name without feeling a violent, potent, animalistic need to murder her with my bare hands. Evie Sommers is the worst kind of human being. A traitor to humanity. An unadulterated sociopath.

"What have you done?" she says again, this time betraying her fear. Her panic. The gun trembles in her fist. Her eyes are wide, crazed, darting from me to Emmaline, still trapped in the tank behind me.

And then—

I see it. I see the moment she realizes I'm not wearing my manacles.

Evie goes pale.

"I haven't done anything," I say softly. "Not yet."

Her gun falls, with a clatter, to the floor.

Unlike Paris, my mother isn't stupid. She knows there's no point trying to shoot me. She *created* me. She knows what I'm capable of. And she knows—I can see it in her eyes—she knows I'm about to kill her, and she knows there's nothing she can do to stop it.

Still, she tries.

"Ella," she says, her voice unsteady. "Everything we did—everything we've ever done—was to try to help you. We were trying to save the world. You have to understand."

I take a step forward. "I do understand."

"I just wanted to make the world a better place," she says. "Don't you want to make the world a better place?"

"Yes," I say. "I do."

She almost smiles. A small, broken breath escapes her body.

Relief.

I take two swift, running steps and punch her through

the chest, ribs breaking under my knuckles. Her eyes widen and she chokes, staring at me in stunned, paralyzed silence. She coughs and blood spatters, hot and thick, across my face. I turn away, spitting her blood out of my mouth, and by the time I look back, she's dead.

With one last tug, I rip her heart out of her body.

Evie falls to the floor with a heavy thud, her eyes cold and glassy. I'm still holding my mother's heart, watching it die in my hands, when a familiar voice calls out to me.

Thank you

Thank you

Thank you

WARNER

I realize, upon quitting the crime scene, that I have no idea where I am. I stand in the middle of the hallway outside the room within which I just murdered my father, and try to figure out my next moves. I'm nearly naked. No socks. Completely barefoot. Far from ideal.

Still, I need to keep moving.

If only.

I don't make it five feet before I feel the familiar pinch of a needle. I feel it—even as I try to fight it—I feel it as a foreign chemical enters my body. It's only a matter of time before it pulls me under.

My vision blurs.

I try to beat it, try to remain standing, but my body is weak. After two weeks of near starvation, constant poisoning, and violent exhaustion, I've run out of reserves. The last dregs of my adrenaline have left me.

This is it.

I fall to the floor, and the memories consume me.

I gasp as I'm returned to consciousness, taking in great lungfuls of air as I sit up too fast, my head spinning.

There are wires taped to my temples, my limbs, the

plastic ends pinching the soft hinges of my arms and legs, pulling at the skin on my bare chest. I rip them off, causing great distress to the monitors nearby. I yank the needle out of my arm and toss it to the floor, applying pressure to the wound for a few seconds before deciding to let it bleed. I get to my feet, spinning around to assess my surroundings, but still feel off-balance.

I can only guess at who must've shot me with a tranquilizer; even so, I feel no urgency to panic. Killing my father has instilled in me an extraordinary serenity. It's a perverse, horrible thing to celebrate, but to murder my father was to vanquish my greatest fear. With him dead, anything seems possible.

I feel free.

Still, I need to focus on where I am, on what's happening. I need to be forming a plan of attack, a plan of escape, a plan to rescue Ella. But my mind is being pulled in what feels like a hundred different directions.

The memories are growing more intense by the minute.

I don't know how much more of this I can take. I don't know how long this barrage will last or how much more will be uncovered, but the emotional revelations are beginning to take their toll on me.

A few months ago, I knew I loved Ella. I knew I felt for her what I'd never felt before for anyone. It felt new and precious and tender.

Important.

But every day—every minute—of the last couple of

weeks I've been bombarded by memories of her I never even knew I had. Moments with her from years ago. The sound of her laughter, the smell of her hair, the look in her eyes when she smiled at me for the first time. The way it felt to hold her hand when everything was new and unknown—

Three years ago.

How could it be possible that I touched her like that three years ago? How could we have known then, without actually knowing *why*, that we could be together? That she could touch me without hurting me? How could any of these moments have been ripped from my mind?

I had no idea I'd lost so much of her. But then, I had no idea there'd been so much to lose.

A profound, painful ache has rooted inside of me, carrying with it the weight of years. Being apart from Juliette—*Ella*—has always been hard, but now it seems unsurvivable.

I'm being slowly decimated by emotion.

I need to see her. To hold her. To bind her to me, somehow. I won't believe a word my father said until I see her and speak with her in person.

I can't give up. Not yet.

To hell with what happened between us back on base. Those events feel like they happened lifetimes ago. Like they happened to different people. Once I find her and get her to safety I will find a way to make things right between us. It feels like something long dead inside of me is being slowly returned to life—like my hopes and dreams are being resuscitated, like the holes in my heart are being slowly, carefully mended. I will find her. And when I do, I will find a way to move forward with her, by my side, forever.

I take a deep breath.

And then I get to my feet.

I brace myself, expecting the familiar sting of my broken ribs, but the pain in my side is gone. Gingerly, I touch my torso; the bruising has disappeared. I touch my face and I'm surprised to discover that my skin is smooth, clean-shaven. I touch my hair and find it's been returned to its original length—exactly as it was before I had to cut it all off.

Strange.

Still, I feel more like myself than I have in a long time, and I'm quietly grateful. The only thing bothering me is that I'm wearing nothing but a dressing grown, under which I'm completely naked.

I'm sick of being naked.

I want my clothes. I want a proper pair of pants. I want—

And then, as if someone has read my mind, I notice a fresh set of clothes on a nearby table. Clothes that look exactly my size.

I pick up the sweater. Examine it.

These are my actual clothes. I know these pieces. Recognize them. And if that wasn't enough, my initials—AWA—are monogrammed on the cuff of the sweater. This was no accident. Someone brought my clothes here. From my own closet.

They were expecting me.

I dress quickly, grateful for the clean outfit regardless of the circumstances, and I'm nearly done with the straps on my boots when someone walks in.

"Max," I say, without lifting my head. Carefully, I step on the needle I'd tossed earlier to the floor. "How are you?"

He laughs out loud. "How did you know it was me?"

"I recognized the rhythm of your footfalls."

He goes quiet.

"Don't bother trying to deny it," I say, hiding the syringe in my hand as I sit up. I meet his eyes and smile. "I've been listening to your heavy, uneven gait for the last two weeks."

Max's eyes widen. "I'm impressed."

"And I appreciate the clean shave," I say, touching my face.

He laughs again, more softly this time. "You were pretty close to dead when I brought you in here. Imagine my surprise to find you nearly naked, severely dehydrated, half-starved, vitamin-deficient. You had three broken ribs. Your father's blood all over your hands."

"Three broken ribs? I thought it was two."

"Three broken ribs," Max says, and nods. "And still, you managed to sever Paris's carotid artery. Nicely done."

I meet his eyes. Max thinks this is funny.

And then I understand.

"He's still alive, isn't he?" I say.

Max smiles wider. "Quite alive, yes. Despite your best efforts to murder him."

"That seems impossible."

"You sound irritated," Max says.

"I am irritated. That he survived is an insult to my skill set."

Max fights back another laugh. "I don't remember you being so funny."

"I'm not trying to be funny."

But Max can't wipe the smile off his face.

"So you're not going to tell me how he survived?" I say. "You're just going to bait me?"

"I'm waiting for my wife," he says.

"I understand. Does she help you sound out the big words?"

Max's eyebrows jump up his forehead. "Watch yourself, Aaron."

"Apologies. Please step out of my way."

"As I said, I'm waiting for my wife. She has something she wants to say to you."

I study him, looking closely at his face in a way I can't remember ever having done. He has dark brown hair, light brown skin, and bright blue-green eyes. He's aged well. On a different day, I might've even described his face as warm, friendly. But knowing now that he's Ella's father—I almost can't believe I didn't notice sooner. She has his eyes.

I hear a second set of footsteps drawing nearer to the door. I expect to see Evie, Supreme Sommers, and instead—

"Max, how long do you think it'll take bef—"

My father. His voice.

I can hardly believe it.

He stops, just inside the doorway, when he sees my face.

He's holding a bloodied towel to his throat. "You *idiot,*" he says to me.

I don't have a chance to respond.

A sharp alarm sounds, and Max goes suddenly rigid. He glances at a monitor on the wall before looking back at my father.

"Go," Anderson says. "I can handle him."

Max glances at me just once before he disappears.

"So," I say, nodding at my father's face, his healing wound. "Are you going to explain?"

He merely stares at me.

I watch, quietly, as he uses his free hand to pull a handkerchief from his pocket. He wipes the remaining blood from his lips, refolds the handkerchief, and tucks it back inside his pocket.

Something between us has changed.

I can feel it. Can feel the shift in his attitude toward me. It takes a minute to piece together the various emotional cues long enough to understand, but when it finally hits me, it hits me hard.

Respect.

For the first time in my life, my father is staring at me with something like respect. I tried to kill him, and instead of being angry with me, he seems pleased. Maybe even impressed.

"You did good work back there," he says quietly. "It was a strong throw. Solid."

It feels strange to accept his compliment, so I don't.

My father sighs.

"Part of the reason I wanted custody of those healer twins," he says finally, "was because I wanted Evie to study them. I wanted her to replicate their DNA and braid it into my own. Healing powers, I realized, were extremely useful."

A sharp chill goes up my spine.

"But I didn't have them under my control for as long as I wanted," he says. "I was only able to extract a few blood samples. Evie did the best she could with the time we had."

I blink. Try to control the expression on my face. "So you have healing powers now?"

"We're still working on it," he says, his jaw tight. "It's not yet perfect. But it was enough that I was able to survive the wounds to the head just long enough to be shipped to safety." He smiles a bitter smile. "My feet, on the other hand, didn't make it."

"How unfortunate," I lie.

I test the weight of the syringe in my hand. I wonder how much damage it could do. It's not substantial enough to do much more than stun, but a carefully angled attack could result in temporary nerve pain that would buy me a sizable amount of time. But then, so might a single, precise stab in the eye.

"Operation Synthesis," my father says sharply.

I look up. Surprised.

"You're ready, Aaron." His gaze is steady. "You're ready for a real challenge. You've got the necessary fire. The drive. I'm seeing it in your eyes for the first time."

I'm too afraid to speak.

Finally, after all these years, my father is giving me praise. He's telling me I'm capable. As a child, it was everything I'd ever wanted.

But I'm not a child anymore.

"You've seen Emmaline," my father says. "But you haven't seen her recently. You don't know what state she's in."

I wait.

"She's dying," he says. "Her body isn't strong enough to survive her mind or her environment, and despite Max and Evie's every effort, they don't know if there's anything else they can do to help her. They've been working for years to prolong her life as much as possible, but they've reached the end of the line. There's nothing left to do. She's deteriorating at a rate they can no longer control."

Still, I say nothing.

"Do you understand?" my father says to me. "Do you understand the importance of what I'm saying to you? Emmaline is not only a psychokinetic, but a telepath," he says. "As her body deteriorates, her mind grows wilder. She's too strong. Too explosive. And lately, without a strong enough body to contain her, she's become volatile. If she's not given a n—"

"Don't you dare," a voice barks, loudly, into the room. "Don't you dare say another word. You thickheaded *fool.*"

I spin around, surprise catching in my throat.

Supreme Commander Ibrahim. He seems taller than I remember him. Dark skin, dark hair. *Angry.*

"It's okay," my father says, unbothered. "Evie has taken care of—"

"Evie is *dead,*" Ibrahim says angrily. "We need to initiate the transfer immediately."

"What?" My father goes pale. I've never seen him pale. I've never seen him terrified. "What do you mean she's dead?"

Ibrahim's eyes flash. "I mean we have a serious problem." He glances at me. "This boy needs to be put back in isolation. We can't trust any of them right now. We don't know what she might've done."

And just as I'm trying to decide my next move, I hear a whisper at my ear.

"Don't scream," she says.

Nazeera.

~~JULIETTE~~

ELLA

I'm running for my life, bolting down hallways and up staircases. A low, insistent alarm has gone off, its high, piercing sound sending shocks of fear through me even as my feet pound the floor. I feel strong, steady, but I'm increasingly aware of my inability to navigate these snaking paths. I could see—could feel—Emmaline growing weaker as I left, and now, the farther I get from her, the dimmer our connection becomes. She showed me, in her memories, how Max and Evie slowly stripped her of control; Emmaline is more powerful than anyone, but now she can only use her powers on command. It took all her strength to push past the failsafes long enough to use her strength at will, and now that her voice has retreated from my mind, I know she won't be back. Not anytime soon. I have to figure out my own way out of here.

I will.

My power is back on. I can get through anything from here. I have to. And when I hear someone shout I spin around, ready to fight—

But the face in the distance is so familiar I stop, stunned, in my tracks.

Kenji barrels into me.

Kenji.

Kenji is hugging me. Kenji is hugging me, and he's uninjured.

He's perfect.

And just as I begin to return his embrace he swears, violently, and launches himself backward. "Jesus, woman— Are you trying to kill me? You can't turn that shit off for a second? You have to go and ruin our dramatic reunion by nearly murdering me even after I've gone to all the trouble of f—"

I launch myself into his arms again and he stiffens, relaxing only when he realizes I've pulled my power back. I forgot, for a second, how much of my skin was exposed in this dress.

"Kenji," I breathe. "You're alive. You're okay. Oh my God."

"Hey," he says. "*Hey.*" He pulls back, looks me in the eye. "I'm okay. You okay?"

I don't really know how to answer the question. Finally, I say, "I'm not sure."

He studies my face for a second. He looks concerned.

And then, the knot of fear growing only more painful in my throat, I ask the question killing me most:

"Where's Warner?"

Kenji shakes his head.

I feel myself begin to unravel.

"I don't know yet," Kenji says quietly. "But we're going to find him, okay? Don't worry."

I nod. My bottom lip trembles and I bite it down but the tremble won't be killed. It grows, multiplies, evolves into a tremor that shakes me from stem to sternum.

"Hey," Kenji says.

I look up.

"You want to tell me where all the blood came from?"

I blink. "What blood?"

He raises his eyebrows at me. "The *blood*," he says, gesturing, generally, at my body. "On your face. Your dress. All over your hands."

"Oh," I say, startled. I look at my hands as if seeing them for the first time. "The blood."

Kenji sighs, squints at something over my shoulder. He pulls a pair of gloves out of his back pocket and tugs them on. "All right, princess, turn your power back on. We have to move."

We break apart. Kenji pulls his invisibility over us both.

"Follow me," he says, taking my hand.

"Where are we going?" I say.

"What do you mean, *where are we going*? We're getting the hell out of here."

"But— What about Warner?"

"Nazeera is looking for him as we speak."

I stop so suddenly I nearly stumble. "Nazeera is here?"

"Uh, yeah— So— It's a really long story? But the short answer is yes."

"So that's how you got in here," I say, beginning to understand. "Nazeera."

Kenji makes a sound of disbelief. "Wow, right off the bat you give me no credit, huh? C'mon, J, you know I love a good rescue mission. I know some things. I can figure things out, too."

For the first time in weeks I feel a smile tug at my lips. A laugh builds and breaks inside my body. I've missed this so much. I've missed my friends so much. Emotion wells in my throat, surprising me.

"I missed you, Kenji," I say. "I'm so happy you're here."

"*Hey,*" Kenji says sharply. "Don't you dare start crying. If you start crying I'll start crying and we do not have time to cry right now. We have too much shit to do, okay? We can cry later, at a more convenient time. Okay?"

When I say nothing, he squeezes my hand.

"Okay?" he says again.

"Okay," I say.

I hear him sigh. "Damn," he says. "They really messed you up in here, didn't they?"

"Yeah."

"I'm so sorry," he says.

"Can we cry about it later? I'll tell you everything."

"Hell yeah we can cry about it later." Kenji tugs gently on my hand to get us moving again. "I have so much shit to cry about, J. So much. We should make, like, a list."

"Good idea," I say, but my heart is in my throat again.

"Hey, don't worry," Kenji says, reading my thoughts. "Seriously. We'll find Warner. Nazeera knows what she's doing."

"But I don't think I can just wait while Nazeera goes searching for him. I can't just stand around— I need to do something. I need to look for him myself—"

"Uh-uh. No way. Nazeera and I split up on purpose. *My* mission is to get you on the plane. *Her* mission is to get

Warner on the plane. That's how math works."

"Wait— You have a plane?"

"How else did you think we got here?"

"I have no idea."

"Well, that's another long story, and I'll fill you in later, but the highlights are that Nazeera is very confusing but helpful, and according to her calculations, we need to be getting the hell out of here yesterday. We're running out of time."

"But wait, Kenji— What happened to everyone? Last time I saw you, you were bleeding. Brendan had been shot. Castle was down. I thought everyone was dead."

Kenji doesn't answer me at first. "You really have no idea what happened, huh?" he says finally.

"I only know that I didn't actually kill all those people at the symposium."

"Oh yeah?" He sounds surprised. "Who told you?"

"Emmaline."

"Your *sister*?"

"Yeah," I say, sighing heavily. "There's so much I have to tell you. But first— Please tell me everyone is still alive."

Kenji hesitates. "I mean, I think so? Honestly, I don't know. Nazeera says they're alive. She's promising to come through on getting them to safety, so I'm still holding my breath. But get this." He stops walking, puts an invisible hand on my shoulder. "You're never going to believe this."

"Let me guess," I say. "Anderson is alive."

I hear Kenji's sharp intake of breath. "How did you know?"

"Evie told me."

"So you know about how he came back to Sector 45?"

"What?" I say. "No."

"Well, what I was about to tell you, right now, was that Anderson came back to base. He's resumed his position as supreme commander of North America. He was there right before we left. Nazeera told me he made up this whole story about how he'd been ill and how our team had spread false rumors while he was recovering—and that you'd been executed for your deception."

"What?" I say, stunned. "That's insane."

"This is what I'm saying."

"So what are we going to do when we get back to Sector 45?" I say. "Where do we go? Where do we stay?"

"Shit if I know," Kenji says. "Right now, I'm just hoping we can get out of here alive."

Finally, we reach the exit. Kenji has a security card that grants him access to the door, and it opens easily.

From there, it's almost too simple. Our invisibility keeps us undetected. And once we're on the plane, Kenji checks his watch.

"We've only got thirty minutes, just so you know. That was the rule. Thirty minutes and if Nazeera doesn't show up with Warner, we have to go."

My heart drops into my stomach.

WARNER

I have no time to register my shock, or to ask Nazeera when on earth she was going to tell me she had the power to turn herself invisible, so I do the only thing I can, in the moment.

I nod, the movement almost imperceptible.

"Kenji is getting Ella onto a plane. I'm going to wait for you just outside this door," she says. "Do you think you can make it? If you go invisible in front of everyone, they'll be on to us, and it'd be better if they think you're just trying to run."

Again, I nod.

"All right then. I'll see you out there."

I wait a second or two, and then I head for the door.

"Hey—" Ibrahim bellows.

I hesitate, turning back slightly, on my heel.

"Yes?"

"Where do you think you're going?" he says. He pulls a gun from the inside of his jacket and points it at me.

"I have to use the bathroom."

Ibrahim doesn't laugh. "You're going to wait here until Max gets back. And then we decide what we're going to do with you."

I tilt my head at him. The gun he's pointing at me looks

suspiciously like one of the guns I stole from my father earlier.

Not that it matters.

I take a quick breath. "I'm afraid that's not how this is going to work," I say, attempting a smile. "Though I'm sure we'll all be seeing each other soon, so I wouldn't worry about missing me too much."

And then, before anyone has a chance to protest, I run for the door, but not before Ibrahim fires his weapon.

Three times.

In close range.

I fight back the urge to cry out as one of the bullets shoots clean through my calf, even as the pain nearly takes my breath away.

Once I'm on the other side of the door, Nazeera pulls her invisibility over me. I don't make it far before I take a sharp breath, slumping against the wall.

"*Shit*," she says. "Did you get shot?"

"Obviously," I bite out, trying to keep my breathing even.

"Dammit, Warner, what the hell is wrong with you? We have to get back to the plane in the next fifteen minutes, or they're going to leave without us."

"What? Why would—"

"Because I told them to. We have to get Ella out of here no matter what. I can't have them waiting around for us and risk getting killed in the process."

"Your sympathy is truly heartwarming. Thank you."

She sighs. "Where did you get shot?"

"In my leg."

"Can you walk?"

"I should be able to in just a minute."

I hear her hesitate. "What does that mean?"

"If I manage to live long enough, maybe I'll tell you."

She's unamused. "Can you really start running in just a minute?"

"Oh, now it's running? A moment ago you were asking if I could walk."

"Running would be better."

I offer her a bitter laugh. It's hard from this distance, but I've been drawing on my father's new ability, harnessing it as best I can from where I am. I feel the wound healing, slowly regenerating nerves and veins and even a bit of bone, but it's taking longer than I'd like.

"How long is the flight back?" I say. "I can't remember."

"We've got the jet, so it should only take about eight hours."

I nod, even though she can't see me. "I don't think I can survive eight hours with an open wound."

"Well, it's a good thing I don't give a shit. I'm giving you two more minutes before I carry you out of here myself."

I grunt in response, focusing all of my energy on drawing up the healing powers into my body. I've never tried to do something like this while wounded, and I didn't realize how demanding it was, both emotionally and physically. I feel drained. My head is throbbing, my jaw aching from the intense pressure I've used to bite back the pain, and my leg feels like it's on *fire*. There's nothing pleasant about the healing process. I have to imagine that my father is on the move—probably searching for me with Ibrahim—because harnessing his power is harder than any of the others I've tried to take.

"We're leaving in thirty seconds," Nazeera says, a warning in her voice.

I grit my teeth.

"Fifteen."

"Shit."

"Did you just swear?" Nazeera says, stunned.

"I'm in an extraordinary amount of pain."

"All right, that's it, we're out of time."

And before I manage to get a word in, she picks me up, off the ground.

And we're in the air.

~~JULIETTE~~
ELLA

Kenji and I have been staring at each other in nervous silence for the last minute. I spent the first ten minutes telling him a little about Emmaline, which was its own stressful distraction, and then Kenji helped me wash the blood off my hands and face with the few supplies we have on board. Now we're both staring into the silence, our combined terror filling the plane.

It's a nice plane, I think. I'm not sure. I haven't actually had the presence of mind to look around. Or to ask him who, exactly, among us even knows how to fly a plane. But none of that will matter, of course, if Nazeera and Warner don't get back here soon.

It won't matter because I won't be leaving without him.

And my thoughts must be easy to read, because suddenly Kenji frowns. "Listen," he says, "I'm just as worried about them as you are. I don't want to leave Nazeera behind and I sure as hell don't want to imagine anything bad happening to her while she's out there, but we have to get you out of here."

"Kenji—"

"We don't have a choice, J," he says, cutting me off. "We have to get you out of here whether you like it or not. The

Reestablishment is up to some shady shit, and you're right in the center of it. We have to keep you safe. Right now, keeping you safe is my entire mission."

I drop my face in my hands, and then, just as quickly, look up again. "This is all my fault, you know? I could've prevented this."

"What are you talking about?"

I look him straight in the eye. "I should've done more research on The Reestablishment. I should've read up on its history—and my history within it. I should've learned more about the supreme commanders. I should've been better prepared. Hell, I should've demanded we search the water for Anderson's dead body instead of just *assuming* he'd sunk with the ship." I shake my head, hard. "I wasn't ready to be supreme commander, Kenji. You knew it; Castle knew it. I put everyone's lives in danger."

"Hey," he says sharply, "I never said you weren't—"

"Only Warner ever tried to convince me I was good enough, but I don't think I ever really believed it."

"J, listen to me. I never said you weren't—"

"And now he's gone. Warner is gone. Everyone from Omega Point might be dead. Everything we built . . . everything we worked toward—" I feel myself break, snap open from the inside. "I can't lose him, Kenji." My voice is shaking. My hands are shaking. "I can't— You don't know— You don't—"

Kenji looks at me with actual pain in his eyes. "Stop it, J. You're breaking my heart. I can't hear this."

And I realize, as I swallow back the lump in my throat, how much I'd needed to have this conversation. These feelings had been building inside of me for weeks, and I'd desperately needed someone to talk to.

I needed my friend.

"I thought I'd been through some hard things," I say, my eyes now filling with tears. "I thought I'd lived through my share of awful experiences. But this— I honestly think these have been the worst days of my life."

Kenji's eyes are deep. Serious. "You want to tell me about it?"

I shake my head, wiping furiously at my cheeks. "I don't think I'll be able to talk about any of it until I know Warner is okay."

"I'm so sorry, J. I really am."

I sniff, hard. "You know my name is Ella, right?"

"Right," he says, his eyebrows pulling together. "Yeah. Ella. That's wild."

"I like it," I say. "I like it better than Juliette."

"I don't know. I think both names are nice."

"Yeah," I say, turning away. "But *Juliette* was the name Anderson picked out for me."

"And *Ella* is the name you were born with," Kenji says, shooting me a look. "I get it."

"Yeah."

"Listen," he says with a sigh. "I know this has been a rough couple of weeks for you. I heard about the memory thing. I heard about lots of things. And I can't pretend to imagine I have any idea what you must be going through right now. But you can't blame yourself for any of this. It's not your fault. None of it is your fault. You've been a pawn at the center of this conspiracy your entire life. The last month wasn't going to change that, okay? You have to be kinder to yourself. You've already been through so much."

I offer Kenji a weak smile. "I'll try," I say quietly.

"Feeling any better now?"

"No. And thinking about leaving here without Warner—not knowing if he'll even make it onto this plane— It's killing me, Kenji. It's boring a hole through my body."

Kenji sighs, looks away. "I get it," he says. "I do. You're worried you won't have a chance to make things right with him."

I nod.

"Shit."

"I won't do it. I can't do it, Kenji."

"I understand where you're coming from, kid, I swear. But we can't afford to do this. If they're not back here in five minutes, we have to go."

"Then you'll have to leave without me."

"No way, not an option," he says, getting to his feet. "I don't want to do this any more than you do, but I know Nazeera well enough to know that she can handle herself out there, and if she's not back yet, it's probably because she's waiting for a safer moment. She'll find her way. And you have to trust that she'll bring Warner back with her. Okay?"

"No."

"C'mon—"

"Kenji, stop." I get to my feet, too, anger and heartbreak colliding.

"Don't do this," he says, shaking his head. "Don't force me to do something I don't want to do. Because if I have to, I will tackle you to the floor, J, I swear—"

"You wouldn't do that," I say quietly. The fight leaves my body. I feel suddenly exhausted, hollowed out by heartache. "I know you wouldn't. You wouldn't make me leave him behind."

"Ella?"

I turn around, a bolt of feeling leaving me breathless. Just the sound of his voice has my heart racing in a way that feels dangerous. The jarring shift from fear to joy has my head pounding, delirious with feeling. I'd been so worried, all this time, and to know now—

He's unharmed.

His face, unmarked. His body, intact. He's perfect and beautiful and he's *here*. I don't know how, but he's here.

I clap my hands over my mouth.

I'm shaking my head and searching desperately for the right words but find I can't speak. I can only stare at him as he steps forward, his eyes bright and burning.

He pulls me into his arms.

Sobs break my body, the culmination of a thousand fears and worries I hadn't allowed myself to process. I press my face into his neck and try, but fail, to pull myself together.

"I'm sorry," I say, gasping the words, tears streaming fast down my face. "Aaron, I'm so sorry. I'm so, so sorry."

I feel him stiffen.

He pulls away, staring at me with strange, scared eyes. "Why would you say that?" He looks around wildly, glances at Kenji, who only shakes his head. "What happened, love?" He pushes the hair out of my eyes, takes my face in his hands. "What are you sorry for?"

Nazeera pushes past us.

She nods at me, just once, before heading to the cockpit. Moments later I hear the roar of the engine, the electric sounds of equipment coming online.

I hear her voice in the speakers overhead, her crisp, certain commands filling the plane. She tells us to take our seats and get strapped in and I stare at Warner just once more, promising myself that we'll have a chance to talk. Promising myself that I'll make this right.

When we take off, he's holding my hand.

We've been climbing higher for several minutes now, and Kenji and Nazeera were generous enough to give us some illusion of privacy. They both shot me separate but similar looks of encouragement just before they slipped off into the cockpit. It finally feels safe to keep talking.

But emotion is like a fist in my chest, hard and heavy.

There's too much to say. Too much to discuss. I almost don't even know where to start. I don't know what happened to him, what he learned or what he remembers. I don't know if he's feeling the same things I'm feeling anymore. And all the unknowns are starting to scare me.

"What's wrong?" he says.

He's turned in his seat to face me. He reaches up, touches my face, and the feeling of his skin against mine is overwhelming—so powerful it leaves me breathless. Feeling shoots up my spine, sparks in my nerves.

"You're afraid, love. Why are you afraid?"

"Do you remember me?" I whisper. I have to force myself to remain steady, to fight back the tears that refuse to die. "Do you remember me the way I remember you?"

Something changes in his expression. His eyes change, pull together in pain.

He nods.

"Because I remember you," I say, my voice breaking on the last word. "I remember you, Aaron. I remember everything. And you have to know— You have to know how sorry I am. For the way I left things between us." I'm crying again. "I'm sorry for everything I said. For everything I put you thr—"

"Sweetheart," he says gently, the question in his eyes resolving to a measure of understanding. "None of that matters anymore. That fight feels like it happened in another lifetime. To different people."

I wipe away my tears. "I know," I say. "But being here— All of this— I thought I might never see you again. And it *killed* me to remember how I left things between us."

When I look up again Warner is staring at me, his own

eyes bright, shining. I watch the movement in his throat as he swallows, hard.

"Forgive me," I whisper. "I know it all seems stupid now, but I don't want to take anything for granted anymore. Forgive me for hurting you. Forgive me for not trusting you. I took my pain out on you and I'm so sorry. I was selfish, and I hurt you, and I'm so sorry."

He's silent for so long I almost can't bear it.

When he finally speaks, his voice is rough with emotion. "Love," he says, "there's nothing to forgive."

WARNER

Ella is asleep in my arms.

Ella.

I can't really think of her as *Juliette* anymore.

We've been in the air for an hour now, and Ella cried until her tears ran dry, cried for so long I thought it might kill me. I didn't know what to say. I was so stunned I didn't know how to soothe her. And only when the exhaustion overcame the tears did she finally go still, collapsing fully and completely into my arms. I've been holding her against my chest for at least half an hour, marveling at what it does to me to just be this close to her. Every once in a while, it feels like a dream. Her face is pressed against my neck. She's clinging to me like she might never let go and it does something to me, something heady, to know that she could possibly want me—or need me—like this. It makes me want to protect her even if she doesn't need protecting. It makes me want to carry her away. Lose track of time.

Gently, I stroke her hair. Press my lips to her forehead.

She stirs, but only slightly.

I had not been expecting this.

Of all the things I thought might happen when I finally saw her, I could never have dreamed a scenario such as this.

No one has ever apologized to me before. Not like this.

I've had men fall to their knees before me, begging me to spare their lives—but I can't remember a single time in my life when someone apologized to me for hurting my feelings. No one has ever cared about my feelings long enough to apologize for hurting them. In my experience, I'm usually the monster. I'm the one expected to make amends.

And now—

I'm stunned. Stunned by the experience, by how strange it feels. All this time, I'd been preparing to win her back. To try to convince her, somehow, to see past my demons. And up until just this moment, I don't think I was ever truly convinced anyone would see me as human enough to forgive my sins. To give me a second chance.

But now, she knows everything.

Every dark corner of my life. Every awful thing I ever tried to hide. She knows and she still loves me.

God. I run a tired hand across my face. She asked me to forgive *her.* I almost don't know what to do with myself. I feel joy and terror. My heart is heavy with something I don't even know how to describe.

Gratitude, perhaps.

The ache in my chest has grown stronger, more painful. Being near her is somehow both a relief and a new kind of agony. There's so much ahead of us, so much we still need to face, together, but right now I don't want to think about any of it. Right now I just want to enjoy her proximity. I want to watch the gentle motions of her breathing. I want to inhale the soft scent of her hair and lean into the steadying warmth of her body.

Carefully, I touch my fingers to her cheek.

Her face is smooth, free from pain and tension. She looks peaceful. She looks *beautiful.*

My love.

My beautiful love.

Her eyes flutter open and I worry, for a moment, that I might've spoken out loud. But then she looks up at me, her eyes still soft with sleep, and I bring my hand to her face, this time trailing my fingers lightly along her jaw. She closes her eyes again. Smiles.

"I love you," she whispers.

A shock of feeling swells inside of me, makes it hard for me to breathe. I can only look at her, studying her face, the lines and angles I've somehow always known.

Slowly, she sits up.

She leans back, stretching out her sore, stiff muscles. When she catches me watching her, she offers me a shy smile.

She leans in, takes my face in her hands.

"Hi," she says, her words soft, her hands gentle as she tilts my chin down, toward her mouth. She kisses me, once, her lips full and sweet. It's a tender kiss, but feeling strikes through me with a sharp, desperate need. "I missed you so much," she says. "I still can't believe you're here." She kisses me again, this time deeper, hungrier, and my heart beats so fast it roars in my ears. I can hardly hear anything else. I can't bring myself to speak.

I feel stunned.

When we break apart, her eyes are worried. "Aaron," she says. "Is everything okay?"

And I realize then, in a moment that terrifies me, that I want this, forever. I want to spend the rest of my life with her. I want to build a future with her. I want to grow old with her.

I want to marry her.

~~JULIETTE~~
ELLA

"Aaron?" I say again, this time softly. "Are you all right?"

He blinks, startled. "Yes," he says, drawing in a sharp breath. "Yes. Yes, I'm perfect."

I manage a small smile. "I'm glad you finally agree with me."

He frowns, confused, and then, as realization hits—

He *blushes*.

And for the first time in weeks, a full, genuine grin spreads across my face. It feels good. Human.

But Aaron shakes his head, clearly mortified. He can't meet my eyes. His voice is careful, quiet when he says, "That's not at all what I meant."

"Hey," I say, my smile fading. I take his hands in mine, squeeze. "Look at me."

He does.

And I forget what I was going to say.

He has that kind of face. The kind of face that makes you forget where you are, who you are, what you might've been about to do or say. I've missed him so much. Missed his eyes. It's only been a couple of weeks, but it feels like forever since the last time I saw him, a lifetime full of horrible revelations that threatened to break us both. I can't believe he's here, that we found each other and made things right.

It's no small thing.

Even with everything else—with all the other horrors we've yet to contend with—being here with him feels like a huge victory. Everything feels new. My mind feels new, my memories, new. Even Aaron's face is new, in its own way. He looks a little different to me now.

Familiar.

Like he's always been here. Always lived in my heart.

His hair, thick and golden and beautiful, is how I remember it best—Evie must've done something to his hair, too, somehow. And even though he looks more exhausted than I'd like, his face is still striking. Beautiful, sharp lines. Piercing green eyes so light and bright they're almost painful to look at. Everything about him is finely crafted. His nose. His chin. His ears and eyebrows. He has a beautiful mouth.

I linger too long there, my eyes betraying my mind, and Aaron smiles. *Aaron.* Calling him Warner doesn't feel right anymore.

"What are you doing, love?"

"Just enjoying the view," I say, still staring at his mouth. I reach up, touch two fingers to his bottom lip. Memories flood through me in a sudden, breathless rush. Long nights. Early mornings. His mouth, on me. Everywhere. Over and over again.

I hear him exhale, suddenly, and I glance up at him.

His eyes are darker, heavy with feeling. "What are you thinking?"

I shake my head, feeling suddenly shy. It's strange, considering how close we've been, that I'd feel shy around him now. But he feels at once old and new to me—like we're still learning about each other. Still discovering what our relationship means and what we mean to each other. Things feel deeper, desperate.

More important.

I take his hands again. "How are you?" I whisper.

He's staring at our hands, entwined, when he says: "My father is still alive."

"I heard. I'm so sorry."

He nods. Looks away.

"Did you see him?"

Another nod. "I tried to kill him."

I go still.

I know how hard it's been for Aaron to face his father. Anderson has always been his most formidable opponent; Aaron has never been able to fight him head on. He's never been able to bring himself to actually follow through with his threats to kill his father.

It's astonishing he even came close.

And then Aaron tells me how his father has semi-functional healing powers, how Evie tried to re-create the twins' DNA for him.

"So your dad is basically invincible?"

Aaron laughs quietly. Shakes his head. "I don't think so. It makes him harder to kill, but I definitely think there's a chink to be found in his armor." He sighs. "Believe it or not, the strangest part of the whole thing was that, afterward, my father was proud of me. Proud of me for trying to kill him." Aaron looks up, looks me in the eye. "Can you imagine?"

"Yes," I whisper. "I can."

Aaron's eyes go deep with emotion. He pulls me close. "I'm so sorry, love. I'm so sorry for everything they did to you. For everything they've put you through. It kills me to know that you were suffering. That I couldn't be there for you."

"I don't want to think about it right now." I shake my head. "Right now all I want is *this*. I just want to be here. With you. Whatever comes next, we'll face it together."

"Ella," he says softly.

A wave of feeling washes over me. Hearing him say my name—my real name—makes everything feel real. Makes *us* feel real.

I meet his eyes.

He smiles. "You know— I feel everything when you touch me, love. I can feel your excitement. Your nervousness. Your pleasure. And I love it," he says quietly. "I love the way you respond to me. I love the way you *want* me. I feel it, when you lose yourself, the way you trust me when we're together. And I feel your love for me," he whispers. "I feel it in my bones."

He turns away.

"I have loved you my entire life." He looks up, looks at me with so much feeling it nearly breaks my heart. "And after everything we've been through—after all the lies and the secrets and the misunderstandings—I feel like we've been given a chance to start fresh. I want to start over," he says. "I never want to lie to you again. I want us to trust each other and be true partners in everything. No more misunderstandings," he says. "No more secrets. I want us to begin again, here, in this moment."

I nod, pulling back so I can see his face more clearly. Emotions well in my throat, threaten to overcome me. "I want that, too. I want that so much."

"Ella," he says, his voice rough with feeling. "I want to spend the rest of my life with you."

My heart stops.

I stare at him, uncertain, thoughts pinwheeling in my head. I touch his cheek and he looks away, takes a sudden, shaky breath.

"What are you saying?" I whisper.

"I love you, Ella. I love you more th—"

"*Wow.* You two seriously couldn't wait until we got back to base, huh? You couldn't spare my eyes?"

The sound of Kenji's voice pulls me suddenly, abruptly out of my head. I turn too quickly, awkwardly disengaging from Aaron's body.

Aaron, on the other hand, goes suddenly white.

Kenji throws a thin airplane pillow at him. "You're welcome," he says.

Aaron chucks the pillow back without a word, his eyes burning in Kenji's direction. He seems both shocked and angry, and he leans forward in his seat, his elbows balanced on his knees, the heels of his hands pressed against his eyes.

"You are a plague upon my life, Kishimoto."

"I said *you're welcome*."

Aaron sighs, heavily. "What I would give to snap your neck right now, you have no idea."

"Hey—*you* have no idea what I just did for you," Kenji says. "So I'm going to repeat myself one more time: You are *welcome*."

"I never asked for your help."

Kenji crosses his arms. When he speaks, he overenunciates each word, like he might be talking to an idiot. "I don't think you're thinking clearly."

"I'm thinking clearer than I ever have."

"You really thought that would be a good idea?" Kenji says, shaking his head. "Here? Now?"

Aaron's jaw clenches. He looks mutinous.

"Bro, this is not the moment."

"And when, exactly, did you become an expert on this sort of thing?"

I look between the two of them. "What is going on?" I say. "What are you guys talking about?"

"Nothing," they say at the same time.

"Um, okay." I stare at them, still confused, and I'm about to ask another question when Kenji says, suddenly:

"Who wants lunch?"

My eyebrows shoot up my forehead. "We have lunch?"

"It's pretty awful," Kenji says, "but Nazeera and I have a

picnic basket we brought with us, yeah."

"I guess I'm up for trying the contents of the mystery basket." I smile at Aaron. "Are you hungry?"

But Aaron says nothing. He's still staring at the floor. I touch his hand and, finally, he sighs. "I'm not hungry," he says.

"Not an option," Kenji says sharply. "I'm pretty sure you haven't eaten a damn thing since you got out of fake prison."

Aaron frowns. And when he looks up, he says, "It wasn't *fake* prison. It was a very real prison. They poisoned me for weeks."

"What?" My eyes widen. "You never t—"

Kenji cuts me off with the wave of his hand. "They gave you food, water, and let you keep the clothes on your back, didn't they?"

"Yes, but—"

He shrugs. "Sounds like you had a little vacation."

Aaron sighs. He looks both annoyed and exhausted as he runs a hand down the length of his face.

I don't like it.

"Hey— Why are you giving him such a hard time?" I say, frowning at Kenji. "Just before he and Nazeera showed up you were going on and on about how wonderful he is, and n—"

Kenji swears, suddenly, under his breath. "Jesus, J." He shoots me a dark look. "What did I say to you about repeating that conversation out loud?"

Aaron sits up, the frustration in his eyes slowly giving

way to surprise. "You think I'm wonderful?" he says, one hand pressed against his chest in mock affection. "That's so sweet."

"I *never* said you were wonderful."

Aaron tilts his head. "Then what, exactly, did you say?"

Kenji turns away. Says nothing.

I'm grinning at Kenji's back when I say, "He said you looked good in everything and that you were good at everything."

Aaron's smile deepens.

Aaron almost never smiles widely enough for me to see his dimples, but when he does, they transform his face. His eyes light up. His cheeks go pink with feeling. He looks suddenly sweet. *Adorable.*

It takes my breath away.

But he's not looking at me, he's looking at Kenji, his eyes full of laughter when he says, "Please tell me she's not serious."

Kenji flips us both off.

Aaron laughs. And then, leaning in—

"You really think I look good in everything?"

"Shut up, asshole."

Aaron laughs again.

"Stop having fun without me," Nazeera shouts from the cockpit. "No more making jokes until I put this thing on cruise control."

I stiffen. "Do planes have cruise control?"

"Um"—Kenji scratches his head—"I don't actually know?"

But then Nazeera saunters over to us, tall and beautiful and unbothered. She's not covering her hair today, which I suppose makes sense, considering it's generally illegal, but I feel a faint panic spread through my body when I realize she's in no hurry to return to the cockpit.

"Wait— No one is flying the plane," I say. "Shouldn't someone be flying the plane?"

She waves me down. "It's fine. These things are practically automatic now, anyway. I don't have to do more than input coordinates and make sure everything is operating smoothly."

"But—"

"Everything is fine," she says, shooting me a sharp look. "We're fine. But someone needs to tell me what's going on."

"Are you sure we're fine?" I ask once more, quietly.

She levels me with a dark look.

I sigh. "Well, in that case," I say. "You should know that Kenji was just admiring Aaron's sense of style."

Nazeera turns to Kenji. Raises a single eyebrow.

Kenji shakes his head, visibly irritated. "I wasn't— Dammit, J, you have no loyalty."

"I have plenty of loyalty," I say, slightly wounded. "But when you guys fight like this it stresses me out. I just want Aaron to know that, secretly, you care about him. I love you both and I want the two of you to be frien—"

"Wait"—Aaron frowns—"What do you mean you love us both?"

I glance between him and Kenji, surprised. "I mean I care about both of you. I love you both."

"Right," Aaron says, hesitating, "but you don't *actually* love us both. That's just a figure of speech, isn't it?"

It's my turn to frown. "Kenji is my best friend," I say. "I love him like a brother."

"But—"

"I love you, too, princess," Kenji says, a little too loudly. "And I appreciate you saying that."

Aaron mutters something under his breath that sounds suspiciously like, *"Unwashed idiot."*

"What did you just say to me?" Kenji's eyes widen. "I'll have you know I wash *all the time—"*

Nazeera places a calming hand on Kenji's arm, and he startles at her touch. He looks up at her, blinking.

"We have another five hours ahead of us on this flight," she says, and her voice is firm but kind. "So I recommend we put this conversation to bed. I think it's clear to everyone that you and Warner secretly enjoy each other's friendship, and it's not doing anyone any good to pretend otherwise."

Kenji blanches.

"Does that sound like a reasonable plan?" She looks around at all of us. "Can we all agree that we're on the same team?"

"Yes," I say enthusiastically. "I do. I agree."

Aaron says, "Fine."

"Great," Nazeera says. "Kenji, you okay?"

He nods and mumbles something under his breath.

"Perfect. Now here's the plan," she says briskly. "We're going to eat and then take turns trying to get some sleep.

We'll have a ton of things to deal with when land, and it's best if we hit the ground running when we do." She tosses a few vacuum-sealed bags at each of us. "That's your lunch. There are water bottles in the fridge up front. Kenji and I will take the first shift—"

"No way," Kenji says, crossing his arms. "You've been up for twenty-four hours straight. I'll take the first shift."

"But—"

"Warner and I will take the first shift together, actually." Kenji shoots Warner a look. "Isn't that right?"

"Yes, of course," Aaron says. He's already on his feet. "I'd be happy to."

"Great," Kenji says.

Nazeera is already stifling a yawn, pulling a bunch of thin blankets and pillows from a storage closet. "All right, then. Just wake us up in a couple of hours, okay?"

Kenji raises an eyebrow at her. "Sure."

"I'm serious."

"Yup. Got it." Kenji offers her a mock salute, Aaron offers me a quick smile, and the two of them disappear into the cockpit.

Kenji closes the door behind them.

I'm staring at the closed door, wondering what on earth is going on between the two of them, when Nazeera says—

"I had no idea you two were so intense."

I look up, surprised. "Who? Me and Aaron?"

"No," she says, smiling. "You and Kenji."

"Oh." I frown. "I don't think we're intense."

She shoots me a funny look.

"I'm serious," I say. "I think we have a pretty normal friendship."

Instead of answering me, she says, "Did you two ever"—she waves a hand at nothing—"date?"

"What?" My eyes widen. A traitorous heat floods my body. "*No.*"

"Never?" she says, her smile slow.

"Never. I swear. Not even close."

"Okay."

"Not that there's anything wrong with him," I hurry to add. "Kenji is wonderful. The right person would be lucky to be with him."

Nazeera laughs, softly.

She carries the stack of pillows and blankets over to the row of airplane seats and begins reclining the backs. I watch her as she works. There's something so smooth and refined about her movements—something intelligent in her eyes at all times. It makes me wonder what she's thinking, what she's planning. Why she's here at all.

Suddenly, she sighs. She's not looking at me when she says, "Do you remember me yet?"

I raise my eyebrows, surprised. "Of course," I say quietly.

She nods. She says, "I've been waiting awhile for you to catch up," and sits down, inviting me to join her by patting the seat next to her.

I do.

Wordlessly, she hands me a couple of blankets and

pillows. And then, when we're both settled in and I'm staring, suspiciously, at the vacuum-sealed package of "food" she threw at me, I say—

"So you remember me, too?"

Nazeera tears open her vacuum-sealed package. Peers inside to study the contents. "Emmaline guided me to you," she says quietly. "The memories. The messages. It was her."

"I know," I say. "She's trying to unify us. She wants us to band together."

Nazeera shakes out the contents of the bag into her hand, picks through the bits of freeze-dried fruit. She glances at me. "You were five when you disappeared," she says. "Emmaline was six. I'm six months older than you, and six months younger than Emmaline."

I nod. "The three of us used to be best friends."

Nazeera looks away, looks sad. "I really loved Emmaline," she says. "We were inseparable. We did everything together." She shrugs, even as a flash of pain crosses her face. "That was all we got. Whatever we might've been was stolen from us."

She picks out two pieces of fruit and pops them into her mouth. I watch as she chews, thoughtfully, and wait for more.

But the seconds pass and she says nothing, and I figure I should fill the silence. "So," I say. "We're not actually getting any sleep, are we?"

That gets her to smile. Still, she doesn't look at me.

Finally, she says, "I know you and Warner got the

absolute worst of it, I do. But if it makes you feel any better, they wiped all of our memories, in the beginning."

"I know. Emmaline told me."

"They didn't want us to remember you," she says. "They didn't want us to remember a lot of things. Did Emmaline tell you she's reached out to all of us? You, me, Warner, my brother—all the kids."

"She told me a little bit, yeah. Have you talked to any of the others about it?"

Nazeera nods. Pops another piece of fruit in her mouth.

"And?"

She tilts her head. "We'll see."

My eyes widen. "What does that mean?"

"I'll know more when we land, that's all."

"So— How did you even know?" I say, frowning a little. "If you'd only ever had memories of me and Emmaline as children—how did you tie it all back to the present? How did you know that I was the Ella from our childhood?"

"You know— I wasn't a hundred percent positive I was right about everything until I saw you at dinner that first night on base."

"You recognized me?" I say. "From when I was five?"

"No," she says, and nods at my right hand. "From the scar on the back of your wrist."

"This?" I say, lifting my hand. And then I frown, remembering that Evie repaired my skin. I used to have faded scars all over my body; the ones on my hands were the worst. My adoptive mom put my hands in the fire, once. And I hurt myself a lot while I was locked up; lots of burns, lots of poorly healed wounds. I shake my head at Nazeera when I say, "I used to have scars on my hand from my time in the asylum. Evie got rid of them."

Nazeera takes my hand, flips it over so my palm is up, open. Carefully, she traces a line from my wrist to my forearm. "Do you remember the one that was here?"

"Yes." I raise my eyebrows.

"My dad has a really extensive sword collection," she says, dropping my hand. "Really gorgeous blades—gilded, handmade, ancient, ornate stuff. Anyway," she says, tapping the invisible scar on my wrist. "I did that to you. I broke into my dad's sword room and thought it'd be fun for us to practice a little hand-to-hand combat. But I sliced you up pretty bad, and my mom just about beat the crap out of me." She laughs. "I will never forget that."

I frown at her, at where my scar used to be. "Didn't you say that we were friends when we were *five*?"

She nods.

"We were five and we thought it would be fun to play with real swords?"

She laughs. Looks confused. "I never said we had a *normal* childhood. Our lives were so messed up," she says, and laughs again. "I never trusted my parents. I always knew they were knee-deep in some dark shit; I always tried to learn more. I'd been trying, for years, to hack into Baba's electronic files," she says. "And for a long time, I only ever accessed basic information. I learned about the asylums. The Unnaturals."

"That's why you hid your abilities from them," I say, finally understanding.

She nods. "But I wanted to know more. I knew I was only scratching the surface of something big. But the levels of security built into my dad's account are unlike anything I'd ever seen before. I was able to get through the first few levels of security, which is how I learned of yours and Emmaline's existence, a few years back. Baba had tons of records, reports on your daily habits and activities, a log with the time and date of every memory they stole from you—and they were all from recent years and months."

I gasp.

Nazeera shoots me a sympathetic look. "There were brief mentions of a sister in your files," she says, "but nothing substantial; mostly just a note that you were both powerful, and had been donated to the cause by your parents. But I couldn't find anything on the unknown sister, which made me think that her files were more protected. I spent the last couple of years trying to break into the deeper levels of Baba's account and never had any success. So I let it go for a while."

She pops another piece of dried fruit in her mouth.

"It wasn't until my dad started losing his *mind* after you almost killed Anderson that I started getting suspicious. That was when I began to wonder if the *Juliette Ferrars* he kept screaming about wasn't someone important." She studies me out of the corner of her eye. "I knew you couldn't have been some random *Unnatural.* I just knew it. Baba went *ballistic.* So I started hacking again."

"Wow," I say.

"Yeah," she says, nodding. "Right? Anyway, all I'm trying to say is that I've been trying to sniff out the bullshit in this situation for a few years, and now, with Emmaline in my head, I'm finally getting close to figuring it all out."

I glance up at her.

"The only thing I still don't know is *why* Emmaline is locked up. I don't know what they're doing with her. And I don't understand why it's such a secret."

"I do," I say.

Her head snaps up. She looks at me, wide-eyed. "Way to bury the lede, Ella."

I laugh, but the sound is sad.

WARNER

As soon as we take our seats, Kenji turns on me. "You want to tell me what the hell is going on?" he says.

"No."

Kenji rolls his eyes. He rips open his little snack bag and doesn't even inspect the contents before he tips the bag directly into his mouth. He closes his eyes as he chews. Makes little satisfied noises.

I manage to fight the impulse to cringe, but I can't stop myself from saying—

"You eat like a caveman."

"No, I don't," he says angrily. And then, a moment later: "Do I?"

I hesitate, feeling his sudden wave of embarrassment. Of all the emotions I hate experiencing, secondhand embarrassment might be the worst. It hits me right in the gut. Makes me want to turn my skin inside out.

And it's by far the easiest way to make me capitulate.

"No," I say heavily. "You don't eat like a caveman. That was unfair."

Kenji glances at me. There's too much hope in his eyes.

"I've just never seen anyone eat food with as much enthusiasm as you do."

Kenji raises an eyebrow. "I'm not enthusiastic. I'm hungry."

Carefully, I tear open my own package. Shake out a few bits of the fruit into my open hand.

They look like desiccated worms.

I return the fruit to the bag, dust off my hands, and offer my portion to Kenji.

"You sure?" he says, even as he takes it from me.

I nod.

He thanks me.

We both say nothing for a while.

"So," Kenji says finally, still chewing. "You were going to propose to her. Wow."

I exhale a long, heavy breath. "How you could have even known something like that?"

"Because I'm not deaf."

I raise my eyebrows.

"It echoes in here."

"It certainly does not echo in here."

"Stop changing the subject," he says, shaking more fruit into his mouth. "The point is, you were going to propose. Do you deny it?"

I look away, run a hand along the side of my neck, massaging the sore muscles. "I do not deny it," I say.

"Then congratulations. And yes, I'd be happy to be your best man at the wedding."

I look up, surprised. "I've no interest in addressing the latter part of what you just said, but— Why offer congratulations? I thought you were vehemently opposed to the idea."

Kenji frowns. "What? I'm not opposed to the idea."

"Then why were you so angry?"

"I thought you were stupid for doing it *here*," he says. "Right now. I didn't want you to do something you would regret. That you'd both regret."

"Why would I regret proposing right now? This seems as good a time as any."

Kenji laughs, but somehow manages to keep his mouth closed. He swallows another bite of food and says, "Don't you want, to, like, I don't know—buy her some roses? Light a candle? Maybe hand her a box of chocolates or someshit? Or, hell, uh, I don't know—maybe you'd want to get her a *ring* first?"

"I don't understand."

"C'mon, bro— Have you never seen, like, a movie?"

"No."

Kenji stares at me, dumbfounded. "You're shitting me," he says. "Please tell me you're shitting me."

I bristle. "I was never allowed to watch movies growing up, so I never picked up the habit, and after The Reestablishment took over, that sort of thing was outlawed anyway. Besides, I don't enjoy sitting still in the dark for that long. And I don't enjoy the emotional manipulations of cinema."

Kenji brings his hands to his face, his eyes wide with something like horror. "You have got to be kidding me."

"Why would— I don't understand why that's strange. I

was homeschooled. My father was very—"

"There are so many things about you that never made sense to me," Kenji says, staring, flabbergasted, at the wall behind me. "Like, everything about you is weird, you know?"

"No," I say sharply. "I don't think I'm weird."

"But now it all makes sense." He shakes his head. "It all makes so much sense. Wow. Who knew."

"*What* makes sense?"

Kenji doesn't seem to hear me. Instead, he says, "Hey, is there anything else you've never done? Like—I don't know, have you ever gone swimming? Or, like, blown out candles on a birthday cake?"

"Of course I've been swimming," I say, irritated. "Swimming was an important part of my tactical training. But I've never—" I clear my throat. "No, I never had my own birthday cake."

"Jesus."

"What is wrong with you?"

"Hey," Kenji says suddenly. "Do you even know who Bruce Lee is?"

I hesitate.

There's a challenge in his voice, but Kenji isn't generating much more in the way of emotional cues, so I don't understand the importance of the question. Finally, I say, "Bruce Lee was an actor. Though he's also considered to be one of the greatest martial artists of our time. He founded a system of martial arts called jeet kune do, a type of Chinese kung fu that eschews patterns and form.

His Chinese name is Lee Jun-fan."

"Well shit," Kenji says. He sits back in his chair, staring at me like I might be an alien. "Okay. I wasn't expecting that."

"What does Bruce Lee have to do with anything?"

"First of all," he says, holding up a finger, "Bruce Lee has everything to do with everything. And second of all, can you just, like, do that?" He snaps his fingers in the direction of my head. "Can you just, like, remember shit like that? Random facts?"

"They're not random facts. It's information. Information about our world, its fears, histories, fascinations, and pleasures. It's my job to know this sort of thing."

"But you've never seen a single movie?"

"I didn't have to. I know enough about pop culture to know which films mattered or made a difference."

Kenji shakes his head, looks at me with something like awe. "But you don't know anything about the *best* films. You never saw the really good stuff. Hell, you've probably never even heard of the good stuff."

"Try me."

"Have you ever heard of *Blue Streak*?"

I blink at him. "That's the name of a movie?"

"*Romeo Must Die*? *Bad Boys*? *Rush Hour*? *Rush Hour 2*? *Rush Hour 3*? Actually, *Rush Hour 3* wasn't that great. *Tangled*?"

"That last one, I believe, is a cartoon about a girl with very long hair, inspired by the German fairy tale 'Rapunzel.'"

Kenji looks like he might be choking. "A *cartoon?*" he says, outraged. "*Tangled* is not a *cartoon*. *Tangled* is one of the greatest movies of all time. It's about fighting for freedom and true love."

"Please," I say, running a tired hand across my face. "I really don't care what kinds of cartoons you like to watch in your free time. I only want to know why you're so certain I was making a mistake today."

Kenji sighs so deeply his shoulders sag. He slumps down in his chair. "I can't believe you've never seen *Men in Black*. Or *Independence Day*." He looks up at me, his eyes bright. "Shit, you'd love *Independence Day*. Will Smith punches an alien in the face, for God's sake. It's so good."

I stare blankly at him.

"My dad and I used to watch movies all the time," he says quietly. "My dad loved movies." Kenji only allows himself to feel his grief for a moment, but when he does, it hits me in a wild, desperate wave.

"I'm so sorry for your loss," I say quietly.

"Yeah, well." Kenji runs a hand over his face. Rubs at his eyes and sighs. "Anyway, do whatever you want. I just think you should buy her a ring or something before you get down on one knee."

"I wasn't planning on getting down on one knee."

"What?" He frowns. "Why not?"

"That seems illogical."

Kenji laughs. Rolls his eyes. "Listen, just trust me and at least pick out a ring first. Let her know you actually thought about it. Think it through for a beat, you know?"

"I did think it through."

"For, what, five seconds? Or did you mean that you were planning this proposal while you were being poisoned in prison?" Kenji laughs. "Bro, you literally saw her—for the first time—*today,* like, two hours ago, after two weeks of being apart, and you think proposing to her is a rational, clearheaded move?" Kenji shakes his head. "Just take some time. Think about it. Make some plans."

And then, suddenly, his reaction makes sense to me.

"You don't think she's going to say yes." I sit back, stunned. Look at the wall. "You think she'll refuse me."

"What? I never said that."

"But it's what you think, isn't it?"

"Listen," he says, and sighs. "I have no idea what she'll say. I really don't. I mean I think it's more than obvious that she loves you, and I think if she's ready to call herself the supreme commander of North America she's probably ready to handle something as big as this, but"—he rubs his chin, looks away—"I mean, yeah, I think maybe you should, like, think about it for a minute."

I stare at him. Consider his words.

Finally, I say, "You think I should get her a ring."

Kenji smiles at the floor. He seems to be fighting back a laugh. "Uh. Yeah, I do."

"I don't know anything about jewelry."

He looks up, his eyes bright with humor. "Don't worry. I'm sure the files in that thick head of yours have tons of information on this sort of thing."

"But—"

The plane gives a sudden, unexpected jolt, and I'm thrown backward in my seat. Kenji and I stare at each other for a protracted second, caution giving way to fear, fear building slowly into panic.

The plane jolts again. This time harder.

And then, once more.

"That's not turbulence," I say.

Kenji swears, loudly, and jumps to his feet. He scans the dashboard for a second before turning back, his head in a viselike grip between his hands. "I can't read these dials," he says, "I have no idea how to read these goddamn dials—"

I shove the cockpit door open just as Nazeera runs forward. She pushes her way past me to scan the dashboard and when she pulls away she looks suddenly terrified. "We've lost one of our engines," she says, her words barely a whisper. "Someone is shooting us out of the sky."

"What? How is that—"

But there's no time to discuss it. And Nazeera and I hardly have a chance to try to figure out a way to fix it before the plane jolts, once more, and this time the emergency oxygen masks fall out of their overhead compartments. Sirens are wailing. Lights overhead blink rapidly, insistent, sharp beeps warning us that the system is crashing.

"We have to try to land the plane," Nazeera is saying. "We have to figure out— Shit," she says. She covers her mouth with one hand. "We just lost another engine."

"So we're just going to fall out of the goddamn sky?" This, from Kenji.

"We can't land the plane," I say, my heart beating furiously even as I try to keep a level head. "Not like this, not when we're missing two engines. Not while they're still shooting at us."

"So what do we do?" she says.

It's Ella, at the door, who says quietly, "We have to jump."

~~JULIETTE~~
ELLA

"What?"

The three of them turn to face me.

"What are you talking about?" Kenji says.

"Love, that's really not a good idea— We don't have any parachutes on this plane, and without them—"

"No, she's right," Nazeera says carefully. She's looking me in the eye. She seems to understand what I'm thinking.

"It'll work," I say. "Don't you think?"

"Honestly, I have no idea," she says. "But it's definitely worth a shot. It might be our only shot."

Kenji is beginning to pace. "Okay, someone needs to tell me what the hell is going on."

Aaron has gone pale. "Love," he says again, "what—"

"Nazeera can fly," I explain. "If we all find a way to secure ourselves to one another, she can use her powers to bolster us, you can use your power to bolster *her* power, and because there's little chance either of you could use that much of your strength while still carrying our combined weight, we'll eventually, slowly, be dragged down to the ground."

Nazeera glances at the dash again. "We're eight thousand feet in the air and losing altitude quickly. If we're going to do this, we should jump now, while the plane is still relatively stable."

"Wait—where are we?" Kenji says. "Where are we going to land?"

"I'm not sure," she says. "But it looks like we're somewhere over the general vicinity of sectors 200 through 300." She looks at Aaron. "Do you have any friends in this region?"

Aaron shoots her a dark look. "I have friends nowhere."

"Zero people skills," Kenji mutters.

"We're out of time," I say. "Are we going to do this?"

"I guess so. It's the only plan we've got," Kenji says.

"I think it's a solid plan," Aaron says, and shoots me a hesitant, but encouraging look. "But I think we should find a way to strap ourselves together. Some kind of harness or something—so we don't lose each other in the air."

"We don't have time for that." Nazeera's calm is quickly giving way to panic. "We'll just have to hold on tight."

Kenji nods, and with a sudden heave, shoves open the airplane door. Air rushes in fast and hard, nearly knocking us off our feet.

Quickly, we all link arms, Nazeera and Aaron holding up the outer edges, and with a few reassuring shouts through the howling wind—

We jump.

It's a terrifying sensation.

The wind pushes up fast and hard and then, all at once, stills. We seem to be frozen in time, whirring in place even as we watch the jet fall, steadily, into the distance. Nazeera and Aaron appear to be doing their jobs almost too well. We're not falling fast enough, and not only is it freezing up here, oxygen is scarce.

"I'm going to drop my hold on your power," Aaron calls out to Nazeera, and she shouts back her agreement.

Slowly, we begin to descend.

I watch as the world blurs around us. We drift downward, unhurried, the wind pushing hard against our feet. And then, suddenly, the bottom seems to drop out from under us, and we go shooting down, hard, into the terrain below.

I give out a single, terrified scream—

Or was that Kenji?

—before we pull to a sudden stop, a foot above the ground. Aaron squeezes my arm and I look at him, grateful for the catch.

And then we fall to the ground.

I land badly on my ankle and wince, but I can put weight on my foot, so I know it's all right. I look around to assess the state of my friends, but realize, too late, that we're not alone.

We're in a vast, wide-open field. This was, once upon a time, almost certainly farmland, but it's now been reduced to little more than ash. In the distance appears a thin band of people, quickly closing in on us.

I harness my powers, ready to fight. Ready to face whatever comes our way. Energy is thrumming inside me, sparking in my blood.

I am not afraid.

Aaron puts his arm around me, pulls me close. "Together," he whispers. "No matter what."

Finally, after what feels like immeasurable minutes, two bodies separate from their group. Slowly, they walk up to us.

My whole body is tense in preparation for an attack, but as they get closer, I'm able to discern their faces.

They're two adults:

One, a slender, stunning woman with closely cropped hair and skin so dark it gleams. She's luminous as she walks, her smile widening with every step. Beside her is another smiling face, but the familiar sight of his brown skin and long dreadlocks sends shock and panic and hope rushing through me. I feel dazed.

Castle.

His presence here could be either good or bad. A thousand questions run through my mind, among them: What is he doing here? How did he get here? The last time I saw him, I didn't think he was on my side at all—has he turned against us completely?

The woman is the first to speak.

"I'm glad to see you're all right," she says. "I'm afraid we had no choice but to shoot your plane out of the sky."

"What? What are y—"

"Castle?" Kenji's quiet, tentative voice reaches out from behind me.

Castle steps forward just as Kenji moves toward him, and the two embrace, Castle pulling him in so tightly I can practically feel the tension from where I'm standing. They're both visibly emotional, and the moment is so touching it puts my fears at ease.

"You're okay," Kenji says. "I thought—"

Haider and Stephan, the son of the supreme commander of Africa, step out of the crowd. Shock seizes my body at the sight of them. They nod at Nazeera and the three of them separate to form a new group, off to the side. They speak in low, hurried whispers.

Castle takes a deep breath. "We have a lot to talk about." And then, to me, he says, "Ella, I'd like you to meet my daughter, Nouria."

My eyebrows fly up my forehead. I glance at Aaron, who seems as stunned as I am, but Kenji lets out a sudden *whoop,* and tackles Castle all over again. The two of them laugh. Kenji is saying, *No way, no way*

Nouria pointedly ignores them and smiles at me. "We call our home the Sanctuary," she says. "My wife and I are the leaders of the resistance here. Welcome."

Another woman separates from the crowd and steps forward. She's petite, with long blond hair. She shakes my hand. "It's an honor to meet you," she says. "My name is Samantha."

I study both of them, Nouria and Samantha standing side by side. Castle's happiness. The smile on Kenji's face. The cluster of Nazeera, Haider, and Stephan off to the side. The larger group crowded in the distance.

"The honor is ours," I say, and smile. Then: "But are we safe out here? Out in the open like this?"

Nouria nods. "My powers allow me to manipulate light in unusual ways," she says. "I've cast a protective shield around us right now, so that if someone were to look in our direction, they'd see only a painful brightness that would force them to look away."

"Whoa." Kenji's eyes widen. "That's cool."

"Thank you," Nouria says. She's practically emanating light, her dark brown skin shimmering even as she stands still. There's something breathtaking about just being near her.

"Are those your people?" I hear Aaron say, speaking for the first time. He's peering over her head, at the small crowd in the distance.

She nods.

"And are they here to make sure we don't hurt you?"

Nouria smiles. "They're here to make sure no one hurts *you*," she says. "Your group is welcome here. You've more than proven yourselves worthy." And then, "We've heard all the stories about Sector 45."

"You have?" I say, surprised. "I thought The Reestablishment buried everything."

Nouria shakes her head. "Whispers travel faster than anyone can control. The continent is buzzing with the news of all you've been doing these past couple of months. It's truly a privilege to meet you," she says to me, and holds out her hand. "I've been so inspired by your work."

I take her hand, feeling at once proud and embarrassed. "Thank you," I say quietly. "That's very kind of you."

But then Nouria's eyes grow somber. "I *am* sorry we had to shoot you out of the sky," she says. "That must've been terrifying. But Castle assured me that there were two among you who would be able to fly."

"Wait, what?" Kenji hazards a look at Castle. "You planned this?"

"It was the only way," he says. "Once we were able to get free of the asylum"—he nods gratefully at Nazeera—"I knew the only place left for us was here, with Nouria. But we couldn't have radioed to tell you to land here; our communication would've been intercepted. And we couldn't have you land at the air base, for obvious reasons. So we've been tracking your plane, waiting for the right moment. Shooting you out of the sky punts the problem straight back to the military. They'll think it was action from another unit, and by the time they begin to figure it out, we'll have destroyed all evidence of our being here."

"So— Wait—" I say. "How did you and Nouria coordinate this? How'd you find each other?" And then: "Castle, if you've abandoned the citizens— Won't Anderson just murder them all? Shouldn't you have stayed to protect them? Tried to fight back?"

He shakes his head. "We had no choice but to evacuate Omega Point members from Sector 45. After the two of you"—he nods at me and Aaron—"were taken, things fell into complete chaos. We were all taken hostage and thrown in prison. It was only because of Nazeera—who connected us with Haider and Stephan—that we were able to make our way here. Sector 45 has since been returned to its original state as a prison." Castle takes a tight breath. "There's a great deal we need to share with each other. So much has happened in the last two weeks it'll be impossible to discuss it all quickly. But it *is* important that you know, right now, a little bit about Nouria's role in all this."

He turns to Nouria and gives her a small nod.

Nouria looks me in the eye and says, "That day you were shot on the beach," she says quietly. "Do you remember?"

I hesitate. "Of course."

"I was the one who issued that order against you."

I'm so stunned I visibly flinch.

"*What?*" Aaron steps forward, outraged. "Castle, are you *insane*? You ask us to take refuge in the home of a person who nearly murdered Ella?" He turns back, stares at me with a wild look in his eyes. "How could y—"

"Castle?" There's a warning in Kenji's voice. "What is going on?"

But Nouria and Castle are staring at each other, and a heavy look passes between them.

Finally, Castle sighs.

"Let's get settled before we keep talking," he says. "This is a long conversation, and it's an important one."

"Let's have it now," Aaron says.

"Yes," Kenji says angrily. "Now."

"She tried to murder me," I say, finally finding my voice. "Why would you bring me here? What arc you trying to do?"

"You've had a long, difficult journey," Castle says. "I

want you to have a chance to get settled. Take a shower and eat some food. And then, I promise—we'll give you all the answers you want."

"But how can we trust that we'll be safe?" I say. "How can we know Nouria isn't trying to hurt us?"

"Because," she says steadily, "I did what I did to help you."

"And how is that plausible?" Aaron says sharply.

"It was the only way I knew how to get a message to you," Nouria says, still staring at me. "I was never trying to kill you—and I knew that your own defenses would help protect you from certain death."

"That was a dangerous bet to make."

"Believe me," she says quietly, "it was a difficult decision to make. It came at great cost to us—we lost one of our own in the process."

I feel myself tense, but otherwise betray no emotion. I remember the day Nazeera saved me—the day she killed my assailant.

"But I had to reach you," Nouria says, her dark brown eyes deep with feeling. "It was the only way I could do it without rousing suspicion."

My curiosity beats out my skepticism. For the moment.

"So— Why? Why did you do it?" I ask. "Why poison me?"

Unexpectedly, Nouria smiles. "I needed you to see what I saw. And according to Castle, it worked."

"What worked?"

"Ella—" She hesitates. "May I call you by your real name?"

I blink. Stare at Castle. "You told her about me?"

"He didn't have to. Things don't stay secret for very long around here," Nouria says. "No matter what The Reestablishment has you believe, we're all finding ways to pass messages to each other. All the resistance groups across the globe know the truth about you by now. And they love you more for it."

I don't know what to say.

"Ella," she says softly, "I was able to figure out why your parents have kept your sister a secret for so long. And I just wanted t—"

"I already know," I say, the words coming out quietly.

I haven't talked to anyone about this yet; haven't told a soul. There's been no time to discuss something this big. No time to have a long conversation. But I guess we're going to have it now.

Nouria is staring at me, stunned. "You know?"

"Emmaline told me everything."

A hush falls over the crowd. Everyone turns to look at me. Even Haider, Stephan, and Nazeera finally stop talking amongst themselves long enough to stare.

"She's kept in captivity," I say. "She lives in a holding tank, where she exists almost permanently underwater. Her brain waves are connected to tidal turbines that convert the kinetic energy of her mind into electricity. Evie, my mother, found a way to harness that electricity—and project it outward. All over the world." I take a deep breath. "Emmaline is stronger than I've ever been or ever will be. She has the power to bend the minds of the people—she can warp and distort realities— Here. Everywhere."

Kenji's face is a perfect encapsulation of horror, and his expression is reflected on dozens of other faces around me. Nazeera, on the other hand, looks stricken.

"What you see here?" I say. "Around us? The decay of society, the broken atmosphere, the birds gone from the sky— It's all an illusion. It's true that our climate has changed, yes—we've done serious damage to the atmosphere, to the animals, to the planet as a whole—but that damage is not irreparable. Scientists were hopeful that, with a careful, concerted effort, we could fix our Earth. Save the future. But The Reestablishment didn't like that angle," he says. "They didn't want the people to hope. They wanted people to think that our Earth was beyond salvation. And with Emmaline they were able to do just that."

"Why?" Kenji says, stunned. "Why would they do that? What do they gain?"

"Desperate, terrified people," Nouria says solemnly, "are much easier to control. They used Ella's sister to create the illusion of irreversible devastation, and then they preyed upon the weak and the hopeless, and convinced them to turn to The Reestablishment for support."

"Emmaline and I were designed for something called Operation Synthesis. She was meant to be the architect of the world, and I was to be the executioner. But Emmaline is dying. They need another powerful weapon with which to control the people. A contingency. A backup plan."

Aaron takes my hand.

"The Reestablishment wanted me to replace my sister," I say.

For the first time, Nouria has gone still. No one knew this part. No one but me. "How?" she says. "You have such different abilities."

It's Castle who says, "It's easy to imagine, actually." But he looks terrified. "If they were to magnify Ella's powers the way they did her sister's, she would become the equivalent of a human atom bomb. She could cause mass destruction. Excruciating pain. Death when they please. Across tremendous distances."

"We have no choice." Nazeera's voice rings out, sharp and clear. "We have to kill Evie."

And I'm looking out, far into the distance, when I say, quietly, "I already did."

A collective gasp goes through the crowd. Aaron goes still beside me.

"And now," I say, "I have to kill my sister. It's what she wants. It's the only way."

WARNER

Nouria's headquarters are both strange and beautiful. They have no need to hide underground, because she's found a way to imbue objects with her power—an evolution of our abilities even Castle hadn't foreseen. The Sanctuary's campsite is protected by a series of twenty-foot-tall pole lights that border the edges of the clearing. Fused with Nouria's power, the lights work together as a barrier that makes it impossible to look in the direction of their campsite. She says her abilities not only have the power to blind, but that she can also use light to warp sounds. So they live here, out in the open, their words and actions protected in plain sight. Only those who know the location can find their way here.

Nouria says that the illusion has kept them safe for years.

The sun begins its descent as we make our way toward the campsite—the vast, unusually green field dotted with cream-colored tents—and the scene is so breathtaking I can't help but stop to appreciate the view. Fire streaks across the sky, golden light flooding the air and earth. It feels both beautiful and bleak, and I shiver as a gust of wind wraps around my body.

Ella takes my hand.

I look at her, surprised, and she smiles at me, the fading

sun glinting in her eyes. I feel her fear, her hope, her love for me. But there's something else, too—something like pride. It's faint, but it's there, and it makes me so happy to see her like this. She *should* be proud. I can speak for myself, at least, when I say that I've never been so proud of her. But then, I always knew she would go on to greatness. It doesn't surprise me at all that, even after everything she's been through—after all the horrors she's had to face—she's still managed to inspire the world. She's one of the strongest people I've ever known. My father might be back from the dead, and Sector 45 might be out of our hands, but Ella's impact can't be ignored. Nouria says that no one really believed that she was actually dead, but now that it's official—now that word has spread that Ella is still alive—she's become more notorious than ever. Nouria says that the rumbles underground are already getting stronger. People are more desperate to act, to get involved, and to stand up to The Reestablishment. Resistance groups are growing. The civilians are finding ways to get smarter—to get stronger, together. And Ella has given them a figure to rally around. Everyone is talking about her.

She's become a symbol of hope for so many.

I squeeze Ella's hand, returning her smile, and when her cheeks flush with color I have to fight back the urge to pull her into my arms.

She amazes me more every day.

My conversation with Kenji is still, despite everything, at the forefront of my mind. Things always feel so desperate these days that I feel a new, nagging insistence that this window of calm might be my only chance at happiness. We're almost constantly at war, either fighting for our lives or on the run—and there's no guarantee of a future. No guarantee that I'll live to see another year. No promise to grow old. It makes me feel li—

I stop, suddenly, and Ella nearly stumbles.

"Are you okay?" she says, squeezing my hand.

I nod. I offer her a distracted smile and vague apology as we begin walking again, but—

I run the numbers once more.

Finally, I say, without looking up, "Does anyone happen to know what day it is?"

And someone responds, a voice from the group I can't be bothered to identify, confirming what I already thought might be true. My father wasn't lying.

Tomorrow is my birthday.

I'll be twenty years old.

Tomorrow.

The revelation thunders through me. This birthday feels like more of a milestone than usual, because my life, exactly one year ago, was nearly unrecognizable. Almost everything in my life is different now. One year ago I was a different person. I was in an awful, self-destructive relationship with a different person. One year ago my anxiety was so crippling that five minutes alone with my own mind would leave me spiraling for days. I relied entirely upon my routines and schedules to keep me tethered to the endless horrors of my job and its demands. I was inflexible beyond reason. I was hanging on to humanity by a thread. I felt both wild and nearly out of my mind, all the time. My private thoughts and fears were so dark that I spent nearly all my free hours either exercising, in my shooting range, or in the bowels of Sector 45, running training simulations that, I'm not proud to admit, I designed specifically to experience killing myself, over and over again.

That was one year ago. Less than a year ago. Somehow, it feels like a lifetime ago. And when I think back on who I was and what that version of myself thought my life would be like today—

I'm left deeply and profoundly humbled.

Today is not forever. Happiness does not *happen*. Happiness must be uncovered, separated from the skin of pain. It must be claimed. Kept close.

Protected.

"Would you prefer a chance to shower and change before reuniting with the others?" Nouria is saying.

Her voice is sharp and clear and it shakes me from my reverie. "Yes," I say quickly. "I'd really appreciate the time to rest."

"No problem. We meet for dinner in the main tent in two hours. I'll show you to your new residences." She hesitates. "I hope you'll forgive me for being presumptuous, but I assumed the two of you"—she looks at me and Ella—"would like to share a space. But of course if that's not—"

"Yes, thank you," Ella says quickly. Her cheeks are already pink. "We're grateful for your thoughtfulness."

Nouria nods. She seems pleased. And then she turns to Kenji and Nazeera and says, "If you'd like, I can arrange to join your separate rooms so that y—"

Kenji and Nazeera respond at the same time.

"What? No."

"Absolutely not."

"*Oh,* I'm so sorry," Nouria says quickly. "My apologies. I shouldn't have assumed."

For the first time ever, Nazeera looks flustered. She can hardly get out the words when she says, "Why would you think we'd want to share a room?"

Nouria shakes her head. She shares a quick, confused glance with Castle, but seems suddenly mortified. "I don't know. I'm sorry. You seemed—"

"Separate rooms are perfect," Kenji says sharply.

"Great," Nouria says a little too brightly. "I'll lead the way."

And I watch, amused, as Castle tries and fails to hide a smile.

Our residence, as Nouria called it, is more than I could've hoped for. I thought we'd be camping; instead, inside of each tent is a miniature, self-contained home. There's a bed, a small living area, a tiny kitchen, and a full bathroom. The furnishings are spare but bright, well made and clean.

And when Ella walks in, slips off her shoes, and throws herself backward onto the bed, I can almost imagine us together like this—maybe, someday—in our own home.

The thought sends a wave of disorienting euphoria through my body.

And then—fear.

It seems like tempting fate to even hope for a happiness like that. But there's another part of me, a small, but insistent part of me, that clings to that hope nonetheless. Ella and I overcame what I once thought impossible. I never dreamed she'd still love me once she knew everything about me. I never dreamed that the heartbreak and horrors of recent events would only bring us closer, or that my love for her could somehow increase tenfold in two weeks. I grew up thinking that the joys of this world were for other people to enjoy. I was certain that I was fated to a bleak, solitary life, forever barred from the contentment offered by human connection.

But now—

Ella yawns soundlessly, hugging a pillow to her chest as she curls up on her side. Her eyes close.

A smile tugs at my mouth as I watch her.

I'm still amazed at how just the sight of her could bring me so much peace. She shifts, again, burrowing more deeply into the pillows, and I realize she must be exhausted. And as much as I'd love to pull her into my arms, I decide to give her space. I back away quietly, and instead use the time to explore the rest of our new, temporary home.

I'm still surprised by how much I like it.

We have more privacy here, in these new headquarters, than we ever did before. More freedom. Here, I'm a visitor, welcome to take my time showering and resting before dinner. No one expects me to run their world. I have no correspondence to attend to. No awful tasks to attend to. No civilians to oversee. No innocents to torture. I feel so much freer now that someone else has taken the reins.

It's both alien and wonderful.

It feels so good to have space with Ella—literal and figurative space—to be ourselves, to be together, to simply be and breathe. Ella and I shared my bedroom back on base, but it never felt like home there. Everything was cold, sterile. I hated that building. Hated that room. Hated every minute of my life. Those walls—my own personal rooms—were suffocating, infused with awful memories. But here, even though the room is small, the tight quarters manage to be cozy. This place feels fresh and new and serene. The future doesn't seem improbable here. Hope doesn't feel ridiculous.

It feels like a chance to begin again.

And it doesn't feel dangerous to dream that one day, Ella might be mine in every way. My wife. My family. My future.

I've never, ever dared to think of it.

But my hope is snuffed out just as quickly as it appeared. Kenji's warnings flash through my mind, and I feel suddenly agitated. Apparently proposing to Ella is more complicated than I'd originally thought it might be. Apparently I need some kind of plan. A ring. A moment on one knee. It all sounds ridiculous to me. I don't even know why it sounds ridiculous, exactly, just that it doesn't feel like *me*. I don't know how to put on a performance. I don't want to make a scene. I'd find it excruciating to be so vulnerable in front of other people or in an unfamiliar setting. I wouldn't know what to do with myself.

Still, these problems seem surmountable in the pursuit of forever with her. I would get on one knee if Ella wanted me to. I'd propose in a room filled with her closest friends if that was what she needed.

No, my fear is something much greater than that.

The thing Kenji said to me today that rattled me to my core was the possibility that Ella might say no. It's *unconscionable* that it never occurred to me that she might say no.

Of course she might say no.

She could be uninterested for any number of reasons. She might not be ready, for example. Or she might not be interested in the institution of marriage as a whole. *Or,* I think, she simply might not want to tether herself to me in such a permanent way.

The thought sends a chill through my body.

I suppose I assumed she and I were on the same page, emotionally. But my assumptions in this department have landed me in trouble more times than I'd like to admit, and the stakes are too high now not to take Kenji's concerns seriously. I'm not prepared to acknowledge the damage it would do to my heart if she rejected my proposal.

I take a deep, sharp breath.

Kenji said I need to get her a ring. So far he's been right about most of the things I've done wrong in our relationship, so I'm inclined to believe he might have a point. But I have no idea where I'd be able to conjure up a ring in a place like this. Maybe if we were back home, where I was familiar with the area and its artisans—

But here?

It's almost too much to think about right now.

There's so much to think about, in fact, that I can't quite believe I'm even considering something like this—at a time like this. I haven't even had a moment to reconcile the apparent regeneration of my father, or literally any of the other new, outrageous revelations our families have thrown at us. We're in the middle of a fight for our lives; we're fighting for the future of the *world*.

I squeeze my eyes shut. Maybe I really am an idiot.

Five minutes ago, the end of the world seemed like the right reason to propose: to take everything I can in this transitory world—and grieve nothing. But suddenly, it feels like this really might be an impulsive decision. Maybe this isn't the right time, after all.

Maybe Kenji was right. Maybe I'm not thinking clearly. Maybe losing Ella and regaining all these memories—

Maybe it's made me irrational.

I push off the wall, trying to clear my head. I wander the rest of the small space, taking stock of everything in our tent, and peer into the bathroom. I'm relieved to discover that there's real plumbing. In fact, the more I look around, the more I realize that this isn't a tent at all. There are actual floors and walls and a single vaulted ceiling in this room, as if each unit is actually a small, freestanding building. The tents seem to be draped over the entire structure—and I wonder if they serve a more practical purpose that's not immediately obvious.

Several years, Nouria said.

Several years they've lived here and made this their home. They really found a way to make something out of nothing.

The bathroom is a nice size—spacious enough for two people to share, but not big enough for a bathtub. Still, when we first approached the clearing I wasn't even sure they'd have proper facilities or running water, so this is more than I could've hoped for. And the more I stare at the shower, the more I'm suddenly desperate to rinse these weeks from my skin. I always took pains to stay clean, even in prison, but it's been too long since I've had a hot shower with steady, running water, and I can hardly resist the temptation now. And I've already stripped off most of my clothes when I hear Ella call my name, her still-sleepy voice carrying over from what serves as our bedroom. Or bed space. It's not really a room as much as it is an area designated for a bed.

"Yes?" I call back.

"Where'd you go?" she says.

"I thought I might take a shower," I try to say without shouting. I've just stepped out of my underwear and into the standing shower, but I turn the dials in the wrong direction and cold water sprays from the showerhead. I jump backward even as I hurry to undo my mistake, and nearly collide with Ella in the process.

Ella, who's suddenly standing behind me.

I don't know whether its habit, instinct, or self-preservation, but I grab a towel from a nearby shelf and quickly press it against my exposed body. I don't even understand why I'm suddenly self-conscious. I never feel uncomfortable in my own skin. I like the way I look naked.

But this moment wasn't one I'd anticipated, and I feel defenseless.

"Hi, love," I say, taking a quick breath. I remember to smile. "I didn't see you standing there."

Ella crosses her arms, pretending to look mad, but I can see the effort she's making to fight back a smile. "Aaron," she says sternly. "You were going to take a shower without me?"

My eyebrows fly up, surprised.

For a moment, I don't know what to say. And then, carefully, "Would you like to join me?"

She steps forward, wraps her arms around my waist, and stares up at me with a sweet, secret smile. The look in her eyes is enough to make me think about dropping the towel.

I whisper her name, my heart heavy with emotion.

She pulls me closer, gently touching her lips to my chest, and I go uncomfortably still. Her kisses grow more intent, her lips leaving a trail of fire across my chest, down my torso, and feeling rushes through my veins, sets me on fire. Suddenly I forget why I was ever holding a towel.

I don't even know when it falls to the floor.

I slip my arms around her, reel her in. She feels incredible, her body fitting against me perfectly, and I tilt her face up, my hand caught somewhere behind her neck and the base of her jaw and I kiss her, soft and slow, heat filling my blood with dangerous speed. I pull her tighter and she gasps, stumbles and takes an accidental step back and I catch her, pressing her against the wall behind her. I bunch up the hem of her dress and in one smooth motion yank it upward, my hand slipping under the material to skim the smooth skin of her waist, to grip her hip, hard. I part her legs with my thigh and she makes a soft, desperate sound deep in her throat and it does something to me, to feel her like this, to hear her like this—to be assaulted by endless waves of her pleasure and desire—

It drives me *insane*.

I bury my face in her neck, my hands moving up, under her dress to feel her skin, hot and soft and sensitive to my touch. I've missed her so much. I've missed her body under my hands, missed the scent of her skin and the soft, featherlight whisper of her hair against my body. I kiss her neck, trying to ignore the tension in my muscles or the hard, desperate pressure driving me toward her, toward madness. There's an ache expanding inside of me and demanding more, demanding I flip her over and lose myself in her here, right now, and she whispers—

"How— How do you always feel so good?" She's clinging to me, her eyes half-lidded but bright with desire. Her face is flushed. Her words are heavy with feeling when she says, "How do you always do this to me?"

I break away from her.

I take two steps backward and I'm breathing hard, trying to regain control of myself even as her eyes widen, her arms going suddenly still.

"Aaron?" she says. "What's—"

"Take off your dress," I say quietly.

Understanding awakens in her eyes.

She says nothing, she only looks at me, carefully, as I watch, imprisoned in place by an acute form of agony. Her hands are trembling but her eyes are willing and wanting and nervous. She shoves the material down, past her shoulders and lets it fall to the floor. I drink her in as she steps out of the dress, my mind racing.

Gorgeous, I think. *So gorgeous.*

My pulse is wild.

When I ask her to, she unhooks her bra. Moments later, her underwear joins her bra on the floor and I can't look away from her, my mind unable to process the perfection of this happiness. She's so stunning I can hardly breathe. I can hardly fathom that she's mine, that she wants me, that she would ever love me. I can't even hear myself *think* over the rush of blood in my ears, my heart beating so fast and hard it seems to thud against my skull. The sight of her standing in front of me, vulnerable and flushed with desire, is doing wild, desperate things to my mind. God, the fantasies I've had about her. The places my mind has gone.

I step forward and pick her up and she gasps, surprised, clinging desperately to my neck as I hitch her legs around my waist, my arms settling under her thighs. I love feeling the weight of her soft curves. I love having her this close to me. I love her arms around my neck and the squeeze of her legs around my hips. I love how ready she is, her thighs already parted, every inch of her pressed against me. But then she runs her hands up my naked back and I have to resist the urge to flinch. I don't want to be self-conscious about the scars on my body. I don't want any part of me to be off-limits to her. I want her to know me exactly as I am, and, as hard as it is, I allow myself to ease into her touch, closing my eyes as she trails her hands up, across my shoulders, down my arms.

"You're so gorgeous," she says softly. "I'm always surprised. It doesn't matter how many times I see you without your clothes on, I'm always surprised. It doesn't seem fair that anyone should be this gorgeous."

She looks at me, stares at me as if expecting an answer, but I can't speak. I fear I might unravel if I do. I want her with a desperate need I've never known before—a desperate, painful need so overwhelming it's threatening to consume me. I need her. Need this. Now. I take a deep, unsteady breath, and carry her into the shower.

She screams.

Hot water hits us fast and hard and I press her against the shower wall, losing myself in her in a way I never have before. The kisses are deeper, more desperate. The heat, more explosive. Everything between us feels wild and raw and vulnerable.

I lose track of time.

I don't know how long we've been here. I don't know how long I've lost myself in her when she cries out, clutching my arms so tightly her fingernails dig into my skin, her screams muffled against my chest. I feel weak, unsteady as she collapses in my arms; I'm intoxicated by the pure, stunning power of her emotions: endless waves of love and desire, love and kindness, love and joy, love and tenderness. So much tenderness.

It's almost too much.

I step backward, bracing myself against the wall as she presses her cheek against my chest and holds me, our bodies wet and heavy with feeling, our hearts pounding with something more powerful than I ever thought possible. I kiss the curve of her shoulder, the nape of her neck. I forget where we are and all we have left to do and I just hold on, hot water rushing down my arms, my limbs still slightly shaking, too terrified to let her go.

~~JULIETTE~~
ELLA

I wake up with a start.

After we got out of the shower, Aaron and I dried off, climbed into bed without a word, and promptly fell asleep.

I have no idea what time it is.

Aaron's body is curled around mine, one of his arms under my head, the other wrapped around my waist. His arms are heavy, and the weight of him feels so good—makes me feel so safe—that, on the one hand, I don't ever want to move. On the other hand—

I know we should probably get out of bed.

I sigh, hating to wake him up—he seems so tired—and I turn around, slowly, in his arms.

He only pulls me tighter.

He shifts so that his chin rests on my head; my face is now pressed gently against his throat, and I breathe him in, running my hands along the strong, deep lines of muscle in his arms. Everything about him feels raw. Powerful. There's something both wild and terrified about his heart, and somehow, knowing this only makes me love him more. I trace the lines of his shoulder blades, the curve of his spine. He stirs, but only a little, and buries his face in my hair, breathing me in.

"Don't go," he says quietly.

I tilt my head, gently kiss the column of his throat. "Aaron," I whisper, "I'm not going anywhere."

He sighs. Says, "Good."

I smile. "But we should probably get out of bed. We have to go to dinner. Everyone will be waiting for us."

He shakes his head, barely. Makes a disapproving sound in his throat.

"But—"

"No." And then, deftly, he helps me turn around. He hugs me close again, my back pressed against his chest. His voice is soft, husky with desire when he says. "Let me enjoy you, love. You feel so good."

And I give in. Melt back into his arms.

The truth is, I love these moments most. The quiet contentment. The peace. I love the weight of him, the feel of him, his naked body wrapped around mine. I never feel closer to him than I do like this, when there's nothing between us.

Gently, he kisses my temple. Pulls me, somehow, even tighter. And his lips are at my ear when he says,

"Kenji said I was supposed to get you a ring."

I stiffen, confused. Try to turn around when I say, "What do you mean?"

But Aaron eases my body back down. He rests his chin on my shoulder. His hands move down my arms, trace the curve of my hips. He kisses my neck once, twice, so softly. "I know I'm doing this wrong," he says. "I know I'm not good at this sort of thing, love, and I hope you'll forgive me for it, but I don't know how else to do it." A pause. "And I'm starting to think it might kill me if I don't."

My body is frozen, even as my heart pounds furiously in my chest. "Aaron," I say, hardly daring to breathe. "What are you talking about?"

He says nothing.

I turn around again, and this time, he doesn't stop me. His eyes flare with emotion, and I watch the gentle movement in his throat as he swallows. A muscle jumps in his jaw.

"Marry me," he whispers.

I stare at him, disbelief and joy colliding. And it's the look in his eyes—the hopeful, terrified look in his eyes—that nearly kills me.

I'm suddenly crying.

I clap my hands over my face. A sob escapes my mouth.

Gently, he pries my hands away from my face.

"Ella?" he says, his words hardly a whisper.

I'm still crying when I throw my arms around his neck, still crying when he says, a little nervously—

"Sweetheart, I really need to know if this means yes or no—"

"Yes," I cry, slightly hysterical. "Yes. Yes to everything with you. Yes to forever with you. *Yes.*"

WARNER

Is this joy?

I think it might kill me.

"Aaron?"

"Yes, love?"

She takes my face in her hands and kisses me, kisses me with a love so deep it releases my brain from its prison. My heart starts beating violently.

"Ella," I say. "You're going to be my wife."

She kisses me again, crying again, and suddenly I don't recognize myself. I don't recognize my hands, my bones, my heart. I feel new. Different.

"I love you," she whispers. "I love you so much."

"That you could love me at all seems like some kind of miracle."

She smiles, even as she shakes her head. "That's ridiculous," she says. "It's very, very easy to love you."

And I don't know what to say. I don't know how to respond.

She doesn't seem to mind.

I reel her in, kiss her, again, and lose myself in the taste and feel of her, in the fantasy of what we might have. What we might be. And then I pull her gently onto my lap and she straddles my body, settling over me until we're pressed together, her cheek against my chest. I wrap my arms around her, spread my hands along her back. I feel her gentle breaths on my skin, her eyelashes tickling my chest as she blinks, and I decide I'm never, ever leaving this bed.

A happy, wonderful silence settles between us.

"You asked me to marry you," she says softly.

"Yes."

"Wow."

I smile, my heart filled suddenly with inexpressible joy. I hardly recognize myself. I can't remember the last time I ever smiled this much. I can't recall ever feeling this kind of pure, unburdened bliss.

Like my body might float away without me.

I touch her hair, gently. Run my fingers through the soft, silky strands. When I finally sit up, she sits up, too, and she blushes as I stare at her, mesmerized by the sight of her. Her eyes are wide and bright. Her lips full and pink. She's perfect, perfect here, bare and beautiful in my arms.

I press my forehead to the curve of her shoulder, my lips brushing against her skin. "I love you, Ella," I whisper. "I will love you for the rest of my life. My heart is yours. Please don't ever give it back to me."

She says nothing for what feels like an eternity.

Finally, I feel her move. Her hand touches my face.

"Aaron," she whispers. "Look at me."

I shake my head.

"Aaron."

I look up, slowly, to meet her eyes, and her expression is

at once sad and sweet and full of love. I feel something thaw inside of me as I stare at her, and just as she's about to say something, a complicated chime echoes through the room.

I freeze.

Ella frowns. Looks around. "That sounds like a doorbell," she says.

I wish I could deny the possibility.

I sit back, even though she's still sitting on my lap. I want this interruption to end. I want to go back to our conversation. I want to stick to my original plan to spend the rest of the night here, in bed, with my perfect, naked fiancée.

The chime sounds again, and this time, I say something decidedly ungentlemanly under my breath.

Ella laughs, surprised. "Did you just swear?"

"No."

A third chime. This time, I stare up at the ceiling and try to clear my head. Try to convince myself to move, to get dressed. This must be some kind of emergency, or else—

Suddenly, a voice:

"Listen—I didn't want to come, okay? I really didn't. I hate being this guy. But Castle sent me to come get you guys because you missed dinner. It's getting super late and everyone is a little worried, and now you're not even answering the door, and—Jesus Christ, open the goddamn door—"

I can't believe it. I can't believe he's here. He's always here, ruining my life.

I'm going to *kill* him.

I nearly trip trying to pull on my pants and get to the door at the same time, but when I do, I rip the door open, practically tearing it off its hinges.

"Unless someone is dead, dying, or we are under attack, I want you gone before I've even finished this sentence."

Kenji narrows his eyes at me, and then pushes past me into the room. And I'm so stunned by his gall that it takes me a moment to realize I'm going to have to murder him.

"J—?" he says, looking around as he walks in. "You in here?"

Ella is holding the bedsheet up to her neck. "Uh, hi," she says. She smiles nervously. "What are you doing here?"

"Hey, is it cool if I still call you J?" he says. "I know your name is Ella and everything, but I got so used to calling you J that it just feels right, you know?"

"You can still call me J," she says. And then she frowns. "Kenji, what's wrong?"

I groan.

"Get out," I snap at him. "I don't know why you're here, and I don't care. We don't wish to be disturbed. *Ever.*"

Ella shoots me a sharp look. She ignores me when she says, to Kenji, "It's okay. I care. Tell me what's wrong."

"Nothing is wrong," Kenji says. "But I know your boyfriend won't listen to me, so I wanted to let *you* know that it's almost midnight and we really need you guys to get down to the dining tent ASAP, okay?" He shoots Ella a loaded look, and her eyes widen. She nods. I feel a sudden rush of excitement move through her, and it leaves me confused.

"What's going on?" I say.

But Kenji is already walking away.

"Bro, you really need to, like, eat a pizza or something,"

he says, slapping me on the shoulder as he leaves. "You have too many abs."

"What?" My eyebrows pull together. "That's not—"

"I'm *joking,*" Kenji says, pausing in the doorway just before he leaves. "Joking," he says again. "It was a joke. Jesus."

And then he slams the door behind him. I turn around.

"What's going on?" I say again.

But she only smiles. "We should get dressed."

"Ella—"

"I promise I'll explain as soon as we get there."

I shake my head. "Did something happen?"

"No— I'm just— I'm really excited to see everyone from Omega Point again, and they're all waiting for us in the dining tent." She gets out of bed still holding the bedsheet to her body, and I have to clench my fists to keep from pulling it away from her. From pinning her against the wall.

And before I even have a chance to respond, she disappears into the bathroom, the sheet dragging on the floor as she goes.

I follow her.

She's looking for her clothes, oblivious to my presence, but her dress is on the floor in a corner she hasn't glimpsed yet, and I doubt she'd want to put that bloodied dress back on anyway. I should tell her that I found a drawer full of simple, standard clothes we're probably allowed to borrow.

Maybe later.

For now, I step behind her, slip my hands around her waist. She startles and the sheet falls to the floor. "Ella," I say softly, tugging her body against mine. "Sweetheart, you have to tell me what's going on."

I turn her around, slowly. She looks down at herself, surprised—always surprised—by the sight of her naked body. "I don't have any clothes on," she whispers.

"I know," I say, smiling as I run my hands down her back, appreciating her softness, her perfect curves. I wish I could store these moments. I wish I could revisit them. Relive them. She shivers in my arms and I pull her closer.

"It's not fair," she says, wrapping her arms around me. "It's not fair that you can sense emotions. That it's impossible to keep secrets from you."

"What's not fair," I say, "is that you're about to put your clothes on and force me to leave this bedroom and I don't know why."

She stares at me, her eyes wide and nervous even as she smiles. I can sense that she's torn, her heart in two places at once. "Aaron," she says softly. "Don't you like surprises?"

"I hate surprises."

She laughs. Shakes her head. "I guess I should've known that."

I stare at her, my eyebrows raised, still waiting for an explanation.

"They're going to kill me for telling you," she says. And then at the look in my eyes, "Not— I mean, not literally. But just—" Finally, she sighs. And she won't look at me when she says—

"We're throwing you a birthday party."

I'm certain I've heard her wrong.

~~JULIETTE~~
ELLA

It took more work than I imagined to get him to believe me. He wanted to know how anyone even knew that tomorrow was his birthday and how we could've possibly planned a party when we had no idea we were going to crash the plane here and why would anyone throw him a party and he wasn't even sure he liked parties and on and on and on

And it wasn't until we literally walked through the doors of the dining tent and everyone screamed happy birthday at him that he finally believed me. It wasn't much, of course. We hadn't really had time to prepare. I knew his birthday was coming up because I'd been keeping track of it ever since the day he told me what his father used to do to him, every year, on his birthday. I swore to myself I would do whatever I could to replace those memories with better ones. That forever and ever I would try to drown out the darkness that had inhaled his entire young life.

I told Kenji, when he found me, that tomorrow was Aaron's birthday, and I made him promise me that, no matter what happened, when we found him we would find a way to celebrate, in some small way.

But this—

This was more than I could've hoped for. I thought

maybe, given our time constraints, we'd just get a group to sing him "Happy Birthday," or maybe eat dessert in his honor, but this—

There's an actual cake.

A cake with candles in it, waiting to be lit.

Everyone from Omega Point is here—the whole crew of familiar faces: Brendan and Winston, Sonya and Sara, Alia and Lily, and Ian and Castle. Only Adam and James are missing, but we have new friends, too—

Haider is here. So is Stephan. Nazeera.

And then there's the new resistance. The members of the Sanctuary that we've yet to meet, all come forward, gathered around a single, modest sheet cake. It reads—

HAPPY BIRTHDAY WARNER

in red icing.

The piping is a little sloppy. The icing is imperfect. But when someone dims the lamps and lights the candles, Aaron goes suddenly still beside me. I squeeze his hand as he looks at me, his eyes round with a new emotion.

There's tragedy and beauty in his eyes: something stoic that refuses to be moved, and something childlike that can't help but feel joy. He looks, in short, like he's in pain.

"Aaron," I whisper. "Is this okay?"

He takes a few seconds to respond, but when he finally does, he nods. Just once—but it's enough.

"Yes," he says softly. "This is okay."

And I feel myself relax.

Tomorrow, there will be pain and devastation to contend

with. Tomorrow we'll dive into a whole new chapter of hardship. There's a world war brewing. A battle for our lives—for the whole world. Right now, little is certain. But tonight, I'm choosing to celebrate. We're going to celebrate the small and large joys. Birthdays and engagements. We're going to find time for happiness. Because how can we stand against tyranny if we ourselves are filled with hate? Or worse—

Nothing?

I want to remember to celebrate more. I want to remember to experience more joy. I want to allow myself to be happy more frequently. I want to remember, forever, this look on Aaron's face, as he's bullied into blowing out his birthday candles for the very first time.

This is, after all, what we're fighting for, isn't it?

A second chance at joy.

Lose yourself in the exhilarating return to the #1 global bestselling Shatter Me universe, set ten years after the fall of The Reestablishment.

SHATTER ME: SERIES TWO
BOOK ONE

ROSABELLE

CHAPTER 1

When I open the cupboard, the shelves are empty.

This is no surprise, of course; the shelves have been empty for weeks. It's for Clara's sake that I make a show of opening them every morning, pretending there might be more than the same skittering cockroach living inside.

I close the cabinet door, then turn to face her. Clara never leaves the bed unless I carry her; today she's sitting up and staring out the icy window, her pale eyes made paler by the blast of early morning light. Her hand trembles as she twitches the threadbare curtain, and a blue glare briefly illuminates the glass.

"We're out of bread," I announce. "I'm heading out."

Some days Clara lets me leave without asking questions. Other days she asks me how I pay for the food I bring home. Today she says, "I dreamed of Mama last night."

I keep my face impassive. "Again?"

Clara turns toward me, so gaunt her eyes appear sunken in her face. "She wasn't well, Rosa. She was suffering."

I step into my boots, shaking my head as I move into a shaft of light. "It was only a dream," I say to her. "The dead don't suffer."

Clara looks away again. "You always say that."

"And you stare at her photograph too much," I say, knotting my laces. My right hand doesn't shake today, and I experience a rush of relief as I straighten, then a flash of terror as I note the dwindling fire in the hearth—and the disappearing pile of firewood beside it. I force the terror down. "Besides," I add, "you hardly knew her."

"Well, you hardly speak of her," Clara counters with a sigh.

Through the window I glimpse a redheaded woodpecker and watch, transfixed, as it hammers its beak into a mossy trunk. It's been just over a decade since the fall of The Reestablishment—just over a decade since we've lived here, on Ark Island—and I, too, wish I could bash my head over and over against a hard surface every day. I take a sharp breath, ignoring the ever-present ache of hunger.

It's still strange to see the birds.

They fill the sky with sound and color, rattling roofs and branches. All around us evergreens spiral skyward, never surrendering to the seasons. It's always damp here; viridescent; cold. Lakes shimmer unprovoked. Distant mountain ranges seem painted in watercolors, layers of teeth made translucent by fog. The warm and well-fed have been known to call this land beautiful.

"I won't be long," I say, buttoning myself into Papa's old coat. Years ago I cut off the military insignias with a dull blade, earning myself a scar in the process. "I'll see about rebuilding the fire when I get back."

"Okay," Clara says quietly. Then: "Sebastian came by yesterday."

I stiffen.

Very slowly I reanimate, wrapping my mother's tattered scarf too tightly around my neck. I was allowed to work at the mill yesterday, and by the time I got home Clara had been asleep.

"He came to deliver the mail," she says.

"The mail," I echo. "He came all this way just to deliver the mail."

Clara nods, then reaches under her pillow to retrieve a folded newspaper and a thick, unmarked envelope, both of which she holds out in offering. I tuck the two into my coat pocket without glancing at either.

"Thank you," I say softly. I imagine, for a moment, how it might feel to slit Sebastian's throat.

Clara tilts her head at me. "He said you missed last week's meeting."

"You were sick."

"I told him that."

I look toward the door. "You don't need to tell him anything."

"He still wants to marry you, Rosa."

I lift my head sharply. "How do you know about that?"

"Would it be so terrible?" She ignores my question, shivering violently. "Don't you like him? I thought you liked him."

I turn to face our little kitchen, the small stove, the rickety table and chairs we never use. The wooden plaque hanging above the sink.

Our society
REESTABLISHED
Our future
REDEFINED

My eyes unfocus.

I was ten when I came home to find a black bear tearing through the last of our food. Clara was three; Mama had been dead three days. I don't remember killing the bear or burying what remained of my mother.

I remember the blood.

I remember the weeks it took to scrub the floorboards. The bars of Clara's crib. The ceiling. Mama's last words to me had been *close your eyes, Rosa,* except that she'd closed her eyes and I'd kept mine open. She put the gun in her mouth just hours after we heard that Papa would no longer be executed for war crimes. He'd traded all of us in for a half-life, selling secrets to the enemy in exchange for a slow rot in prison. I used to think Mama killed herself because she couldn't withstand the shame. Now I'm certain it was because she knew she'd be forced to pay for Papa's treason.

Maybe she thought they'd spare her children.

I grab the bear pelt from its hook and drape it around Clara's trembling limbs. She hates the pelt. She says the bear's pain still lingers in the cottage, that it makes her retch even after all these years. So when she allows the fur to settle on her shoulders without protest, I know the situation is dire.

"If you married Sebastian, things would be better," Clara says, suppressing another shiver. She pauses to cough, and the hacking sound drives a hole through my head. "They'd lift the sanctions. You wouldn't have to pretend we have food in our cupboards every morning."

Slowly, I meet her eyes.

I remember when Clara was born, when I'd looked at her and wondered whether Mama had given birth to a doll. Only later did I realize I must've looked just as strange when I was born: all ghost and glass. I study her often when she sleeps, or when the illness overtakes her so completely she slips into a coma. At thirteen, she's tender and optimistic; nothing like I was at her age. Still, despite the seven years between us, she and I are physically similar: shockingly pale; hair so blond it's nearly white; eyes a disorienting shade of cold. Staring at Clara is like staring into the past, at what I used to be, who I could've been.

I was soft once, too.

"I really think he loves you," she says, her eyes brightening with feeling. "You should've heard the way he talked about you— Rosa, wait—"

I don't say goodbye to my sister.

I reach for the automatic rifle tucked away in the entry, pulling the strap over my head before tugging a battered balaclava over my face. I step into the cold, and thick flakes catch in my eyelashes just as the front door slams shut behind me, the sound briefly drowning out his voice. It's my only explanation for being startled.

"Rosabelle," he says, cutting in front of me with a smile. "Still dead inside?"

ROSABELLE

CHAPTER 2

I sidestep Lieutenant Soledad, absently running my hand along the cold weapon slung across my chest. Soledad is no longer a lieutenant the way he once was; the title is a relic of another time. In this newly imagined world he's the head of our island's security, which makes him nothing more than a glorified busybody. And a tyrant.

I nod at familiar faces as they pass, their eyes anxiously tracking between myself and Soledad, who's fallen into step beside me. Snow is beginning to stick to the ground; spirals of smoke curl away from stacked chimneys, smudging the skies like errant brushstrokes. I adjust the balaclava on my face; the wool is old and itchy. I am impatient.

"I thought our appointment was for tomorrow," I say flatly.

"I thought I'd surprise you," he says. "Impromptu interrogations often yield interesting results."

I come to a halt, turning to face him.

I remember when Soledad was young and fit and full of bravado—when he served under my father, the chief commander and regent of Sector 52. Now he's somehow barrel-chested but soft; stooped. His skin is waxy, his hair thinning. He wears the stale air of another time, the only lingering evidence of that epoch imprinted on his face. A soft blue glow pulses at his temples, his dark eyes occasionally brightening, then dimming.

Unbidden, my right arm trembles.

Quietly I change course for the day, feeling the pressure of a single, physical key tucked inside in the false pocket sewn into Papa's old coat. The only lock I own is bolted to the shed camouflaged in the wilds beyond the cottage—which I meant to visit first, and which I'll now have to avoid. No one in the pit knows about the lock because the lock is illegal; the homes in the pit are meant to be borderless. Our minds, too, are meant to be open at all times for inspection. It was the way of our parents, the way of The Reestablishment.

Surveillance is security, Papa used to say. *Only criminals need privacy.*

I glance at Soledad, who still wears his old military fatigues, the front pocket adorned with the tricolored emblem of a buried era. He lost an arm during the post-revolution skirmishes and wears his prosthetic proudly, one sleeve rolled up to reveal the silver gleam of muscular machinery.

"So," he says. "We can set up here, or we can head back to central. Your choice."

I cast a furtive glance around the pit, which comprises a cluster of cottages, square windows aglow in the gray morning light. People scurry along, heads down, avoiding eye contact with Soledad, who's never paid the pit a visit without doing some damage. Those who live here have been sanctioned—cut off from the community for any number of infractions—but no one has lived here longer than Clara and me, who've never known another home on the island. In the chaotic weeks after our supreme commanders were slaughtered, Papa sent us here with Mama, promising to follow as soon as he could. It turned out Papa had stayed behind on purpose, voluntarily surrendering to the rebels. As a reward, we were sanctioned upon arrival.

"Do we have to do this now?" I ask, thinking of Clara, shivering and starved. "I'd rather keep our appointment for tomorrow."

"Why, you have plans this morning?" He says this like it's a joke. "You're not allowed a shift at the mill today."

A sharp pang of hunger cuts through me then, nearly taking my breath away. "Just some things to do."

Soledad grabs my chin and I suppress a flinch, steadying myself as he forces me to look at him. He stares into my eyes for a long beat before letting go, and I kill the flare of revulsion in my chest, compelling my racing heart to slow.

I remind myself that I am dead inside.

"So strange not to know what you're thinking," he says, a notch forming between his brows. "All these years and I still haven't gotten used to it. Makes it hard to believe you're always telling the truth."

Another slight tremor moves through my right hand. I'm the only person here unconnected to the Nexus. Even Clara was brought online before Papa was arrested. Just before the end, all civilians under the directive of The Reestablishment had been connected to the neural network, a program quickly dismantled by the new regime. Soledad and the others like to remind us that the reason we lost the war was because the rebels hadn't been chipped.

I have no acceptable excuse.

"Pity we can't seem to get you online again," Soledad says finally. "Things might've been easier for you."

Memories flare to life: cold metal; muted screams; drug-induced nightmares. With Mama dead, there was no one to beg them to stop. No one who cared whether their experiments would eventually kill me.

"I couldn't agree more," I lie.

Soledad shifts his weight. Blue veins of light pulse through his metal arm, silver fingers flashing as they flex and curl. "So," he says. "Why'd you miss the meeting last week?"

Just like that, an unofficial interrogation has begun. Here, in the freezing cold. While my neighbors watch.

Clara, I realize, can probably see us from the window.

There's a sudden chorus of shouts and my heart stutters, steadying only when I spot Zadie's twin boys, Jonah and Micah, tackling each other in the snow. One of them punches the other in the gut, this accomplishment punctuated by peals of laughter. I catch the drifting scent of breakfast meat from a nearby cottage and my knees nearly give out.

I return my eyes to Soledad. "Clara was sick."

"Coma?"

"No." I look away. "She spent most of the night throwing up."

"Food?"

"Blood," I clarify.

"Right." Soledad laughs. He sizes me up through Papa's overlarge coat. "That makes more sense, considering the fact that you're both starving."

"We're not starving." Another lie.

A fresh circus of sound short-circuits my nervous system. A murder of crows lands heavily on a nearby roof, eerie calls clamoring, wings flapping. I'm watching them, fascinated a moment by an iridescent sheen of black feathers when two earsplitting shots ring out.

I stiffen on impulse—then force myself to thaw, my fingers to unclench, my pulse to slow.

"Fucking birds," Soledad mutters.

He walks over to the duo of fallen bodies, then stomps on their small, hollow bones, smearing blood and feathers into the snow. I blink, exhaling softly into the cold. I've been dead inside for years, I remind myself.

Most people here hate the birds for what they represent. The birds mean that The Reestablishment has been dethroned, that the project has all but failed. The New Republic and its traitorous leaders—the children of our fallen supreme commanders—have been a ripe source of hatred for as long as I can remember.

Clara, I realize, will have questions about the gunshots.

"I've got real work for you, if you're interested," says Soledad, now wiping his boots on a clean patch of ground.

I look up. Realization is swift. "You didn't come here for an interrogation."

Soledad smiles at me, but his eyes are unreadable. "Never misses a thing, this one. I've always hated that about you."

"How many this time?" I ask, my heart beginning a traitorous rhythm.

"We've got four altogether. Three have been processed already. New one came through last night and he's definitely—" Soledad's eyes brighten, glazing over in an inhuman shade of blue. Suddenly he whips around, marches over to the twins still grappling in snow, grabs one of them—Micah—by the scruff of his neck, and shoves him, angrily, to the ground. "You've just lost your rations for the week."

Jonah darts forward. "But— We were only playing around—"

"He was going to take your eye out," Soledad barks, then jerks his head in a familiar motion.

Micah screams.

Jonah stills, but his eyes are fixed on his brother, who's lying on the ground, now silent and twitching violently. There's the slam of a door, a sudden cry, and his mother, Zadie, comes running. Soledad shakes his head in disgust, and Micah is released from his paralysis. With some effort, the boy revives in his mother's arms.

"Sorry, sir," says Micah, his chest heaving. "I didn't mean—"

Soledad directs his next words to Zadie. "If you can't get these two idiots to stop acting like animals, you'll spend another year in the pit. Is that clear?"

Heads appear, then disappear, in neighboring windows.

Zadie nods, mumbling something inarticulate, then grabs her boys and bolts.

In the quiet aftermath Soledad returns to my side, scanning me for a reaction, but I'm careful, as always, to betray no emotion. It's the only way I've survived here, where I'm surveilled not only by the system but also through the eyes of everyone I encounter—even my own sister.

Surveillance is security, Rosa.

Only criminals need privacy.

Only criminals need privacy.

For so many years I used to believe everything my father said.

Those were the years when Soledad was a friend to our family; the years we lived in a warm, comfortable home, when food was abundant, when Nanny would dress me in silks before braiding my hair. I'd sneak downstairs during my mother's dinner parties just to hear the sound of her laughter.

"How many more before you'll lift the sanctions?" I ask, ripping the balaclava off my head. I feel the static of my hair; the compression of my chest. Brisk wind batters my face but the icy air is welcome against my heated skin.

Soledad shakes his head. "I can't answer that. Your father is still alive, still feeding secrets to the enemy. For as long as we can't know your mind, you'll always be a question mark." He shrugs, then looks away. "We all make sacrifices for the security of our nation, Rosabelle. For the security of our future. This is your sacrifice—and it may never end."

He returns his eyes to me.

"Look," he says. "You can kill them all at once or one at a time. I'll let you decide. When you're done, I'll see about getting Clara some medicine."

"And food," I say too quickly, then pause, taking a moment to compose my face. "And firewood."

"All at once, then," he says, narrowing his eyes.

"All at once," I agree. "And right now."

Soledad raises his eyebrows. "You sure? One of them won't stop screaming. She had a bad reaction to the sedative."

I feel unseasonably warm. Overdressed. I distract myself by stuffing the balaclava into Papa's coat pocket, and the thick envelope from earlier kisses me with a paper cut. The pain focuses my thoughts.

It's not necessary to kill them like this.

We have among our ranks some of the best medics and scientists in the world; we possess far more advanced and humane ways to kill the rare spies who manage to breach Ark Island.

Of course, murdering them isn't meant to be humane.

"Do you care how I kill them?" I ask, and my voice is mercifully steady.

The electric hum of the helicopter pulls my attention skyward. Clara will see it. She'll know what it means.

"I don't care how you do it." Soledad smiles now; a real smile. "You've always been creative."